WJ X to C

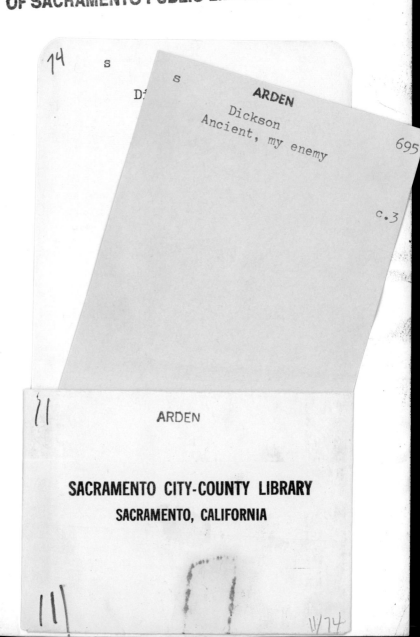

74   s

s

D   ARDEN

                Dickson
        Ancient, my enemy   695

                                        c.3

11

ARDEN

SACRAMENTO CITY-COUNTY LIBRARY
SACRAMENTO, CALIFORNIA

111

11/74

Ancient, My Enemy

Ancient, My Enemy

GORDON R. DICKSON

DOUBLEDAY & COMPANY, INC.
GARDEN CITY, NEW YORK
1974

Library of Congress Cataloging in Publication Data

Dickson, Gordon R
Ancient, my enemy.

CONTENTS: Ancient, my enemy.—The odd ones.—The monkey wrench.
[etc.]
1. Science fiction, American.   I. Title.
PZ4.D553An   [PS3554.I328]   813'.5'4
ISBN 0-385-05202-2
Library of Congress Catalog Card Number 74-4871

Contents

Ancient, My Enemy

Ancient, My Enemy

They stopped at the edge of the mountains eight hours after they had left the hotel. The day was only a dim paling of the sky above the ragged skyline of rock to the east when they set up their shelter in a little level spot—a sort of nest among the granitic cliffs, ranging from fifty to three hundred meters high, surrounding them.

With the approach of dawn the Udbahr natives trailing them had already begun to seek their own shelters, those cracks in the rock into which they would retreat until the relentless day had come and gone again and the light of the nearer moon called them out. Already holed up high among the rocks, some of the males had begun to sing.

"What's he saying? What do the words mean?" demanded the girl graduate student, fascinated. Her name was Willy Fairchild and in the fading light of the nearer moon she showed tall and slim, with short whitish-blond hair around a thin-boned face.

Kiev Archad shrugged. He listened a moment.

He translated:

> *You desert me now, female*
> *Because I am crippled,*
> *And yet all my fault was*
> *That I did not lack courage.*
> *Therefore I will go now to the*
> *high rocks to die,*
> *And another will take you.*

For what good is a warrior
Whose female forsakes him?

Kiev stopped translating.

"Go on," said Willy. The song was still mournfully falling upon them from the rocks above.

"There isn't any more," said Kiev. "He just keeps singing it over and over again. He'll go on singing until it's time to seal his hole and keep the heat from drying him up."

"Oh," said Willy. "Is he really crippled, do you think?"

Kiev shrugged again.

"I doubt it," he said. "If he were really hurt he'd be keeping quiet, so none of the other males could find him. As it is, he's probably just hoping to lure another one of them close— so that he can kill himself a full meal before the sun rises."

She gasped.

He looked at her. "Sorry," he said. "If you weren't printed with the language, maybe you weren't printed with the general info—"

"Like the fact they're cannibals? Of course I was," she said. "It doesn't disturb me at all. Cannibalism is perfectly reasonable in an environment like this where the only other protein available is rock rats—and everything else, except humans, is carbohydrates."

She glanced at one of the several moonplants growing like outsize mushrooms from the rocky rubble of the surface beside the shelter's silver walls. They had already pulled their petals into the protection of horny overhoods. But they had not yet retreated into the ground.

"After all," she said into his silence, "my field's anthropopathic history. People who disturb easily just don't take that up for a study. There were a number of protein-poor areas back on Earth and so-called primitive local people became practical cannibals out of necessity."

"Oh," said Kiev. He wriggled his wide shoulders briefly

against the short pre-dawn chill. "We'd better be getting inside and settled. You'll need as much rest as you can get. We'll have to strike the shelter so as to start our drive at sunset."

"Sunset?" She frowned. "It'll still be terribly hot, won't it? What drive?"

He turned sharply to look at her.

"I thought—if you knew about their eating habits—"

"No," she said, interested. "No one said anything to me about drives."

"We've been picking up a gang of them ever since we left the hotel," he said. "And we're protein, too, just as you say. Or at least, enough like their native protein for them to hope to eat us. Sooner or later, if there get to be enough of them, they'll attack—if we don't drive them first."

"Oh, I see. You scare them off before they can start something."

"Something like that—yes." He turned, ran his finger down the closure of the shelter and threw back the flap. "That's why Wadjik and Shant came this far with us—so we could have four men for the drive. Come on, we've got to get inside."

She went past him into the shelter.

Inside, Johnson and the other prospecting team of Wadjik and Shant—who would split with them next evening—were already cozy. Johnson was hunched in his thermal sleeping bag, reading. Wadjik and Shant were at a card table playing bluet. Johnson turned his dark face to Kiev and Willy as they came in.

He said, "I laid your bags out for you—beyond the stores."

"Regular nursemaid," said Wadjik without looking up from his cards.

"Wad," said Johnson, quietly. "You and Shany can shelter up separately if you want." His bare arms and chest swelled with muscle above the partly open slit of his thermal bag. He was not as big as Wadjik or Kiev but he was the oldest and knew the mountains better than any of them.

"Two more cards," said Wadjik looking to Shant.

The gray-headed man dealt.

Kiev led the way around the card table. Two unrolled thermal bags occupied the floor space next to the entrance to the lavatory partition that gave privacy to the shelter's built-in chemical toilet. Kiev gave the one nearest to the partition to Willy and unrolled the other next to the pile of stores.

The pile was really not much as a shelter divider. By merely lifting himself on one elbow, once he was in his bag, Kiev was able to see the other three bags and Johnson, reading. The card players, sitting up at their table, could look down on both Kiev and Willy—but, of course, once it really started to heat up, they would be in their sacks too.

Kiev undressed within his thermal bag, handing his clothes out as he took them off and keeping his back turned to the girl. When at last he turned to her he saw that, while she was also in her bag, she still wore a sort of light blouse or skivvy shirt—he had no idea what the proper name for it was.

"That's all right for now," he said, nodding at the blouse. "But later on you'll be wanting to get completely down into the bag for coolness, anyhow, so it won't matter for looks. And any kind of cloth between you and the bag's inner surface cuts its efficiency almost in half."

"I don't see why," she answered stiffly.

"They didn't tell you that either?" he asked. "Part of the main idea behind using the thermal bag is that we don't have to carry too heavy an air-conditioning unit. If you take heat from anything, even a human body, you've got to pump it somewhere else. That's what an air-conditioning unit does. But these bags are stuffed between the walls with a chemical heat-absorbent—"

He went on, trying to explain to her that the bag could soak up the heat from her naked body over a fourteen-hour period without getting so full of heat it lost its cooling powers. But the lining of the bag was built to operate in direct contact with the human skin. Anything like cloth in between caused a build-up of stored heat that would overload the bag before the fourteen hours until cool-off was over. It was not just a matter of comfort—she would be risking heat prostration and even death.

She listened stiffly. He did not know if he had convinced her or not. But he got the feeling that when the time finally came she would get rid of the garment. He lay back in his own bag, closed his eyes and tried to get some sleep. In another four hours sleep would be almost impossible even in the bags.

Wadjik and Shant were fools with their cards. A man could tough out a drive with only a couple of hours of sleep; but what if some accident during the next shelter stop kept him from getting any sleep at all? He could be half-dead with heat and exhaustion by the following cool-off, his judgment gone and his reflexes shot. One little bit of bad luck could finish him off. Characters like Johnson had survived in the mountains all these years by always keeping in shape. After four trips into the grounds Kiev had made up his mind to do the same thing.

He slept. The heat woke him.

He found he had instinctively slid down into his bag and sealed it up to the neck without coming fully awake. Opening his eyes now, feeling the blasting dryness and quivering heat of the air against his already parched face, he first pulled his head down completely into the bag and took a deep breath. The hot air from above, pulled momentarily into the bag, cooled on his dust-dry throat and mouth. He worked some saliva into existence, swallowed several times and then, sitting up, pushed his head and one arm out of the bag. He found his salve and began to grease his face and neck.

He glanced over at Willy as he worked. She was lying muffled in her thermal bag, watching him, her features shining with salve.

"You take that shirt off?" he asked.

She nodded briefly. He looked over past the deserted card table at the three other thermal bags. Johnson, encased to his nose, slept with the ease of an old prospector, his upper face placidly shining with salve. Shant was out of sight in his bag—all but his close-cut cap of gray hair. Wadjik was propped up against a case from the stores, his heavy-boned face under its uncombed black hair absent-eyed, staring at and through Kiev.

"Wad," said Kiev, "better get Shanny up out of that. He'll overload his sack in five hours if he goes to sleep breathing down there like that."

Wadjik's eyes focused. He grinned unpleasantly and rolled over on his side. He bent in the middle and kicked the foot of his thermal bag hard against the side of Shant's. Shant's head popped into sight.

"You go to sleep down there," Wad snarled, "and you won't live until sunset."

"Oh—sure, Wad. Sorry," Shant said, quickly.

A short silence fell. Wadjik had gone back to staring through unfocused eyes. Johnson woke but the only sign he gave was the raising of his eyelids. He did not move in his bag. Around them all, now, the heat was becoming a living thing—an invisible but sentient presence, a demon inside the shelter who could be felt growing stronger almost by the second. The shelter's little air-conditioner hummed, keeping the air about them moving and just below unbreathable temperature.

"Kiev," said Wadjik, suddenly. "Was that old Hehog you and Willy were listening to out there, just before dawn?"

"Yes," said Kiev.

"This time we'll get him."

"Maybe," said Kiev.

"No maybe. I mean it, man."

"We'll see," said Kiev.

A movement came beside Kiev. Willy sat up in her bag.

"Mr. Wadjik—"

"Joe. I told you—Joe."

Wadjik grinned at her.

"All right. Joe. Do you mean you don't know which Udbahr male that was—the one who was singing? Don't you know why I'm going to these prospecting grounds of yours? Don't you know about the remains of a city there built by these same Udbahrs?"

"Sure, I've seen it. What of it?"

"I'm telling you what of it! They had a high level of civilization once—or at least a higher level than now. But that doesn't mean anything to you—"

"They degenerated. That's what it means to me. They're cannibal degenerates. And you want me to treat them like human beings—"

"I want you to treat them like intelligent beings—which they are. Even an uneducated, brutal, stupid man like you ought to understand—"

"Listen to who's talking. The kid historian speaks. I thought you were still in school, writing a thesis. You didn't tell me you'd been at this for years—"

"I may be only a graduate student but I've learned a few things you never did—"

Looking past Wadjik's heat-reddened face, flaming under its salve, Kiev saw the upper part of Johnson's countenance beyond. Johnson seemed to be calmly listening. There was nothing to do, Kiev knew, but listen. It was the heat—the sickening intoxication of the deadly heat in the shelter—that was making the argument. When the heat reached its most relentless intensity only the instinct keeping men in their thermal bags stopped them from killing each other.

Wadjik finally broke off the argument by drawing down into his bag and rolling across the floor of the shelter to the lavatory door. He pressed the bottom latch through his bag, opened the door, rolled inside and shut himself off from the rest of the room. Willy fell silent.

Kiev looked sideways at her.

"It's no use," he whispered to her. "Save your energy."

She turned and glared at him.

"And I thought you were different!" she spat and slid down, head and all, into her bag.

Kiev backed into his own cocoon. Fueled by the feverishness induced by the heat, his mind ran on. They were all a little crazy, he thought, all who had taken up prospecting. Crazy or they had something to hide in their pasts that would keep them from ever leaving this planet.

But a man who was clean elsewhere could become rich in five years if he kept his head—and kept his health—both on the trips and back in civilization. On Kiev's first trip into the mountains, two years ago, he had not known what he was after. Just a lot of money, he had thought, to blow back at the hotels. But now he knew better. He was going to take it cool and calm, like Johnson—who could never leave the planet.

Kiev meant to keep his own backtrail clear. And he would leave when the time came with enough to buy him citizenship and a good business franchise back on one of the Old Worlds. He had his picture of the future clear in his mind. A modern home on a settled world, a steady, good income. Status. A family.

He had seen enough of the wild edges of civilization. Leave the rest of it to the new kids coming out. He was still young but he could look ahead and see thirty up there waiting for him.

His thoughts rambled on through the deadly hours as his body temperature was driven slowly upward by the heat. In the end his mind rambled and staggered. He awoke suddenly.

He had passed from near-delirium into sleep without realizing it. The deadly heat of mid-afternoon had broken toward cool-off and with the first few degrees of relief within the shelter he, like all the rest, had dropped immediately into exhausted slumber. By now—he glanced at the wristwatch on the left sleeve of his outergear—the hour was nearly sunset.

He looked about the shelter. Willy, Shant, Wadjik, Johnson were still sleeping.

"Hey," he croaked at them, speaking above a whisper for the first time in hours. "Time for the drive. Up and at 'em."

In forty-five minutes they were all dressed, fed and outside, with the shelter folded and packed, along with the other equipment, on grav-sleds ready to travel. Wadjik and Shant took off to the north, towing their own grav-sled. Kiev and Johnson were left with their sled and the girl. They looked at her thoughtfully. The sun was already down below the peaks to the west. But three-quarters of the sky above them was still white with a glare too bright to look at directly and the heat, even with outersuit and helmet sealed, made every movement a new cause for perspiration. The climate units of the suits whined with their effort to keep the occupants dry and cool.

"I'm not going to join you," Willy snapped. "I won't be a party to any killing of the natives."

"We can't leave you behind," Kiev answered. "Unless you can handle a gun—and will use it. If any of the males break away from the drive they'll double back and you'd make an easy meal."

Inside the transparent helmet her face was pale even in the heat.

"You can stick with the grav-sled," said Kiev. "You don't have to join the drive. Just keep up."

She did not look at him or speak. She was not going to give him the satisfaction of an answer, he thought.

"Move out, then," said Johnson.

They began to climb the cliffs toward the brightness in the sky, the grav-sled trailing behind them on slave circuit, its load piled high. Willy, looking small in her suit, trudged behind it. Under the crown of the cliffs they turned about, deployed to cover both sides of the clearing below and began their drive.

They worked forward, each man firing into every rock niche or cranny that might have an Udbahr sealed up within it. Deep, booming sounds—made by the air and moisture within each cranny exploding outward—began to echo between the cliffs. Soon a shout came over Kiev's suit intercom in Johnson's deep voice.

"One running! One running! Eleven o'clock, sixty meters, down in the cleft there."

Kiev jerked his gaze ahead and caught a glimpse of an adult-sized, humanlike, brown figure with a greenishly naked, round skull and large tarsierlike eyes, vanishing up a narrow cut.

"No clothing," called Kiev over the intercom. "Must be a female, or a young male."

"Or maybe old Hehog playing it incognito—" Johnson began but was interrupted.

"One running! One running!" bellowed Wadjik's voice distantly over the intercom. "Two o'clock, near clifftop."

"One running! Deep in the pass there at three o'clock!" chimed in Johnson, again. "Keep them moving!"

The sounds of the blasting attack now were routing out Udbahrs who had denned up for the day. Most were females or young, innocent of either clothing or weapons. But here and there was a heavier, male figure, running with spear or throwing-stick in hand and wearing anything from a rope of twisted rock vines or rat furs around his waist to some tattered article of clothing, stolen, scavenged—or just possibly taken as a war prize—from the dead body of a human prospector.

The males were slowed by their insistence on herding the females and the young ahead of them. They always did this, even though nearly all prospectors made it a point to kill only the grown males—the warriors who were liable to attack if left alive. The pattern was old, familiar—one of the things that made most prospectors swear the Udbahrs had to be animal rather than intelligent. The females and young were gathering into a herd as they ran, joining up beyond the screen of the males following them. When the herd was complete—when all who should be in it had been accounted for— the males would choose their ground, stop and turn to fight and hold up the pursuers while the females and young escaped.

They always reacted the same way, no matter whether the tactic were favorable or not in the terrain where they were being driven, Kiev thought suddenly. Everything the Udbahrs did was by rote. And strange to creatures who reasoned like men. No matter what Willy said, it was hard to think of them as any kind of people—let alone people with whom you could become involved. For example, if he, Johnson, Shant and Wadjik quit driving the natives now and pulled back, the Udbahr males would immediately turn around and start trying to kill each other. It was only when they were being driven or were joining for an attack on prospectors that the males had ever been known to cooperate.

So, as it always went, it went this sunset hour on the Udbahr Planet. By the time the last light of the day star was beginning to evaporate from the western sky and the great ghostly circle of the nearer moon was beginning to be visible against a more reasonably lighted sky, some half dozen of the Udbahr males disappeared suddenly among the boulders and rocks at the mouth of a pass down which the herd of females and young were vanishing.

"Hold up," Johnson gasped over the intercom. "Hold it up. They've forted. Stop and breathe."

Kiev checked his weary legs and collapsed into sitting position on a boulder, panting. His body was damp all over in spite of the efforts of his suit to keep him dry. His head rang with a headache induced by exhaustion and the heat.

The Udbahr males hidden among the rocks near the mouth of the pass began to sing their individual songs of defiance.

Kiev's breathing eased. His headache receded to a dull ache and finally disappeared. The last of the daylight was all but gone from the sky behind them. The nearer moon, twice as large as the single moon of Earth by which all moons were measured, was sharply outlined, bright in the sky, illuminating the scene with a sort of continuing twilight.

"What're you waiting for?" Willy's voice said dully in his earphones. "Why don't you go and kill them?"

He turned to look for her and was astonished to find her, with the grav-sled, almost beside him. She had sat down on the ground, her back bowed as if in deep discouragement, her face turned away and hidden from him within the transparent helmet.

"They'll come to us," he muttered without thinking.

Suddenly she curled up completely into a huddled ball of silver outerwear suit and crystalline helmet. The sheer, unutterable anguish of her pose squeezed at his throat.

He dropped down to his knees beside her and put his arms around her. She did not respond.

"You don't understand—" he said. And then he had the sense to tongue off the interphone and speak to her directly and privately through the closeness of their helmets, alone. "You don't understand."

"I do understand. You like to do this. You like it."

Her voice was muffled, dead.

His heart turned over at the sound of it and suddenly, unexpectedly, he realized that he had somehow managed to fall in love with her. He felt sick inside. It was all wrong—all messed up. He had meant to go looking for a woman—but eventually, after he'd made his stake and gone back to some civilized world. He had not planned anything like this involvement with a girl he had known only five days and who had all sorts of wild notions about how things should be. He did not know what to do except kneel there, holding her.

"If you don't like it why do you do it?" her voice said. "If you really don't like it—then don't do it. Now. Let these go."

"I can't," he said.

The singing broke off suddenly in a concerted howl from the Udbahr males, mingled with a triumphant cry over the intercom from Wadjik.

"Got one." And then: "Look out. Stones."

Kiev jerked into the shelter of a boulder, dragging Willy with him. Two rocks, each about half the size of his fist, dug up the ground where they had crouched together.

"You see?"

He pushed her roughly from him and drew his sidearm. Leaning around the boulder, he searched the rocks of the slope below the pass, watching the vernier needle of the heat-indicator slide back and forth on the weapon's barrel. It jumped suddenly and he stopped moving.

He peered into the gun's rear sights, thumbing the near lens to telescopic. He held his aim on the warm location, studying the small area framed in the sight screen. Suddenly he made it out—a tiny patch of brown between a larger boulder and a bit of upright, broken rock.

He aimed carefully.

"Don't do it."

He jerked involuntarily, sending his beam wide of the mark at the sound of her voice. A patch of bare gravel boomed and flew. The bit of brown color disappeared from between the rocks. He leaned the front of his helmet wearily against the near side of the boulder before him.

"Damn you," he said helplessly. "What are you doing to me?"

"I'm trying to save you," she said fiercely, "from being a murderer."

Another stone hit the top of the boulder behind which they hid and caromed off their heads.

"How about saving me from that?" he said emptily. "Don't you understand? If we don't kill them they'll try to kill us—"

"I don't believe it." She, too, had shut off her intercom. Her voice came to him distantly through two thicknesses of transparent material. "Have you ever tried? Has anyone ever tried?"

Another sudden volley of stones was followed by more dull explosions as the heat of the human weapons found and destroyed live targets. Shant and Wadjik were howling in triumph and shooting steadily.

"We got five—they're on the run." Shant whooped. "Kiev! Johnson! They're on the run."

The explosions ceased. Kiev peered cautiously around his boulder, stood up slowly. Wadjik, Shant, and Johnson had risen from positions in a semicircle facing the distant pass.

"Any get away?" Johnson was asking.

"One, maybe two—" Shant cut himself short. "Look out—duck. Twelve o'clock, fifty meters."

At once Kiev was again down behind his boulder. He dragged down Willy, tongued on his intercom.

"What is it?"

"That chunk of feldspar about a meter high—"

Kiev looked down the slope until his eyes found the rock. A glint that came and went behind and above it, winking in the waxing light of the nearer moon that now seemed as bright as a dull, cloudy day back on Earth. The flash came and went, came and went.

Kiev recognized it presently as a reflection from the top curve of a transparent helmet bobbing back and forth like the head of someone dancing just behind the boulder. A male Udbahr's voice began to sing behind the rock.

> *Man with a head-and-a-half,*
> *come and get your half-head.*
> *Man with a head-and-a-half*
> * Come so I can kill you.*
> * Ancient, my enemy.*
> * Ancient, my enemy—*

"Hehog," snapped Johnson's voice over the helmet intercom.

Silence held for a minute. Then Wadjik's voice came thinly through the phones.

"What are you waiting for, Kiev?"

Kiev said nothing. The transparent curve of the helmet top, rose again, bobbed and danced behind the boulder. It danced higher. Within it now was a bald, round, greenish skull with reddish, staring tarsier eyes and—finally revealed—the lipless gash of a fixedly grinning mouth.

"What is it? What's Wadjik mean?" Willy asked.

Her voice rang loud in Kiev's helmet phones. She had reactivated her intercom.

"It's Hehog down there," Kiev said between stiff jaws. "That's my helmet he's wearing. He's had it ever since he first took it off me my first trip into the mountains."

"Took it off you?"

"I was new. I'd never been on a drive before," muttered Kiev. "I got hit in the chest by a stone, had the wind knocked out of me. Next thing I knew Hehog was lifting off my helmet. My partners came up shooting and drove him off."

"What about it, Kiev?" The voice was Johnson's. "Do you want us to spread out and get behind him? Or you want to go down and get the helmet by yourself?"

Kiev grunted under his breath, took his sidearm into his left hand and flexed the cramped fingers of his right. They had been squeezing the gunbutt as if to mash it out of all recognizable shape.

"I'm going alone," he said over the intercom. "Stay back."

He got his heels under him and was ready to rise when he was unexpectedly yanked backward to the gravel. Willy had pulled him down.

"You're not going."

He tongued off his intercom, turned and jerked her hand loose from his suit.

"You don't understand," he shouted at her through his hel-

met. "That's the trouble with you. You don't understand a
damn thing."

He pushed her from him, rose and dived for the protection
of a boulder four meters down the slope in front of him and a
couple of meters to his right.

A flicker of movement came from below as he moved—the
upward leap of a throwing-stick behind the rock where Hehog
hid. Kiev glimpsed something dark racing through the air
toward him. A rock fragment struck and burst on the boulder-
face, spraying him with stone chips and splinters.

Reckless now, he threw himself toward the next bit of rocky
cover farther down the slope. His foot caught on a stony outcropping in the shale. He tripped and rolled, tumbling helplessly to a stop beside the very boulder behind which Hehog
crouched, throwing-stick in one hand, stone-tipped spear in
the other.

Kiev sprawled on his back. He stared helplessly up into the
great eyes and humorlessly grinning mouth looming over him
inside the other helmet less than an arm's length away. The
spear twitched in the brown hand—but that was all.

Hehog stared into Kiev's eyes. Kiev was aware of Willy and
the others shouting through his helmet phones. A couple of
shots blasted grooves into the boulder-top above his head. And
with a sudden, wordless cry Hehog bounded to his feet and
dodged away among the boulders toward the pass.

The bright beams of shots from the human guns followed
him but lost him. He vanished into the pass.

Kiev climbed to his feet, shaking inside. He awoke to the
fact that he was still holding his sidearm. A bitter understanding broke upon him with the hard, unsparing clarity of
an Udbahr Planet dawn.

He could have shot Hehog at pointblank range during the
moment he had spent staring frozenly at the spear in Hehog's
hand and at the great-eyed, grinning head within the helmet.

Hehog had to have seen the gun. And that would have been why he had not tried to throw the spear.

Kiev cursed blackly. He was still cursing when the others slid down the loose rock of the slope to surround him.

"What happened?" demanded Shant.

"He—" Kiev discovered that his intercom was still off. He tongued it on. "He got away."

"We know he got away," said Wadjik. "What we want to know is how come?"

"You saw," Kiev snapped. "I fell. He had me. You scared him off."

"He had you? I thought you had *him*, damn it!"

"All right, he's gone," Johnson said. "That's the main thing. Leave the other bodies for whoever wants to eat them. We've had a good drive. We'll split up, now." He looked at Wadjik and Shant. "See you back in civilization."

Wadjik cursed cheerfully.

"Team with the heaviest load buys the drinks," he said. "Come on, Shanny."

The two of them turned away, dragging their loaded gravsled through the air behind them.

Kiev, Willy and Johnson reached Dead City a good two hours before dawn. They had time to pick out one of the empty, windowless houses, half-cave, half-building, to use as permanent headquarters. Tomorrow night they would cut stone to fill the open doorway but for today the shelter, fitted double-thick into the opening, would do well enough.

No singing came from the surrounding cliffs. Johnson crawled in. Kiev lingered to speak to Willy.

"You don't have to worry." The words were not what he had planned to say. "The Udbahrs are scared of this place."

"I know." She did not look at him. "Of course. I know more about this city and the Udbahrs than even Mr. Johnson does. There's a taboo on this place for them."

"Yes." Kiev looked down at his gloved right hand and spread the fingers, still feeling the hard butt of his sidearm clamped inside them. "About earlier tonight, with Hehog—"

"It's all right," she said softly, looking unexpectedly up at him. Her intercom was off and her voice came to him through her helmet. In the combination of the low-angled moonlight and the first horizon glow of the dawn, her face seemed luminescent. "I know you did it for me—after all."

He stared at her.

"Did what?"

She still spoke softly: "I know why you let that Udbahr male live. It was because of what I'd said, wasn't it? But you need to be ashamed of nothing. You simply haven't gone bad inside, like the others. Don't worry—I won't tell anyone."

She took his arm gently with both hands and lifted her head as if—had they been unhelmeted—she might have kissed his cheek. Then she turned and disappeared into the cave.

He followed her after some moments. A small filter panel in the shelter had let a little of the terrible daylight through for illumination. Here artificial lighting had to be on. Kiev saw by it that she had piled stores and opened some of her own gear to set up a four-foot wall that gave her individual privacy.

He laid out his own thermal bag. The heat was quite bearable behind the insulation of the thick-walled building as the day began. Kiev fell into a deep, exhausted sleep that seemed completely dreamless.

He awoke without warning. Instantly alert, he rose to an elbow.

The light was turned down. He heard no sound from Willy. Johnson snored.

Kiev remained stiffly propped on one elbow. A feeling of danger prickled his skin. He found his ears were straining for some noise that did not belong here.

He listened.

For a long moment he heard only the snoring and beyond it silence. Then he heard what had awakened him. It came again, like the voice of some imprisoned spirit—not from beyond the wall but from under the stone floor on which he lay.

> *Man with a head-and-a-half,*
> *come and get your half-head.*
> *Man with a head-and-a-half,*
> *Come, so I can kill you.*
> *Ancient, my enemy.*
> *Ancient, my enemy*

The singing broke off suddenly. Kiev jerked bolt upright and the thermal bag fell down around his waist. Suddenly more loudly through the rock, and nearer, the voice echoed in the dim interior of the stone building:

> *Only for ourselves is the killing*
> *of each other!*
> *Man with a head-and-a-half,*
> *come and get your half-head.*
> *Man with a head-and-a-half . . .*

The singing continued. Fury uprushed like vomit in Kiev. He swore, tearing off his thermal bag and pawing through his piled outerwear. His fingers closed on the butt of the weapon. He jerked it clear, aimed it at the section of floor from which the singing was coming and pressed the trigger.

Light, heat and thunder shredded the sleeping quiet of the dimly lit room. Kiev held the beam steady, a hotter rage inside him than he could express with the rock-rending gun. He felt his arm seized. The sidearm was torn from his grip. He whirled to find Johnson holding the weapon out of reach.

"Give me that," Kiev said thickly.

"Wake up," Johnson said, low-voiced. "What's got into you?"

"Didn't you hear?" Kiev shouted at him. "That was Hehog
—Hehog! Down there!"

He pointed at the hole with its melted sides, half a meter
deep into the floor of the building.

"I heard," said Johnson. "It was Hehog, all right. There
must be tunnels under some of these buildings."

Willy chimed in.

"But Udbahrs don't—"

Kiev and Johnson turned to see her staring at them over
the top of her barricade. Kiev became suddenly conscious that,
like Johnson, he was completely without clothes.

Willy's face disappeared abruptly. Kiev turned back to look
at the hole his gun had burned in the stone. It showed no
breakthrough into further darkness at the bottom.

"All right," he said shakily. "I'm sorry. I woke up hearing
him and just jumped—that's all. We can shift to another
building tomorrow. And sound for tunnels before we move
in."

Johnson turned and returned to his thermal bag. Kiev re-
sumed his cocoon. He lay on his back, hands behind his
head, staring up at the shadowy ceiling.

. . . *Ancient, my enemy . . . ancient, my enemy . . .*

The memory of Hehog's chant continued to run through
his head.

You and me, Hehog. I'll show you, Udbahr . . .

After some time he fell asleep.

They moved camp the next night, as soon as the sun was
down. Kiev and Johnson quarried large chunks of rock from
the wall of an adjoining building, melted them into place to
fill up the new door opening, except for the entrance unit,
which was set up double as a heat lock and fitted into place.

Now the shelter air-conditioner could keep the whole interior of the new building comfortable all day long. The night
was half over by the time they finished.

Kiev and Johnson had some four hours left to trek to their

prospecting area. The gold ore deposits in the neighborhood of Dead City were almost always in pipes and easily worked out in a few days by men with the proper equipment.

Kiev hesitated.

"I'll stay," he said. "With Hehog around, someone's got to stay with Miss Fairchild."

Johnson regarded him thoughtfully.

"You're right. If we leave her here alone Hehog's sure to get her. And who would sell us gear for our next trip if word got out about how we left her to be killed?" He hesitated. "Tell you what—we'll draw straws."

Kiev said, "I'll stay. Drop back in a week. I'll tell you then if I need you to take over."

Johnson nodded. He turned away and began his packing—food, weapons, equipment, a water drill for tapping the moonflower root systems. Also, a breathing membrane for sealing the caves they would be denning up in by day. Kiev, squatting, making a final check of the seal around the entrance, saw a shadow fall across a seam he was examining.

He stood up, turned and saw Willy down the street, taking solidographs of one of the buildings. Johnson stood just behind him, equipment already on his backpack.

"We haven't had a chance to talk," Johnson said.

"No."

"Let me say now what I've wanted to say. Why don't you pack up and go back—and take the girl with you?"

"I've got my stake to make out here—like everybody else."

"You know there's more to the situation. Hehog's changed everything. Also, there's the girl—we both know what I mean. And there's something else—something I don't think you're aware of."

"What?"

"You've heard how sometimes the males—if they've just fed so they aren't hungry and there's only one of them around—will come into your camp and sit down to talk?"

Kiev frowned at him.

"I've heard of it," he said. "It's never happened to me."

"It's happened to me," said Johnson. "They ask you things that'd surprise you. Surprise you what they tell you, too. You know why Hehog's broken taboo and come right into Dead City?"

"Do you?"

Johnson nodded.

"There's a thing the Udbahrs believe in," Johnson said. "They figure that when they eat someone they eat his soul, too?"

"Sure," said Kiev. "And that soul stays inside them until they're killed. Then, when they die, if no one else eats them right away, all the souls of all the bodies they've eaten in their lives fly loose and take over the bodies of pups too young to have strong souls of their own."

Johnson nodded. He tilted his head at the distant figure of Willy.

"You've been learning from her," he said.

"Her? As a matter of fact, I have," said Kiev. "But you were the one told me about Udbahr cannibalism—a year or more ago."

"Did I?" Johnson looked at him. "Did I tell you about Ancient Enemies?"

Kiev shook his head.

"Once in a while a couple of males get a real feud going. It's not an ordinary hate. It's almost a noble thing—if you follow me. And from then on the feud never stops, no matter how many times they both die. Every time one is killed and born again—when he grows up it's his turn to kill the other one. The next time the roles are reversed. You follow me?"

Kiev frowned.

"No."

"Figure both souls live forever through any number of bodies. They take turns killing each other physically." Johnson looked strangely at Kiev. "The only thing is that no soul ever remembers from one body to the next—they never know whose turn it is to be killed and which one's to be the killer. So they just keep running into each other until the soul of one of them tells him, 'Go!' Then he kills the other and goes off to wait to die."

Johnson stopped speaking. Kiev stared.

"You mean Hehog thinks he and I—he thinks we're these Ancient Enemies?"

"Night before last," said Johnson, "you and he were face to face, both armed—and neither one of you killed the other. Yesterday—while we were denned up—he showed up here in the Dead City where it's taboo for him to be. Being Ancient Enemies is the only thing that'd set him free of a taboo like that. What do you think?"

Kiev turned for a second look down the street at Willy.

"Hehog's not going to leave you alone if I'm right," said Johnson. "And he's smart. He might even get away with killing one or two of us so he could stay close to you. And the easiest one for him to kill would be that girl. And it's true what I said. We lose a human woman out here and no supplier's going to touch us with a ten-foot pole."

"Yeah," said Kiev.

"I'm not afraid of Hehog, myself. But I've got no place else to go. I plan to die out here some day—but not yet for a few trips. Take the girl and head back. Give up the mountains while you still can. Kiev—I mean it."

"You can't make us leave," Kiev said slowly.

"No," said Johnson. His face looked old and dark as weather-stained oak. "But you keep that girl here and Hehog'll get her. She doesn't know anything but books and she doesn't understand someone like Hehog. She doesn't even understand us." He took a step back. "So long, partner," he said. "See you in three nights—maybe."

He turned and walked away slowly, leaning forward against the weight of the pack, until he was lost among the rocks of the western cliffs.

Kiev turned and saw the small shape of Willy even farther down the street, still taking pictures.

He continued to think for the next two days and nights, which were quiet. He spent most of his time studying the aerial maps of areas near Dead City he had planned to work during this trip. Actually he was getting his ideas in order for explanation to Willy, who seemed to be having the time of her life. She was measuring and photographing Dead City inch by inch, as excited over it as if it were one large Christmas present. She had changed toward him, too, teasing him and doing for him, by turns.

Hehog did not sing from underground in the new building.

On the third night Kiev invited himself along on her work with the City.

He realized now that what Johnson had told him was true. Johnson's words had been the final shove he had needed to make up his mind. The fact that he and Willy had met less than a week ago meant nothing. Out here things were different.

He had worried about how he would bring up the subject of his future—and hers. But it turned out that he had no need to bring it up. It was already there. Almost before he knew it they were talking as if certain things were understood and taken for granted.

He said, "I've got at least five more trips to make to get the stake I need for a move back to the Old Worlds. You'd have to wait."

"But you don't need to keep coming back here," she said. "I know how you can make the rest of the money you need without even one more trip. I know because a publishing company talked to me about doing something like it. There's a steady market for information about humanoids like the Udbahrs. Books, lectures. Acting as industrial and economic consultant—"

He stared at her.

"I couldn't do anything like that," he said. "I'm no good with words and theories—"

"You don't have to be. All you have to do is tell what you've seen and done on these trips of yours. You'll collect enough on advance bookings alone for us to go back to any Old World you want—after I get my doctorate, of course—and settle down there. Don't forget I've got my work, too. I'll be teaching." She stared at him eagerly. "And think of what you'll be achieving. Intelligent natives are being killed off or exploited on new worlds like this one simply because there's no local concern over them and because our civilization hasn't understood them enough to make the necessary concessions for them to accept it. You could be the one to get the ball rolling that could save the Udbahrs from being hunted down and killed off—"

"By people like me, you mean," he said, a little sourly.

"Not you. You haven't yet been infected with the sort of killing lust Wadjik and Shant—and even Johnson—have."

"It isn't a lust. Out here you have to kill the Udbahrs to keep them from killing you."

She looked at him sharply.

"Yes—if you're a savage," she said. "As the Udbahrs are savages. I couldn't love an Udbahr. I could only love a man who was civilized—able to keep the savage part inside him chained up. That Ancient Enemy business Hehog sang at you—that's the way a savage thinks. I don't expect you not to have the psychological capacity to lust for killing—but if you're a healthy-minded man you can keep that sort of Ancient Enemy locked up inside you. You don't have to let him take you over."

He opened his mouth to make one more stubborn effort to explain himself to her, then closed it again rather helplessly. He found a certain uncomfortable rightness in part of what she was saying. Although from that rightness she went off into left field somewhere to an area where he was sure she was wrong. While he groped for words to express himself the still air around him was suddenly torn by the sound of a gun-bolt explosion.

He found himself running toward the building they had set up as their headquarters, sidearm in his hand, the sound of Willy's voice and footsteps following him. The distance was not great and he did not slow down for her. Better if he made it first—or if she did not come at all until he knew what had happened.

He rounded the corner of the building and saw the shelter entrance hanging in blackened tatters. He dove past it. By some miracle the light was still burning against the ceiling but the interior it illuminated was a scene of wreckage. Concussion and heat from the bolt had torn apart or scorched everything in the place.

With a wild coldness inside him, he pawed swiftly through the rubble for whatever was usable. Two thermal sleeping bags were still in working condition, though their outer covering was charred in spots and stinking of burned plastic. Food containers were ripped open and their contents destroyed. The water drill was workable and most of one air membrane was untouched.

"What happened? Who did it? Kiev—"

He awoke to the fact that Willy was with him again, literally pulling at him to get his attention. He came erect wearily.

"I don't know," he said, dully. "Maybe some prospector has gone out of his head entirely. Or—"

He hesitated.

"Or what?"

He looked at her.

"Or an Udbahr male has gotten hold of the gun of a dead prospector."

Her face thinned and whitened under the light of the overhead lamp.

"A dead—"

She did not finish.

"That's right," he said. "One of our people, it could be—Wadjik, Shant or Johnson."

"How could a savage who knows only sticks and stones kill an experienced, armed man?"

Willy sounded outraged.

"All sorts of animals kill people." He felt sick inside, hating himself for not having set up at least a trigger wire to guard the building area. "We've got to get out of here. We can't spend another night in a building, anyway, without a shelter entrance."

"Where'll we go?"

"We'll head toward Johnson," Kiev said. "He isn't digging so far away that we shouldn't be able to make it before dawn —if he isn't dead."

They started out on the bearing Johnson had taken and soon left the city behind them. Fully risen moonflowers—some of them giants over three meters high—surrounded them. They were lost in a forest of strange, pale beauty, where by day there would only be the bare, heat-blasted mountainside.

"Aren't we likely to pass him and not even see him?" asked Willy.

"No," Kiev said absently. "He'll be following contours at a constant elevation. So are we. When he gets close enough, we'll hear static in our earphones."

He did not again mention the possibility of Johnson's being dead—partly because he wanted to be easy on himself.

They tramped on in silence. Kiev's mind was busy among the number of problems opened up by their present situation. After about an hour he heard the hiss of interference in his helmet phones that signaled the approach of another transmitting unit.

He stopped so suddenly that Willy bumped into him. He rotated his helmet slowly, listening for the maximum noise. When he found it, he spoke.

"Johnson? Johnson, can you hear me?"

"Thought it was you, Kiev." Johnson's voice came distorted and weakened by rocky distance. "The girl with you? What's up?"

"Somebody fired a gun into our building," said Kiev. "I scraped together a sort of maintenance kit out of what was left—but I'm carrying all the salvage."

"I see." Johnson did not waste breath on speculation. "Stop where you are and wait for me. We better head back toward Wad's and Shanny's diggings as soon as we're together. No point your burning energy trying to meet me halfway."

"Right."

Kiev loosened his pack and sat down with his back to the trunk of a moonflower. Willy sat beside him. She said nothing and, busy with his own thoughts still, he hardly noticed her silence.

By the time Johnson found them Kiev had already worked out the new compass heading from their present location to the diggings where Wadjik and Shant had planned to work. A little over three hours of the night remained.

"Do you think we can make it before dawn?" Kiev asked as the three of them started out on the new heading. "You've been through that area before, haven't you?"

Johnson nodded.

"I don't know," he said. "It'll be faster going once the moonflowers are down." He looked at Willy. "We'll be pushing on as fast as we can. Think you can keep up?"

"Yes," she said without looking at him. Her voice was dull.

"Good. If you start really to give out, though, speak up. Don't overdo it to the point where we have to carry you. All right?"

"Yes."

They continued their march. Soon the moonflowers had drawn in their petals until they were hardly visible under the hoods and begun their retreat into the ground. The men were now able to see, across the tops of the hoods, the general shape of the terrain and pick the most direct route from contour point to contour point. Willy walked between them. The moonflower hoods still stood above her head—tall as she was for a woman—but did not seem to bother her. She looked at nothing.

Johnson glanced at Kiev across the top of her helmet, and tongued off his helmet phones. He let her walk slightly ahead, then leaned toward Kiev until their helmets touched.

"I told you," Johnson said softly through the helmet contact. "She didn't understand or believe. We were something out of books to her—so were the Udbahrs. Now she's trying hard to keep on not believing. You see why I told you yesterday to get her out of here?"

Kiev said nothing.

Johnson pulled back his helmet, tongued his intercom back on, kept walking.

After a while the sky began to whiten ominously. The nearer moon was low and paling on the horizon behind. Johnson halted. Kiev and Willy also stopped.

"It's no good," said Johnson, over the intercom to Kiev. "We're going to have to take time to find a hole to crawl into before day. We're going to have to quit now and wait for night."

Kiev nodded.

"A hole?" echoed Willy.

Kiev looked at Johnson. Johnson shrugged. The message of the shrug was clear—there were no caves in this area. But they hunted until Johnson called a halt.

"This will have to do."

He pointed to a crack in a rock face. He and Kiev attacked the crack with mining tools and their guns.

Twenty minutes' work hollowed out a burrow three meters in circular diameter, with an entrance two feet square. Above the entrance the crack had been sealed with melted rock. The trio crawled inside and fitted the breathing membrane in place against the opening.

Kiev waited until all were undressed and in their thermal bags before setting the light he had saved from the building in place against the rocky ceiling. The cramped closeness of their enclosure came to solid life around them. The den was beginning to heat up.

The place had no air-conditioning unit—the shelter had been a palace by comparison. Even Kiev had to struggle against the intoxicating effect of the heat and the claustrophobic panic of the enclosed space. Willy went out of her head before noon. Kiev and Johnson had to hold her in her thermal bag. Shortly after that she went into snycope and stayed unconscious until cool-off.

Haggard with exhaustion, Kiev leaned on one elbow above her, staring down into her face, now smoothed out into natural sleep. Teetering on the verge of irresistible unconsciousness himself, he felt in him the strange clearheadedness of utter weariness. She had been right, he thought, about that primitive part in him and all men—the Ancient Enemy. The prospectors did not so much fight the Udbahr males out here as something in themselves that corresponded to its equivalent in the Udbahrs. The lust for killing. A lust that could get you to the point where you no longer cared if you were killed yourself.

Kiev never finished the thought. When he opened his eyes the membrane was down from the entrance and outside was the cool and blessed moonlight.

He crawled out to find Willy and Johnson already packing gear.

"Got to move, Kiev," said Johnson, seeing him. "If Wad and Shanny are alive and headed home we want to take out after them as soon as possible. One long night's walk can put us back at the hotel."

"The hell you say." Kiev was astonished. "They didn't come all the way out with us and then cut that far back to find a digging area."

"No," Johnson said, "but from here we can hit a different

pass through the border range. Going back that way makes the hypotenuse of a right triangle. Coming out we would have dog-legged it to reach this point like doing the triangle's other two sides. You understand?"

Within half an hour they were on their way. And within an hour, as they were coming around a high spire of rock, Johnson put out his arm and stopped.

"Wait here, Willy," Johnson said. "Come on, Kiev."

The two men rounded the rock and stopped, staring down into a small open area. They saw the scattered remains of working equipment and of Wadjik and Shant. At least one day under the open sun had mummified their bodies. Wadjik lay on his back with the broken shaft of a spear through his chest. But Shant had been pegged out and left to die.

Their outerwear and guns were gone.

"I thought I saw sign of at least half a dozen males back there," Johnson said. "Hehog, all right—with help. He must be swinging some real clout with the other males to have kept them from eating these two right away." He glanced hard at Kiev. "And all for you."

Kiev stared.

"Me? You mean Hehog tied Shanny up and left him like that on purpose—just so I could come along and see it?"

"You begin to see what Ancient Enemy means?" he responded. "We're in trouble, Kiev. Two guns missing and one of the local males grown into a real hoodoo. We'll get moving for civilization right now."

"You're going to bury them first," Willy said.

The men swung around. She was standing just behind them, looking at them. Her gaze dropped, fixed on the bodies below. For a second Kiev thought that the sight had sent her completely out of her mind. Then he saw that her eyes were clear and sane.

Johnson said, "We haven't time—and, anyway, the Udbahrs would come back to dig them up again when they were hungry enough."

"He's right, Willy," said Kiev. "We've got to go—fast." He

thought of something else and swung back to Johnson. "That pass you talked about—they'll be laying for us there, Hehog and the other males he's got together. It's the straightest route home, you say, and they know prospectors always head straight out of the mountains when they get into trouble."

Johnson shook his head.

"Don't think so," he said. "You're his Ancient Enemy, looking for that one spot where you and he come face to face and one of you gets the word to kill the other. He'll be right around this area, waiting for us to start hunting for him. If we move fast we've got as good a chance as anyone ever had to get out of these mountains alive."

Johnson set a hard pace. Several times—before the nearer moon was high in the sky and the moonflowers were stretching to full bloom—Willy tripped and would have gone down if Kiev had not caught her. But she did not complain. In fact, she said nothing at all. Shortly after midnight, they broke out from under the umbrellas of a clump of moonflower petals and found themselves in the pass Johnson had talked about.

"We made it," said Johnson, stopping. Kiev also stopped. Willy, stumbling with weariness, blundered into him. She clung to him like a child—and at that moment a thin, bright beam came from among the trunks of the moonflowers behind them.

The side of Johnson's outerwear burst in dazzle and smoke.

Johnson lunged forward. Kiev and Willy ran behind him. Three more bright beams flickered around them as they lurched over the lip of the pass, took half a dozen long, staggering, tripping strides down the far side and dived to shelter behind some waist-high chunks of granite.

Male Udbahr voices began to sing on the far side of the pass.

Johnson coughed. Kiev looked at him and Johnson quickly turned his helmet away, so that the face plate was hidden.

"Move out," Johnson said, in a thick voice, like that of a man with a frog in his throat.

"Are you crazy?"

Kiev had his sidearm out. He sighted around the granite boulder before him and sent a beam high into the rock wall beyond the lip of the pass, on the other side. The rock boomed loudly and flew in fragments. The singing stopped. After a moment it started again.

"I can't help you now," Johnson said, still keeping his face turned away. "Move out, I tell you."

"You think I'm going to leave you?"

Kiev sent off another bolt into the rock face beyond the lip of the pass. This time the singing hardly paused.

"Don't waste your charges," Johnson said hoarsely. "Get out. An hour puts you—hotel."

He had to stop in mid-sentence to cough.

"Forget it, partner," said Kiev. "With my gun and yours I can hold that pass until morning. They can't come through."

Johnson gave an ugly laugh.

"What partner?" he asked. "This partnership's dissolved. And what'll you do when dawn comes? Cook? You're still a good hour's trek from the hotel."

Kiev became aware that Willy was tugging at his arm. She motioned with her head for him to follow her. He did. She slid back down among the rocks until they were a good four meters from where Johnson lay, head toward the pass.

Willy tongued off her intercom and touched her helmet to his.

"He's dying," she said to him through the helmets.

"All right."

Kiev stared at her as if she were Hehog himself.

"You couldn't get him to the hotel in time to save his life even if there weren't any Udbahrs behind us. And we'll never make the hotel unless he stays there and keeps them from following us."

"So?"

She took hold of his shoulders and tried to shake him but he was too heavy and too unmoving with purpose.

"Be sensible." She was almost crying. "Don't you see it's something he wants to do? He wants to save us—"

Kiev stared at her stonily.

"Shanny's dead," Kiev said. "Wad's dead. You want me to leave Johnson?"

She did begin to cry at that, the tears running down her pale face inside her helmet.

"All right, hate me," she said. "Why shouldn't I want to live? This is all your fault—not mine. I didn't kill your partners. I didn't make Hehog your special enemy. All I did was love you. If you were back there I wouldn't leave you, either. But that wouldn't make my staying sensible."

"Go on if you want," he said coldly.

"You know I can't find the hotel by myself!" she said. "You know I'm not going to leave you. Maybe you've got a right to kill yourself—maybe you've even got a right to kill me. But have you got the right to kill me for something that's got nothing to do with me?"

He closed his eyes against the sight of her face. After seconds he opened his eyes, looked away from her, and began to crawl back up the slope until he once more lay beside Johnson.

"It's Willy," he said, not looking at the other man.

"Sure. That's right," said Johnson hoarsely.

A flicker of dark movement came from one side of the pass and his gun spat. The pass was clear of pursuers again.

"Damn you both," Kiev said, emptily.

"Sure, boy," said Johnson. "Don't waste time, huh?"

Kiev lay where he was. The nearer moon was descending in the sky a little above and to the right of the pass.

"I'll leave my gun," Kiev said at last.

"Don't need it," Johnson said.

Kiev reached out and took Johnson's gloved hand in his own. Through the fabric the return pressure of the other man's grip was light and feeble.

"Get out," said Johnson. "I told you I figured on ending out here."

"You told me not for some trips yet."

"Changed my mind." Johnson let go of Kiev's hand and closed his eyes. His voice was not much more than a whisper. "I think instead I'll make it this trip."

He did not say any more. After a long minute Kiev spoke to him again.

"Johnson—"

Johnson did not answer. Only the gun in his hand spat light briefly into the wall of the pass. Kiev stared a second longer, then turned and went sliding down the hill to where Willy crouched.

"We go fast," said Kiev.

They went away without looking back. Twice they heard the sound of a gun behind them. Then intervening rocks cut off whatever else they might have heard. They walked without pausing. After about an hour Willy began to stumble with exhaustion and clung to him. Kiev put his arm around her; they hobbled along together, leaning into the pitch of the upslopes, sliding in the loose rock of downslopes.

The moon was low on the stony horizon behind them. Ahead came the first whitening in the sky that said dawn was less than two hours away. Willy staggered and leaned more heavily upon Kiev. Looking down at her face through the double transparencies of both helmets, Kiev saw that she was stumbling along with her eyes tightly closed, her face hardened into a colorless mask of effort. A strand of hair had fallen forward over one closed eye and his heart lurched at the sight of it.

Not from the first had he ever thought of her as beautiful.

Now, gaunt with effort, hair disarrayed, she was less so than
ever—and yet he had never loved and wanted her more. It
was because of the mountains, he though. And Hehog, Wad,
Shanny—and Johnson. Each time he had paid out one of
them for her, the worth of her had gone up that much. Now
she was equal to the total of all of them together.

She stumbled again, almost lost her footing. A wordless
little sound was jolted out from between her clenched teeth,
though her eyes stayed closed.

"Walk," he said savagely, jerking her upright and onward.
"Keep walking." They were on the Track, now, the curving
trail that all the prospectors took out of the valley of the
Border Hotel. "Keep walking," he muttered to her. "Just
around the curve there—"

A bolt from a gun behind them boomed suddenly against
the cliff-base to their right. Rock chips rained down Willy's
knees. She lurched toward the shelter of the nearest boulder.

He jerked her upright.

"Run for it. Run—"

Jolting, stumbling, they ran while bolts from the gun
boomed.

"They can't shoot worth—" Kiev muttered through his
teeth.

He stopped talking. Because at that moment they rounded
a curve and saw the sprawling concrete shape of the Border
Hotel and its grounds—and saw Hehog, holding a sidearm,
stepping out from behind a rock twenty feet ahead.

In that instant time itself seemed to hesitate. Kiev's weary
legs had checked at his sight of Hehog. He started forward
again at a walk, half-carrying Willy. Her eyes were still
closed.

He thought, *She doesn't see Hehog.*

He marched on. Hehog brought up the gun, aimed it—but
he, too, seemed caught in the suspension of time. He wore
the helmet he had taken from Kiev two years before and now
he also wore the white jacket of Shant's outerwear suit—which

almost fit him. He stood waiting, one sidearm in a jacket pocket, one in his hand, aimed.

Kiev stumped toward him, bringing Willy. Kiev's eyes were on the bulging eyes of Hehog. Their gazes locked. The only sound was the noise of Kiev's boots scuffing the rock underfoot. From the hotel in the valley below, no sound. From the other Udbahr males that had been firing at them from behind, no sound.

Kiev marched on, Hehog growing before him. The great eyes danced in Kiev's vision. There was a wild emptiness in Kiev now, an insane certainty. He did not move aside to avoid Hehog. They were ten feet apart—they were five— they would collide—

Hehog stepped back. Without shifting the line of his advance an inch, without moving his eyes to follow Hehog, Kiev marched past him. The trail to the hotel sloped suddenly more sharply under Kiev's feet and now he looked only at what was manmade. All the Udbahrs were behind him. And behind him he heard Hehog beginning to sing softly.

> *Man with a head-and-a-half,*
> *come and get your half-head.*
> *Man with a head-and-half,*
> *Come, so I can kill you . . .*

The song faded behind him until his stumbling feet carried him in through the great airdoor of the hotel and all things ended at once.

He was nearly four days recovering and three days after that sitting around the Border Hotel, making plans for the future with Willy. They had adjoining rooms, each with a balcony looking out to the dawnrise side of the hotel. Heavy filterglass doors shut out the sunlight and protected the rooms' air-conditioned interiors during the daytime. Kiev had agreed to go back to the Old Worlds with Willy, to get married and write and tell what he knew. There was nothing wrong with making a living any way you could back on the Old Worlds, even if it meant writing and lecturing. Only once did Willy bring up the subject of the mountains.

"Why did Hehog let us pass?" she asked.

He stared at her.

"I thought that your eyes were closed."

"I opened them when you halted. I closed them when I saw him. I thought it was all over then—and that he was going to kill us both. But you started walking and he let us pass. Why?"

Kiev looked down at the thick brown carpet.

"Hehog's never going to get the message," he said to the carpet.

"What?"

"Ancient Enemies—Johnson told me. Hehog thinks he and I are something special to each other with this Ancient Enemies business. We're doomed to have one of us kill the other. We're supposed to keep coming together until one of us gets the message to kill. Then the other just lets it happen. Because he's doomed—there's nothing he can do about it."

He stopped talking. For a minute she said nothing, either, as if she was waiting for him to go on explaining.

"Hehog didn't get the message when we walked past him?" she asked, at last. "Is that it?"

"He'll never get the message," said Kiev dully. "He had two clear chances at me and he didn't do anything. It means he thinks he's the one who's doomed. He's waiting to die—for me to kill him."

"To kill him? Why would he want you to kill him?"

Kiev shrugged.

"Answer me."

"How do I know?" Kiev said exhaustedly. "Maybe he's getting old. Maybe he thinks its just time for him to die—maybe his mate's dead."

There was momentary, somehow ugly silence. Then Willy spoke again.

"Kiev."

"What?"

"Look up here," she said, sharply. "I want you to look at me."

He raised his gaze slowly from the thick carpet and saw her face as stiffly fixed as it had been in the helmet on the last long kilometer to the hotel.

"Listen to me, Kiev," she said. "I love you and I want to live with you more than anything else for the rest of my life—and I'll do anything for you I can do. But there's one thing I can't do. I just can't."

He frowned at her, uneasy and restless.

"I can't help it," she said. "I thought we were getting away from it here and that it wouldn't matter. But it does. If I can feel it there in you I go dead inside—I just can't love you any more. That's all there is to it."

"What?" he asked.

Her hands made themselves into ineffective small fists in her lap, then uncurled and lay limp.

"There are so many things I love about you," she said emptily, "I thought I could ignore this one thing. But I can't think so any more. Not since we saw those two dead men—and not since the walk back here. Our love is just never going to work if you still want—want to kill. Do you understand? If you're still wanting to kill it just won't work out for us. Do you understand, Kiev?"

The bottom seemed to fall out of his stomach. He was abruptly sick.

"I told you that's all over!" he shouted furiously at her. "I don't want to kill anything!"

"You don't have to promise." She rose to her feet, her face still tight. "It doesn't matter if you promise. It only matters if you're telling the truth."

She turned and walked to the door of his hotel room.

"It's almost dawn," she said. "I'm going down to see if the authorization for our spaceship tickets has come through for today's flight—before the sun shuts off communications. I'll be back in half an hour."

She went out. The door made no noise closing behind her.

He turned and flopped on the bed, stared up at the ceiling. Everything was wonderful—or was it? He tried to think about the future in safety of the Old Worlds but his mind would not focus. After a bit he rose and walked out to the balcony.

Before him stood the ramparts of the cliffs. On the balcony was an observation scope. He bent over it and fiddled with its controls until the boulders a kilometer away seemed to hang a dozen meters in front of him.

He turned the sound pick-up on.

It was nearly time for the Udbahrs to be hunting their dens for the day but he heard no singing. He panned the scope, searching the rocks. There it came—a faint wisp of melody.

He searched the rock. The stone blurred before him. He lost then found the song again and closed in on it until the image in the screen of the scope locked on the figure of a male Udbahr standing deep between two tall boulders—an Udbahr wearing a transparent helmet and white jacket, with a sidearm in his hand.

The song came suddenly loud and clear.

> *Ancient, my enemy. Ancient,*
>   *my enemy.*
> *No one but ourselves has the*
>   *killing of each other . . .*
> *Man with a head-and-a-half,*
> *come and get your half-head.*
> *Man with a head-and-a-half*

Kiev stepped back from the scope. His head pounded suddenly. His stomach knotted. His throat ached. A fever blazed through him and his skin felt dry, dusty. He turned and strode across the room to his bag. He plowed through it, throwing new shoes, pants and shirts aside.

His hand closed on the last hard item at the bottom. His gun. He jerked out the weapon, snatched up the long barrel for distance shooting and was snapping it into position on the gun even as he was striding toward the balcony.

He applied the magnetic clamp of the gunbutt to the scope and thumbed up the near lens of the telescope sight. The red cross-hairs wavered, searched, found Hehog. It was a long shot. The lenses of the sight held level on the Udbahr in a straight line; but below them, on their gimbals, the barrel of the automatically sighting weapon was angled so that it seemed to point clear over the cliffs at the day that was coming. Kiev's dry and shaking fingers curled around the butt. His forefinger reached toward the firing button and instantly all the shaking was over.

His grip was steady. His blood was ice but the fever still burned in his brain. As clearly as a vision before him, he saw the mummified figures of Wadjik and Shant—and Johnson as he had last seen the older man.

Kiev pressed the firing button.

From the cliffside came the sound of a distant explosion. A puff of rockdust plumed toward the whitening sky. A rising murmur, a mounting buzz of voices began beyond the walls of his room. People began to appear on the surrounding balconies.

Kiev faded back two steps, silent as a thief. Hidden in the shadows of the balcony he could still see what the others could not.

Hehog lay beside one of the two boulders between which he had been standing. A blackish stain was spreading on the right side of his white jacket and the sidearm had fallen from his grip.

He was plainly dying. But he was not yet dead. He began
to sing again.

> Man with a head-and-a-half
> . . . . come and get your . . .
> half-head.
> Man with a head-and-a. . . .

Through the pick-up of the scope Kiev, frozen in the
shadows, could hear the Udbahr's voice weakening. Then the
door to the room slammed open behind him.

"Kiev, did you hear it? Someone shot from the Hotel—"
Willy's voice broke off.

He turned and saw her just inside the door. She was gazing
past him at the scope with its picture of Hehog and the sound
of Hehog's weakening song coming from it. She stared at it.
Then, slowly, as if she was being forced against her will, her
eyes shifted until they met his.

All the feeling in him that the sight of Hehog had triggered
into life went out of him with a rush, leaving him empty as a
disemboweled man.

"Willy—"

He took a step toward her. Her face twitched as if with a
sudden, sharp, unbearable pain and her hand came up re-
flexively as if to push him away, though they were still more
than half a room apart.

Her throat worked but she made no sound. She struggled
for an instant, then shook her head briefly. Still holding up
her hand as if to fend him off, she backed away from him. The
door opened behind her and let her out.

The door closed, leaving him alone. He swung slowly back
to face the scope. Hehog still lay framed in the lens and above
that image the ominous light of day was fast whitening the
sky.

Hehog was still feebly singing; but the song had changed.
Now it was the song Willy had asked Kiev to translate when
she had first heard an Udbahr male. Kiev turned and flung

himself facedown on the bed, his arms over his head to shut out the sound. But the song came through to him.

You desert me now, female,
Because I am crippled.
And yet, all my fault was
That I did not lack courage.
Therefore I will go now to the
high rocks to die.
And another will take you . . .

The slow rumble of the heavy, opaque, thermal glass, sliding automatically across the entrance to the balcony, silenced the song in Kiev's ears. Beyond the dark glass the sun of day broke at last over the rim of the cliffs and sent its fierce light slanting down. There was no mercy in that relentless light and all living things who did not hide before it died. •

The Odd Ones

The Lut and the Snorap were witnessing something new . . .

Said the Snorap, sitting down with a thump, "This I do not understand."

"They are young," replied the Lut, settling on his haunches beside the Snorap. "Young and stupid."

"I agree they are young," said the Snorap. "I am not yet convinced they are stupid. But how can they expect to persist?"

They were of different races these two; but equally old and experienced in the ways of the universe. Both had evolved to cope with the varying conditions to be found in space and on many different worlds, and though the end product of each race's evolution had resulted in some difference, in essence they were similar. Neither of them, for example, required an atmosphere; and they could fuel their bodies with almost any chemical compound which would give off energy in the process of being broken down into its component parts. At a pinch, they could even get by on solar radiation, though this was an unsatisfying form of diet. Fleshed and muscled to meet truly fantastic gravities, pressures, and temperature extremes, they were at home just about anywhere.

These were the common points. In appearance each race had settled on a form of its own. The Snorap strongly resembled a very fat and sleepy lizard about ten feet in length—a sort of unterrifying, overstuffed dragon of the kind who would prefer a pleasant nap in a soft chair to eating maidens, any day in the week. His hide was heavy and dark and ridged like armor-plating.

The Lut, on the other hand, was built more on the model of an Earthly tiger, except that he was longer—being fully as long as the Snorap—and thicker, with an almost perfectly round body, rather like a big sewer main. He was tailless, his head was big and flat of face, and he possessed an enormous jaw which could crunch boulders like hard candy. His eyes had a fierce green glint to them and he was covered with very fine, but incredibly tough, small glassy scales which would have permitted him to take an acid shower every morning and never notice it at all. But in spite of his appearance, he was just as civilized, just as intelligent, and just as much a gentleman as the Snorap; which put them both, as a matter of fact, several notches above the two humans they were watching, in all those respects.

The two aliens were philosophical engineers, an occupation it is hard to explain in human terms. It might be attempted by saying that every living being, no matter how far down the intelligence scale it may be, has a sort of inherent philosophy of survival. When the philosophies of all life forms on one world balance nicely, there is no problem. When they fall out of balance with one another, the philosophical engineer moves in, hoping to correct the situation and incidentally, gain new knowledge.

These two, the Snorap and the Lut, had discovered this world they were on to be a new one, not heretofore checked, and they had just spent the last eighty years or so in going over it. Their own ship—which was more of a space-sled than a ship, being completely open, except for an energy shield for meteor protection—was clear on the other side of the planet, they having wandered away from it completely in the past half-century of philosophy-testing. Now they had just stumbled on a pair of human immigrants. These soft little bipeds were a new experience to the Snorap and the Lut, neither of their races having encountered the type before; and they sat in the obscurity of the vegetation that hemmed the little clearing where the human ship had landed, conversing in something that was not verbal speech, sign language, nor telepathy, but a mixture of all three—and they marveled.

"I do not understand it," repeated the Snorap. "I literally fail to comprehend. They will most certainly perish."

"Undoubtedly," replied the Lut, blinking his green eyes. "They believe in their machines, I think." He indicated the domed metal hut and the low hydroponics tank-building, like the top half of a loaf of bread cut off and set close to the ground, and the small ship beyond, from which the two human figures were laboring to extract the motors for their power plant. The planet was at the hot end of its summer and the temperature was above a hundred and forty degrees fahrenheit, a fact the Snorap and the Lut did not even notice. The humans sweated in conditioned clothing and face masks.

"I give them four months," said the Lut, snapping his heavy jaws closed.

"I'm afraid so," said the Snorap. "Their home world must be badly out of balance if they take the easy way of machines instead of trying to adapt. There can be no endurance, no philosophical strength in such creatures. Their original planet must be very badly off. I wonder where it is?"

"When the machines break down, they will have to leave," said the Lut. "We will follow."

And with entirely inhuman patience, the two settled themselves in the shadow and shelter of the vegetation to wait.

"What are they doing now?" asked the Lut.

He had been napping for the past two weeks; leaving the Snorap to observe. The Snorap, who slept only during the process of regrowing a lost limb, was quite obviously fascinated.

"They've been getting ready for winter," he answered.

"Oh, winter," said the Lut, getting up and stretching himself like the big cat he somewhat resembled. "That's right."

The planet they were on did not tilt on its axis, but had an orbit that carried it quite well out from its sun during the shorter part of the year. The result was a brief, but very severe winter. The temperature had, in fact, fallen a good hundred degrees since they had first sighted the human clearing; but neither the Snorap nor the Lut paid any attention to this, a difference so minor hardly registered on their senses.

Under a heavy, gray sky, the humans were working feverishly to bank up the living dome, the hydroponics tank-building and the ship. They had set up the ship's motors in a little structure off to one side, with a thick pipe-like affair running from it to the dome and off to the hydroponics building. The Lut cocked his eye at the banks of earth.

"Why?" he asked.

"Insulation, I would imagine," replied the Snorap.

"It won't work," said the Lut. "The blizzards will blow it away."

"Not if it freezes first," said the Snorap. "They are ingenious."

"Now I suppose they'll go inside and hole up until the warmth comes," said the Lut. "An underground sort of existence." He looked across the chill earth to where the two humans were laboring with hand shovels to pile the crumbly brown soil of the planet against the side of the motor building. "How do you tell them apart?"

"They are almost identical, aren't they?" said the Snorap. "However, if you take the trouble to figure it out, you'll notice one has a slightly greater mass than the other. I call them the Greater Biped Colonist and the Lesser Biped Colonist. Great and Less for short. That's Great going around the corner of the motor building right now. And Less is still digging."

"I wonder why there are two of them?" said the Lut thoughtfully.

"There are two of us," said the Snorap.

"Of course," said the Lut, "but there's reason for that. We're different life forms. Our senses and abilities complement each other. But these two are exact duplicates. Doesn't make sense."

"Nonsense," retorted the Snorap. "There could be all sorts of possible explanations. For instance one might be a spare."

"A spare?"

"What's so fantastic about that?" said the Snorap. "Consider how fragile they are; and how far they are, undoubtedly, from their home world."

"All the same," said the Lut, snapping his big jaws shut, "I cannot agree with such a hypothesis. It is immoral in the extreme."

"I merely offered it as one possible explanation of why there were two of them," replied the Snorap, glancing at his friend and companion. "While you've been napping I've devoted a lot of time to close observation of them. Do you know what I deduce?"

"Don't ask rhetorical questions," grumbled the Lut.

"They haven't been civilized for more than eight or ten thousand years."

"What? Ridiculous!" snorted the Lut. "Obviously they're young; but eight to ten thousand is utterly fantastic."

"Not when you stop to consider this philosophical imbalance that has driven them to the production of machines for any and every possible use. That in itself is the worst possible danger signal. Undoubtedly it has sapped all of their moral fiber."

"I might point out," said the Lut, "that, to migrate to a world like this when you are like that, takes a certain amount of moral fiber."

"Ah, but there we come to another question," persisted the Snorap, interlocking the big, blunt claws of his forepaws together like a pedantic old man. "What reason can they have for coming here? They show no intellectual interest in the planet. Their senses are obviously very limited. They seem to have no purpose in being here other than to exist."

"Under great difficulties," said the Lut.

"Granted," answered the Snorap, "under great difficulties. Which merely confirms my belief in their unbalance."

The Lut was by nature a contrary creature; and in addition he was always snappish after a nap.

"And I," he retorted, "prefer to assume that there may be some good reason which you and I are too dull-witted to understand."

"My dear fellow—" protested the Snorap, aghast.

"Why not?" The Lut sat down rather complacently. "Simply because you and I know and understand the philosophies of some hundreds of thousands of different intelligent life forms, it does not necessarily follow that we will be able to know and understand this one. Now does it?"

"No, but—but—" the Snorap was actually floundering in the sea of the Lut's sophistical argument.

"You will have to admit," said the Lut, "that there is room for reasonable doubt. Let us clarify the argument. You say that machines have sapped their moral fiber. Therefore, it is clear that without their machines they will show no instinct or capability for survival. Is this not so?"

"Exactly," said Snorap, sternly.

"And I," went on the Lut, "disagree. I do not understand, any more than you do, what they are doing here, why there are two of them, or what their philosophy of life is. But I claim that no members of a race which has made a migration to a world where conditions are so inhospitable to them, as this one, can be lacking in moral fiber. Now, I propose that we abandon our work on this planet temporarily, and observe these two instead—until we come to a conclusion."

"And if I should turn out to be right," countered the Snorap, stiffly, "do you agree to locating their home planet and doing a thorough job of philosophical re-balancing on this race?"

"I do," replied the Lut. "But what if I should turn out to be right? What concession will you make?"

"Concession?" said the Snorap, blinking.

"Certainly," said the Lut. "It's only fair that I should stand to gain something as well. If I am right, do you agree to introducing ourselves to them; and introducing them to the fact that many other intelligent races exist, of radically different philosophies?"

"I do," said the Snorap. He turned his heavy lizard-like muzzle to the sky. "And here comes the winter to seal the bargain and administer the first environmental test to our subjects."

From the dark sky, a first few snowflakes were falling. Around the buildings, Great and Less, the two odd little bipeds, tamped their last shovels-full of earth into place; and went inside the domed living quarters. The day wore on and darkness came swiftly. The ground was covered now with snow and the air was thick with swirling flakes.

Two weeks later, by the planet's local time, the snow ceased blowing, the distant winter sun came out, and the temperature dropped sharply to about eighty degrees below zero fahrenheit. Behind the denuded branches of the vegetation surrounding the clearing, but almost as well shielded by their twisted tangle as they had been when leaves sprouted from the black limbs, the Snorap and Lut sat in the snow, watching the dome.

"What are they doing in there?" the Lut kept asking. The Snorap's sense of hearing was more adaptable than that of the tigerish alien; and he had been keeping his companion posted on what went on out of their sight.

"They're talking," replied the Snorap.

"Still?" said the Lut, registering astonishment. "How can a strictly verbal language contain enough concepts to permit of prolonged discussion?"

"I don't understand it myself," answered the Snorap. He

had been trying to learn the biped language from what he could overhear. "A lot of their talk doesn't make sense."

"Take a rest," suggested the Lut. "Forget about them for a while and let's have a talk about relative gravitic strains in a forty-body system."

Gravitic strains were the Snorap's hobby at the present and had been for the past two hundred years. Grumbling, he allowed himself to be persuaded. He and the Lut withdrew their attention from the clearing.

Great and Less grew sleepy and went to bed.

Unnoticed by human or alien, a pipe in the hydroponics building that was too close to the deadly cold of the outer wall, burst. Liquid sprayed from it onto the floor of the building; and gradually, but with an inexorable steadiness, the level of the nutrient fluid in the planting tanks began to go down.

"I blame myself," said the Snorap, miserably. "I blame myself."

"What for?" snapped the Lut. "We aren't here to protect them. We're waiting around to see if they have any moral fiber. I should think you'd be pleased by the whole thing."

They had just been watching Great and Less as they struggled in temperatures that were now below the hundred-below-zero mark, to transfer what could be salvaged from the hydroponics building to their living-dome. Helmeted and bundled in heavy suits, they had been losing ground in their salvage effort. Finally, in desperation they had cut down on clothing and had substituted improvised face masks. This permitted them to carry more on each trip, but rendered them more vulnerable to the cold. Less had collapsed twice before giving up; and Great had finished the job alone. Apparently he had a touch of frostbite in his lungs, though. Less was doing what their meager stock of medical equipment permitted, to mend the condition.

"Are you convinced now?" asked the Lut.

The Snorap shook himself back into a less emotional frame of mind.

"No," he said. "No. They didn't sit down and fold their hands when their machine failed, true. But we—I—am concerned with a matter of proper racial philosophy. What strength have these creatures aside from the strength of their machines and their own strength to make more? What else have they? Here we have only one machine that has failed. What if they all failed? What if the *idea* of machines failed? They must prove that it is more than their pride in their ability to build that has given them reason to think that they can successfully dare strange worlds."

"Humph!" said the Lut.

"But a race cannot *grow* without a proper philosophy, you know that," said the Snorap, almost pleading with him.

"Well—" growled the Lut. "I think I'll go for a walk. Need some exercise." He turned and loped off into the snow. When he reached a level spot out of sight of the Snorap he turned on the speed, and the barren winter plains were treated to the sight of him burning up his ill-humor at the rate of better than a hundred miles an hour. For the Lut was in a bad temper and did not quite like to ask himself why.

The Snorap, left alone, looked doubtfully at the buildings in the clearing.

"I don't think I'm too hard on them," he said. "I don't *think* I am—"

The short winter wore itself out; and spring came in with a rush. The snow disappeared; and the ground around the buildings became brown mud. Great, fully recovered, and Less could be seen daily extending the clearing in the direction of a stream that ran from the hills west of their buildings down onto the plain below.

"Now, what's the point of that?" the Lut asked the Snorap.

"I'm not sure," answered the Snorap. "It has something to do with the hydroponics building."

They found out a few days later, when Great and Less began to plant in the muddy soil the seeds and shoots from the vegetable things they had saved. The soil itself they treated with chemicals and other necessary ingredients from the ruined building.

"Very clever," approved the Lut. He turned to the Snorap. "How do you like that?"

"Very good," said the Snorap. "But may I point out that if they are to prove themselves by doing without their machines, they'll have to do without all of them?"

"If the crops prosper, they can extend their planting," the Lut pointed out.

"That is true."

"—And with the long summer they have on this world they can probably get in two or three more crops before the next winter."

"The possibility," said the Snorap politely, "had not entirely escaped my notice."

The year warmed gradually. For a matter of weeks there was anxiousness in human and alien hearts alike, until the first shoots of the planted things began to show their heads above the brown soil.

"Beautiful," said the Snorap, one dark night, looking over the field with the Lut. He bent down to touch the soft firmness of a soft green spear-tip. His night vision, like the Lut's was fully equal to the task of appreciating it in full color, although the humans would hardly have been able to see their hands before their faces. "Here indeed is beauty, and strength and purpose. In alien soil it fights as valiantly toward the light of a strange sun as ever it fought for light of its native star from the womb of its natural earth."

"It and the bipeds are probably sons of the same mother world," remarked the Lut.

"Almost undoubtedly," answered the Snorap, abandoning the plant and straightening up. "But there are good and bad on all worlds, as you well know, my friend."

The ice-green eyes of the Lut softened to turquoise.

"Except on Lut," he said.

"And Snorap," added the Snorap. "And some few others where the creatures have grown older and attained wisdom . . ." His words trailed off; and they stood together in silence for a moment, each thinking of the world that was his home.

They were feeling the weight of the universe as all thinking beings do, when they open their souls to the unknown. In their hearts they stood with bowed heads before the Mother of all Mysteries, the great and final *Why?* which is never answered, but merely moved back a step by those who win knowledge. The mood lasted for perhaps the space of five minutes; and then they had come back to their ordinary selves again.

"I gave them four months," said the Lut. "That time is up already."

"And I at least," said the Snorap, "am no closer to understanding their basic philosophy, if, truly, it is not that the machine is the answer to all problems."

"They have a strong will toward survival."

"I must admit it," replied the Snorap. "But that by itself is pure animal, non-thinking animal. And while we do not condemn the animal, we do not reach out our hands to him in friendship as you want us to do with these bipeds."

"I have a hunch," said the Lut.

"Real or wishful?" asked the Snorap. They were talking about a subconscious reasoning process that both knew to exist, but both instinctively distrusted.

"I don't know," said the Lut. "But their pattern of living is at odds with the conditions here. I foresee trouble."

Summer approached. The earth dried under a swelling sun and thrust forth the fruit of the bipeds' planting. Great and Less harvested feverishly under a cloudless sky, while the south winds that blew steadily now, grew stronger and warmer, day by day.

Finally the crops were all in and the ground re-planted. From the wreckage of the hydroponics building they had constructed a granary; and this was stocked with all that they had brought in. With the strengthening winds and the heat came dust storms blown up over the empty plains and carried up the slopes into the shallow hills where Great and Less had built. Behind the screen of the new-grown vegetation behind the clearing, the Lut and the Snorap watched an area in which the humans were seldom seen. Heat as fierce in its own way as the cold of the winter past, held them virtual prisoners in the dome.

"It is not good for them," the Snorap informed the Lut.

"Why?" asked the Lut. An eighty-mile-an-hour gale was sand-blasting away at his scales, without apparently affecting them, beyond polishing them up so that they shone more brightly.

"The wind. The sound of the wind," said the Snorap. "And the fact that they cannot go outside. They are often nervous and angry at one another without reason."

"The season will pass," said the Lut indifferently. "One day the winds will start to drop; and then it will be fall."

—And, of course, eventually it happened. The bipeds came forth at last into a temperature of a little over a hundred degrees. The wind had dropped steadily for nearly a week. Now it shifted suddenly to the north—and the rains came.

Gently at first; and then with increasing violence, they poured down on the dusty earth. The ground puffed, soaked, and steamed in the short intervals of sunshine. And after several weeks the two went out to examine the fields they had planted for the second growing season.

They found a muddy desert.

With time growing short before the winter, they had to break into the stored treasure of the granary and gamble that one more crop could be gotten in before the frost came.

"Do you think they'll have time?" the Lut asked Snorap.

"I don't know," replied the Snorap. "Theoretically they should. But will these crops grow as fast as those planted at the start of the summer?"

"Hum," said the Lut, thoughtfully. "Well, they've got an even chance, anyway."

Over the months, the Lut and the Snorap had grown sensitive to small changes in the two bipeds. But they were not perceptive enough to sense that the constant struggle for existence had strained the nerves of both humans to the breaking point. Indeed, they were living together now, through this second planting, like two caged animals, avoiding each other as much as possible for fear that a chance word would bring them into open conflict. This, the two aliens did not sense. Only the physical elements got through to them.

"Their mass has gone down," the Lut remarked critically to the Snorap one afternoon in late summer as the two sat watching the bowed figures readying the clearing for the approaching winter.

"Possibly they do not have enough food," answered the Snorap.

"I don't think that's it," said the Lut thoughtfully. "More likely it is overexertion. They are exercising themselves for long hours these last few weeks."

"They talk less," said the Snorap.

"And they do not laugh," added the Lut, who had finally gotten around to mastering the biped language and was able to grasp the difference between laughter and speech. "But maybe when the crop starts to show itself above ground they will cheer up."

"The visual emergence of new life into the world always has a stimulating effect," said the Snorap. "For those capable of understanding, it connotes the ever-fresh wonder of existence renewed."

"I was thinking more," said the Lut, "of what those crops mean to them in terms of food through the winter."

"That, of course, too," agreed the Snorap, a little miffed at being interrupted in his philosophizing.

But the first of the second crop pushing its way through the brown soil did have the good effect the Lut had anticipated. The two bipeds relaxed and fell once more into an easy, happy relationship between themselves. This second harvest came more slowly, indeed, but the growth was strong and hardy; and the yield, if anything, a shade heavier.

But now, with the ripening of the planted things, the native life of the planet came to prey upon the growing fields. Where they had been during the sterile winter, and through the fresh spring and the blasting heat of mid-summer, it was impossible to tell. It seemed vaguely to Great and Less that they had noticed some native life around before, but never paid a great deal of attention to it. The smallest came first— insects of all sizes and tiny animals; and the two bipeds, working late, dug a deep moat around their planted ground and filled it with water diverted from the stream beyond the fields. After these came larger animals; and for a few nights one or the other was always on duty all night long with a missile-hurling device that the Lut and the Snorap recognized as a weapon—for the larger animals came only in the hours of darkness when the bipeds were not visible in the fields.

This last fact finally struck home to the mind of Great, and the Lut and the Snorap saw him out in the fields one day, setting posts about their perimeters. On each post was a short, thick tube and from each post to the next ran what looked like heavy black rope. That night they went forth to investigate after dark.

"Cable," said the Snorap, picking up a section of it, "designed to conduct some form of energy. Come to think of it, I did notice Less working around the power-house; but I was

so interested in what Great was doing out here, I didn't pay
much attention. Now I wonder—"

At that moment, at the furthest end of the field, one of
the tubes atop a post seemed suddenly to explode and throw
out colored balls of fire at a great rate. It was, in fact, nothing
more than a self-refueling roman candle, although that particular comparison did not occur to either the Snorap nor the
Lut, in spite of the fact that they understood the nature of
the thing almost instantly. Hardly had the pyrotechnics of
the first ceased, when the next one up the border of the
field burst out and lit up its own section. The Lut and the
Snorap drew back into the darkness.

"There!" said the Lut in triumph. "You see the difference?
The biped does not depend on the machine. It is a tool that
he uses as he sees fit."

The Snorap turned his heavy head and looked at his companion.

"Well?" demanded the Lut. "You must admit that I'm
right. Listen!" The sensitive hearing of the two ranged out
into the darkness behind them. "The wild ones are frightened
and drawing away."

"I admit it," said the Snorap ponderously. "But all through
this business you have made it a practice to misunderstand
me. It is not how the biped uses the tool that is important.
It is whether he can lay aside the tool. It is whether he can
attempt something where the tool will not aid him. It is his
ability to conceive of meeting a problem without tools. When
he shows evidence of that, and only then will I be willing
and proud to face him and call him brother."

The Lut's eyes glowed with green anger.

"You are being unfair," he said. "The centuries past have
taught me your nature. You mistrust your own softness of
emotion which kindles an instinctive fellow feeling between
you and the bipeds. In your efforts to be impartial you lean
over backwards and place the benefit of the doubt against
them."

There was enough truth in this to make the Snorap wince inwardly.

"After all those same centuries," he retorted bitterly, "must we descend to personal criticism?"

"Truth is truth!" said the Lut. And his great jaws rang shut together. "Your conclusions are your own."

"And I stand by them!" said the Snorap.

"And I by mine!"

For a moment they stood facing each other. Then the Snorap turned away and headed back to the shelter of their accustomed vegetation. The Lut stood watching him go for a minute; then he also turned and headed out away from the clearing, to run the plains and think himself back to reasonableness.

In the dome, the two exhausted humans slept their first good night of sleep in weeks.

Two days later they began their harvesting. By the end of the first day they had gathered in the produce of perhaps a fifth of their fields. And on the second day of harvesting, Less staggered suddenly and sat down. Watching in a mutual silence from which the old friendly warmth was still missing, the Lut and the Snorap saw Great break off his own work and run to the fallen biped.

"For God's sake, don't quit now!" they heard him say.

"One day—" Less forced the words through worn lips "let's take one day off. I can't go any more, I tell you!"

"Something may go wrong—"

Less stirred and weakly rose; then turned toward the dome.

"The weather's good. The gadget you made will keep the beasts out. There's no point to killing ourselves. I've got to get some sleep."

For a long moment Great stood watching the other biped move slowly off toward the dome. Suddenly, he cursed. He threw down the tool he was holding and followed.

The Snorap and the Lut turned to look at each other.

"They are giving up," said the Snorap. "They are leaving the machine to guard the field."

The Lut faced him.

"I don't blame them," he said.

"To me," replied the Snorap, "they are failures."

They stood looking at each other.

"I think," said the Lut at last, "I think that we no longer possess the mutual understanding necessary to our partnership."

The Snorap bowed his head.

"I cannot disagree," he said.

"Our association in the past has been a long and good one," said the Lut. "I will remember it."

"Nor will I forget," said the Snorap. He paused. "I will wait here a little while yet to see the end of this."

"I will wait also, then," the Lut answered.

They stood facing each other. Suddenly, the Snorap raised his head and tilted it, listening to the southward. After a second the Lut's head followed suit.

—"And the end comes now," said the Snorap.

There are monsters on all young worlds. The creature that came northward over the plains, migrating with the seasons from tropics to temperate zone, was a proof of that statement. Vegetarian but vast, in size and strength beyond all natural enemies of his world, his body was all head, horns and stomach, balanced on four pillar-like legs; and he followed the comfortable temperatures of cool autumns northward, gleaning the land as he went.

From far out on the dark plains, he had scented the bipeds' crops. But because he stood at that time up to his tremendous midlegs in soft second growth grass, he had not turned immediately but had continued to feed where he was. When dawn came he had slept, standing with rock-like motionlessness upon his pillar legs. But when the midday breeze brought a scent of the ripe growing stuff once more to his flaring nostrils, he had stirred out of his sleep and methodically began to feed toward the clearing.

The beast came out toward the edge of the field, moving with inexorable ponderousness. Some fifty yards away impatience seemed to break through his normal calm, and abandoning his slow feeding pace, he lifted his head and broke into a sudden trot toward the orderly rows of cultivation.

In the dome, the vibration reached through the fogs of Great's sleep, and stirred him. He moved, groaned, and opened his eyes. He lay on his back, listening, with his eyes open.

The monster had reached the edge of the field. He slowed and halted, the burnt metal smell of the roman candle pots stirred his little brain to caution. Slowly he moved up the line of cable to the nearest one and sniffed at it, the sound of his heavy snuffling audible to the Snorap and Lut behind their screen of branches.

Suddenly he screamed—a fantastic sound that rolled and re-echoed between open earth and empty sky. And, lifting himself on his hind legs, he pounded with both forelegs on the post, driving it into the dusty ground. And, as if this action had set loose the fires of his rage, he began almost to dance on the remains of the heavy post, mashing it to matchstick wood.

From the dome, Great and Less came tumbling. Less, half-asleep and reeling with fatigue, Great cursing and trying to arm the weapon he carried—the gun the Snorap and Lut had seen him use when he tried to drive away the night predators on the fields. Finally dropping on one knee he fired at the monster. A puff of dust rose from behind the creature's heavy shoulder, and it turned to charge the human.

Great fired again—this time for the head. And the missile ricocheted from the heavy bone plates as from a granite boulder.

The second shot had caused the monster to hesitate. Now weaving its head back and forth, it caught sight of Less and turned after this new quarry. Less took one panic-stricken glance at the towering creature; and ran blindly into the open space that separated the clearing from the fields.

Great fired twice more before the gun jammed. By that time, the monster was upon Less. But, fantastically, because of its speed and huge bulk, it overran the fleeing biped, and Less stumbled and fell without being touched.

For perhaps two seconds, while the monster was slowing and turning, Great continued to wrestle with the weapon. Then seizing it by the barrel and swinging it like a club, he ran forward the creature.

"What is this?" cried the Snorap.

The monster had wheeled now and stood confronting them both. Great passed the fallen Less, shouting "Get to the dome. Get to the dome! I'll hold him!"

The monster screamed his fury and turned to follow; and Great ran on, a living lure to give Less time to reach safety.

"No moral fiber, eh?" snarled the Lut, leaping to his feet. He started to spring from concealment, but the Snorap gripped him.

"I will go!" cried the Snorap. "I was wrong. It's my responsibility."

"But my pleasure!" growled the Lut. "You take care of the bipeds."

He crossed the distance separating himself from the monster like one long flash of glittering light. Reaching up with a forelimb as he passed he dealt it a blow that staggered it. For a second it stood dazed; then it raised its head and screamed.

The Lut stood looking at it, from a few feet before it. His ice-green eyes caught the wild black ones of the creature and held them.

The creature roared and shifted uncertainly, feeling an uneasiness that it could not understand. For a moment it fought for decision—then it charged.

The Lut shot from the ground like a projectile and met it head to head. There was a sound like a tree breaking in a high wind. The heavy bone that had warded off the missile from Great's gun, gave like cardboard before the fantastic stuff of which the Lut's body was constructed. The creature tumbled backwards, lay for a moment, then slowly struggled to its feet and reeled off like something half-conscious. Its huge forehead was caved in and dark fluid dripped from it and dropped on the ground as it went.

"It will live," said the Lut, looking after it.

He turned to look at the bipeds. The Snorap had come up and Great, with Less shoved behind him, was frantically trying to unjam the gun and shoot at them.

"Put that thing away," said the Lut. "We're friends."

The man froze, his hands on the breech of his weapon. The Lut was forming the human words by swallowing air and forcing it back through his capable throat muscles; and the result was a deep, growling bass that did not at first identify itself with rational speech.

"I said we're friends," said the Lut. "We've been watching you for a year now. Besides, your weapon there can't hurt us." He turned to the Snorap. "Say something to reassure them that you're not a wild animal."

"I have been guilty of badly misjudging you," said the Snorap humbly to the humans. He was talking by the same process and the humans looked from him to the Lut as if they suspected the latter of being a ventriloquist.

"Who—who are you?" asked Great at last.

"We," said the Lut, "are individual members of two old and respected races, from elsewhere than this system. You might refer to me as a Lut and to my friend as a Snorap. And you call yourselves—?"

The man laughed a little wildly. Exchanging introductions with two nightmare beings after a hair-breadth escape from death, has a tendency to make anyone a bit hysterical.

"We're humans," he said. "I'm Jos Parner. This is my wife, Gela."

"What is a wife?" asked the Lut.

"Why—a wife—" answered the human in astonishment. "I'm a man, she's a woman. Male—female—"

"You mean," demanded the Lut, "that your race is bisexual?"

"Of course," answered the man. "Isn't everything? Aren't you—" He broke off and stared at them. "You mean it's not usual?"

The Lut turned his head slowly and looked at the Snorap, who sat down in the dust.

"I am an old fool," said the Snorap, penitently, "I am a senile old idiot who ought to have my brains examined. Sitting here engaged in high speculation about the source of their racial philosophy and questioning their moral basis, when all the time they were loving each other and complementing each other's character-traits right under my very nose. What else would be the basis of colonization in a bisexual race but the family unit? Where but in the urge to build a home would their drive lie? What would be their courage, but love transformed?" He sat with head hanging. "I am an old fool."

The Lut crossed over to him and hung his heavy head on the Snorap's shoulder.

"Friend of many years past and yet to come," he said. "We are old fools together."

The Monkey Wrench

Cary Harmon was not an ungifted young man. He had the intelligence to carve himself a position as a Lowland society lawyer, which on Venus is not easy to do. And he had the discernment to consolidate that position by marrying into the family of one of the leading drug-exporters. But, nevertheless, from the scientific viewpoint, he was a layman; and laymen, in their ignorance, should never be allowed to play with delicate technical equipment; for the result will be trouble, as surely as it is the first time a baby gets its hands on a match.

His wife was a high-spirited woman; and would have been hard to handle at times if it had not been for the fact that she was foolish enough to love him. Since he did not love her at all, it was consequently both simple and practical to terminate all quarrels by dropping out of sight for several days until her obvious fear of losing him for good brought her to a proper humility. He took good care, each time he disappeared, to pick some new and secure hiding place where past experience or her several years' knowledge of his habits would be no help in locating him. Actually, he enjoyed thinking up new and undiscoverable bolt-holes, and made a hobby out of discovering them.

Consequently, he was in high spirits the gray winter afternoon he descended unannounced on the weather station of Burke McIntyre, high in the Lonesome Mountains, a jagged, kindless chain on the deserted shorelands of Venus' Northern Sea. He had beaten a blizzard to the dome with minutes to spare; and now, with his small two-place flier safely stowed away, and a meal of his host's best supplies under his belt, he sat reveling in the comfort of his position and listening to the hundred-and-fifty-mile-per-hour, subzero winds lashing impotently at the arching roof overhead.

"Ten minutes more," he said to Burke, "and I'd have had a tough time making it."

"Tough!" snorted Burke. He was a big, heavy-featured blond man with a kindly contempt for all of humanity aside from the favored class of meteorologists. "You Lowlanders are too used to that present day Garden of Eden you have down below. Ten minutes more and you'd have been spread over one of the peaks around here to wait for the spring searching party to gather your bones."

Cary laughed in cheerful disbelief.

"Try it, if you don't believe me," said Burke. "No skin off my nose if you don't have the sense to listen to reason. Take your bug up right now if you want."

"Not me," Cary's brilliant white teeth flashed in his swarthy face. "I know when I'm comfortable. And that's no way to treat your guest, tossing him out into the storm when he's just arrived."

"Some guest," rumbled Burke. "I shake hands with you after the graduation exercises, don't hear a word from you for six years and then suddenly you're knocking at my door here in the hinterland."

"I came on impulse," said Cary. "It's the prime rule of my life. Always act on impulse, Burke. It puts the sparkle in existence."

"And leads you to an early grave," Burke supplemented.

"If you have the wrong impulses," said Cary. "But then if you get sudden urges to jump off cliffs or play Russian Roulette then you're too stupid to live, anyway."

"Cary," said Burke heavily, "you've a shallow thinker."

"And you're a stodgy one," grinned Cary. "Suppose you quit

insulting me and tell me something about yourself. What's this hermit's existence of yours like? What do you do?"

"What do I do?" repeated Burke. "I work."

"But just how?" Cary said, settling himself cozily back into his chair. "Do you send up balloons? Catch snow in a pail to find how much fell? Take sights on the stars? Or what?"

Burke shook his head at him and smiled tolerantly.

"Now what do you want to know for?" he asked. "It'll just go in one ear and out the other."

"Oh, some of it might stick," said Cary. "Go ahead, anyhow."

"Well, if you insist on my talking to entertain you," he answered, "I don't do anything so picturesque. I just sit at a desk and prepare weather data for transmission to the Weather Center down at Capital City."

"Aha!" Cary said, waggling a lazy forefinger at him in reproof. "I've got you now. You've been laying down on the job. You're the only one here; so if you don't take observations, who does?"

"You idiot!" said Burke. "The machines does, of course. These stations have a Brain to do that."

"That's worse," Cary answered. "You've been sitting here warm and comfortable while some poor little Brain scurries around outside in the snow and does all your work for you."

"Oh, shut up!" Burke said. "As a matter of fact you're closer to the truth than you think; and it wouldn't do you any harm to learn a few things about the mechanical miracles that let you lead a happy ignorant life. Some wonderful things have been done lately in the way of equipping these stations."

Cary smiled mockingly.

"I mean it," Burke went on, his face lighting up. "The Brain we've got here now is the last word in that type of installation. As a matter of fact, it was just put in recently— up until a few months back we had to work with a job that was just a collector and computer. That is, it collected the

weather data around this station and presented it to you.
Then you had to take it and prepare it for the calculator,
which would chew on it for a while and then pass you back
results which you again had to prepare for transmission downstairs to the Center."

"Fatiguing, I'm sure," murmured Cary, reaching for the
drink placed handily on the end table beside his chair.
Burke ignored him, caught up in his own appreciation of the
mechanical development about which he was talking.

"It kept you busy, for the data came in steadily; and you
were always behind since a batch would be accumulating
while you were working up the previous batch. A station like
this is the center-point for observational mechs posted at
points over more than five hundred square miles of territory;
and, being human, all you had time to do was skim the cream
off the reports and submit a sketchy picture to the calculator.
And then there was a certain responsibility involved in taking
care of the station and yourself.

"But now"—Burke leaned forward determinedly and
stabbed a thick index finger at his visitor—"we've got a new
installation that takes the data directly from the observational
mechs—all of it—resolves it into the proper form for the calculator to handle it, and carries it right on through to the end
results. All I still have to do is prepare the complete picture
from the results and shoot it downstairs.

"In addition, it runs the heating and lighting plants, automatically checks on the maintenance of the station. It makes
repairs and corrections on verbal command and has a whole
separate section for the consideration of theoretical problems."

"Sort of a little tin god," said Cary, nastily. He was used to
attention and subconsciously annoyed by the fact that Burke
seemed to be waxing more rhapsodic over his machine than
the brilliant and entertaining guest who, as far as the meteorologist could know, had dropped in under the kind impulse
to relieve a hermit's boring existence.

Unperturbed, Burke looked at him and chuckled.

"No," he replied. "A *big* tin god, Cary."

The lawyer stiffened slightly in his chair. Like most people who are fond of poking malicious fun at others, he gave evidence of a very thin skin when the tables were turned.

"Sees all, knows all, tells all, I suppose," he said sarcastically. "Never makes a mistake. Infallible."

"You might say that," answered Burke, still with a grin on his face. He was enjoying the unusual pleasure of having the other on the defensive. But Cary, adept at verbal battles, twisted like an eel.

"Too bad, Burke," he said. "But those qualities alone don't quite suffice for elevating your gadget to godhood. One all-important attribute is lacking—invulnerability. Gods never break down."

"Neither does this."

"Come now, Burke," chided Cary, "you mustn't let your enthusiasm lead you into falsehood. No machine is perfect. A crossed couple of wires, a burned out tube and where is your darling? Plunk! Out of action."

Burke shook his head.

"There aren't any wires," he said. "It uses beamed connections. And as for burned out tubes, they don't even halt consideration of a problem. The problem is just shifted over to a bank that isn't in use at the time; and automatic repairs are made by the machine itself. You see, Cary, in this model, no bank does one specific job, alone. Any one of them—and there's twenty, half again as many as this station would ever need—can do any job from running the heating plant to operating the calculator. If something comes up that's too big for one bank to handle, it just hooks in one or more of the idle banks—and so on until it's capable of dealing with the situation."

"Ah," said Cary, "but what if something *did* come up that

required all the banks and more too? Wouldn't it overload them and burn itself out?"

"You're determined to find fault with it, aren't you, Cary," answered Burke. "The answer is no. It wouldn't. Theoretically it's possible for the machine to bump into a problem that would require all or more than all of its banks to handle. For example, if this station suddenly popped into the air and started to fly away for no discernible reason, the bank that first felt the situation would keep reaching out for help until all the banks were engaged in considering it, until it crowded out all the other functions the machine performs. But, even then, it wouldn't overload and burn out. The banks would just go on considering the problem until they had evolved a theory that explained why we were flying through the air and what to do about returning us to our proper place and functions."

Cary straightened up and snapped his fingers.

"Then it's simple," he said. "I'll just go in and tell your machine—on the verbal hookup—that we're flying through the air."

Burke gave a sudden roar of laughter.

"Cary, you dope!" he said. "Don't you think the men who designed the machine took the possibility of verbal error into account? You say that the station is flying through the air. The machine immediately checks by making its own observations; and politely replies, 'Sorry, your statement is incorrect' and forgets the whole thing."

Cary's eyes narrowed and two spots of faint color flushed the tight skin over his cheekbones; but he held his smile.

"There's the theoretical section," he murmured.

"There is," said Burke, greatly enjoying himself, "and you could use it by going in and saying 'consider the false statement or data—this station is flying through the air' and the machine would go right to work on it."

He paused, and Cary looked at him expectantly.

"But—" continued the meteorologist, triumphantly, "it

would consider the statement with only those banks not then in use; and it would give up the banks whenever a section using real data required them."

He finished, looking at Cary with quizzical good humor. But Cary said nothing; only looked back at him as a weasel might look back at a dog that has cornered it against the wall of a chicken run.

"Give up, Cary," he said at last. "It's no use. Neither God nor Man nor Cary Harmon can interrupt my Brain in the rightful performance of its duty."

And Cary's eyes glittered, dark and withdrawn beneath their narrowed lids. For a long second, he just sat and looked, and then he spoke.

"I could do it," he said, softly.

"Do what?" asked Burke.

"I could gimmick your machine," said Cary.

"Oh, forget it!" boomed Burke. "Don't take things so seriously, Cary. What if you can't think of a monkey wrench to throw into the machinery? Nobody else could, either."

"I said I could do it," repeated Cary.

"Once and for all," answered Burke, "it's impossible. Now stop trying to pick flaws in something guaranteed flawless and let's talk about something else."

"I will bet you," said Cary, speaking with a slow, steady intensity, "five thousand credits that if you will leave me alone with your machine for one minute I can put it completely out of order."

"Forget it, will you?" exploded Burke. "I don't want to take your money, even if five thousand *is* the equivalent of a year's salary for me. The trouble with you is, Cary, you never could stand to lose at anything. Now, forget it!"

"Put up or shut up," said Cary.

Burke took a deep breath.

"Now look," he said, the beginnings of anger rumbling in his deep voice. "Maybe I did wrong to needle you about the machine. But you've got to get over the idea that I can be bullied into admitting that you're right. You've got no conception of the technology that's behind the machine, and no idea of how certain I am that you, at least, can't do anything to interfere with its operation. You think that there's a slight element of doubt in my mind and that you can bluff me out of proposing an astronomical bet. Then, if I won't bet, you'll tell yourself you've won. Now listen, I'm not just ninety-nine point nine, nine, nine, nine, per cent sure of myself. I'm one hundred per cent sure of myself and the reason I won't bet you is because that would be robbery; and besides, once you'd lost, you'd hate me for winning the rest of your life."

"The bet still stands," said Cary.

"All right!" roared Burke, jumping to his feet. "If you want to force the issue, suit yourself. It's a bet."

Cary grinned and got up, following him out of the pleasant, spacious sitting room, where warm lamps dispelled the gray gloom of the snow-laden sky beyond the windows, and into a short, metal-walled corridor where the ceiling tubes blazed in efficient nakedness. They followed this for a short distance to a room where the wall facing the corridor and the door set in it were all of glass.

Here Burke halted.

"There's the machine," he said, pointing through the transparency of the wall and turning to Cary behind him. "If you want to communicate with it verbally, you speak into that grille there. The calculator is to your right; and that inner door leads down to the room housing the lighting and heating plants. But if you're thinking of physical sabotage, you might as well give up. The lighting and heating systems don't even have emergency manual controls. They're run by a little atomic pile that only the machine can be trusted to handle—that is, except for an automatic setup that damps the pile in case lightning strikes the machine or some such thing. And you couldn't get through the shielding in a week. As for breaking through to the machine up here, that panel

in which the grille is set is made of two-inch-thick steel
sheets with their edges flowed together under pressure."

"I assure you," said Cary. "I don't intend to damage a
thing."

Burke looked at him sharply, but there was no hint of
sarcasm in the smile that twisted the other's thin lips.

"All right," he said, stepping back from the door. "Go
ahead. Can I wait here, or do you have to have me out of
sight?"

"Oh, by all means, watch," said Cary. "We machine-gim-
mickers have nothing to hide." He turned mockingly to
Burke, and lifted his arms. "See? Nothing up my right
sleeve. Nothing up my left."

"Go on," interrupted Burke roughly. "Get it over with. I
want to get back to my drink."

"At once," said Cary, and went in through the door, closing
it behind him.

Through the transparent wall, Burke watched him approach the panel in line with the speaker grille and stop some
two feet in front of it. Having arrived at this spot, he became
utterly motionless, his back to Burke, his shoulders hanging
relaxed and his hands motionless at his side. For the good
part of a minute, Burke strained his eyes to discover what
action was going on under the guise of Cary's apparent
immobility. Then an understanding struck him and he
laughed.

"Why," he said to himself, "he's bluffing right up to the
last minute, hoping I'll get worried and rush in there and
stop him."

Relaxed, he lit a cigarette and looked at his watch. Some
forty-five seconds to go. In less than a minute, Cary would
be coming out, forced at last to admit defeat—that is, unless
he had evolved some fantastic argument to prove that defeat
was really victory. Burke frowned. It was almost pathological,
the way Cary had always refused to admit the superiority of

anyone or anything else; and unless some way was found to
soothe him he would be a very unpleasant companion for
the remaining days that the storm held him marooned with
Burke. It would be literally murder to force him to take off
in the tornado velocity winds and a temperature that must
be in the minus sixties by this time. At the same time, it
went against the meteorologist's grain to crawl for the sake
of congeniality—

The vibration of the generator, half-felt through the floor
and the soles of his shoes, and customarily familiar as the
motion of his own lungs, ceased abruptly. The fluttering
streamers fixed to the ventilator grille above his head ceased
their colorful dance and dropped limply down as the rush of
air that had carried them, ceased. The lights dimmed and
went out, leaving only the gray and ghostly light from the
thick windows at each end of the corridor to illuminate the
passage and the room. The cigarette dropped unheeded from
Burke's fingers and in two swift strides he was at the door and
through it.

"What have you done?" he snapped at Cary.

The other looked mockingly at him, walked across to the
nearer wall of the room and leaned his shoulder blades neg-
ligently against it.

"That's for you to find out," he said, his satisfaction
clearly evident.

"Don't be insane—" began the meteorologist. Then, check-
ing himself like a man who has no time to lose, he whirled
on the panel and gave his attention to the instruments on
its surface.

The pile was damped. The ventilating system was shut off
and the electrical system was dead. Only the power in the
storage cells of the machine itself was available for the operating light still glowed redly on the panel. The great outside
doors, wide enough to permit the ingress and exit of a two-
man flier, were closed, and would remain that way, for they

required power to open or close them. Visio, radio, and teletype were alike, silent and lifeless through lack of power.

But the machine still operated.

Burke stepped to the grille and pressed the red alarm button below it, twice.

"Attention," he said. "The pile is damped and all fixtures besides yourself lack power. Why is this?"

There was no response, though the red light continued to glow industriously on the panel.

"Obstinate little rascal, isn't it?" said Cary from the wall.

Burke ignored him, punching the button again, sharply.

"Reply!" he ordered. "Reply at once! What is the difficulty? Why is the pile not operating?"

There was no answer.

He turned to the calculator and played his fingers expertly over the buttons. Fed from the stored power within the machine, the punched tape rose in a fragile white arc and disappeared through a slot in the panel. He finished his punching and waited.

There was no answer.

For a long moment he stood there, staring at the calculator as if unable to believe that, even in this last hope, the machine had failed him. Then he turned slowly and faced Cary.

"What have you done?" he repeated dully.

"Do you admit you were wrong?" Cary demanded.

"Yes," said Burke.

"And do I win the bet?" persisted Cary gleefully.

"Yes."

"Then I'll tell you," the lawyer said. He put a cigarette between his lips and puffed it alight; then blew out a long streamer of smoke which billowed out and hung cloudily in the still air of the room, which, lacking heat from the blowers, was cooling rapidly. "This fine little gadget of yours may be all very well at meteorology, but it's not very good at logic. Shocking situation, when you consider the close relation between mathematics and logic."

"What did you do?" reiterated Burke hoarsely.

"I'll get to it," said Cary. "As I say, it's a shocking situation. Here is this infallible machine of yours, worth, I suppose, several million credits, beating its brains out over a paradox."

"A paradox!" the words from Burke were almost a sob.

"A paradox," sang Cary, "a most ingenious paradox." He switched back to his speaking voice. "Which, in case you don't know, is from Gilbert and Sullivan's 'Pirates of Penzance.' It occurred to me while you were bragging earlier that while your little friend here couldn't be damaged, it might be immobilized by giving it a problem too big for its mechanical brain cells to handle. And I remembered a little thing from one of my pre-law logic courses—an interesting little affair called Epimenides Paradox. I don't remember just how it was originally phrased—those logic courses were dull, sleepy sort of businesses, anyway—but for example, if I say to you 'all lawyers are liars' how can you tell whether the statement is true or false, since I am a lawyer and, if it is true, must be lying when I say that all lawyers are liars? But, on the other hand, if I am lying, then all lawyers are not liars, and the statement is false, i.e., a lying statement. If the statement is false, it is true, and if true, false, and so on, so where are you?"

Cary broke off suddenly into a peal of laughter.

"You should see your own face, Burke," he shouted. "I never saw anything so bewildered in my life—anyway, I just changed this around and fed it to the machine. While you waited politely outside, I went up to the machine and said to it 'You must reject the statement I am now making to you, because all the statements I make are incorrect.'"

He paused and looked at the meteorologist.

"Do you see, Burke? It took that statement of mine in

and considered it for rejecting. But it could not reject it without admitting that it was correct, and how could it be correct when it stated that all statements I made were incorrect. You see . . . yes, you do see, I can see it in your face. Oh, if you could only look at yourself now. The pride of the meteorology service, undone by a paradox."

And Cary went off into another fit of laughter that lasted for a long minute. Every time he would start to recover, a look at Burke's wooden face, set in lines of utter dismay, would set him off again. The meteorologist neither moved, nor spoke, but stared at his guest as if he were a ghost.

Finally, weak from merriment, Cary started to sober up. Chuckling feebly, he leaned against the wall, took a deep breath and straightened up. A shiver ran through him, and he turned up the collar of his tunic.

"Well," he said. "Now that you know what the trick was, Burke, suppose you get your pet back to its proper duties again. It's getting too cold for comfort and that daylight coming through the windows isn't the most cheerful thing in the world, either."

But Burke made no move toward the panel. His eyes were fixed and they bored into Cary as unmovingly as before. Cary snickered a little at him.

"Come on, Burke," he said. "Man the pumps. You can recover from your shock sometime afterwards. If it's the bet that bothers you, forget it. I'm too well off myself to need to snatch your pennies. And if it's the failure of Baby, here, don't feel too bad. It did better than I expected. I thought it would just blow a fuse and quit work altogether, but I see it's still busy and devoting every single bank to obtaining a solution. I should imagine"—Cary yawned—"that it's working toward evolving a theory of types. *That* would give it the solution. Probably could get it, too, in a year or so."

Still Burke did not move. Cary looked at him oddly.

"What's wrong?" he asked irritatedly.

Burke's mouth worked, a tiny speck of spittle flew from one corner of it.

"You—" he said. The word came tearing from his throat like the hoarse grunt of a dying man.

"What—"

"You fool!" ground out Burke, finding his voice. "You stupid idiot! You insane moron!"

"Me? Me?" cried Cary. His voice was high in protest, almost like a womanish scream. "I was right!"

"Yes, you were right," said Burke. "You were too right. How am I supposed to get the machine's mind off this problem and on to running the pile for heat and light, when all its circuits are taken up in considering your paradox? What can I do, when the Brain is deaf, and dumb, and blind?"

The two men looked at each other across the silent room. The warm breath of their exhalations made frosty plumes in the still air; and the distant howling of the storm, deadened by the thick walls of the station, seemed to grow louder in the silence, bearing a note of savage triumph.

The temperature inside the station was dropping very fast—

Tiger Green

I

A man with hallucinations he cannot stand trying to strangle himself in a home-made straitjacket is not a pretty sight. But after a while, grimly thought Jerry McWhin, the *Star Scout's* navigator, the ugly and terrible seem to backfire in effect, filling you with fury instead of harrowing you further. Men in crowds and packs could be stampeded briefly, but after a while the individual among them would turn, get his back up, and slash back.

At least—the hyper-stubborn individual in himself had finally so reacted.

Determinedly, with fingers that fumbled from lack of sleep, he got the strangling man—Wally Blake, an assistant ecologist —untangled and into a position where it would be difficult for him to try to choke out his own life, again. Then Jerry went out of the sickbay storeroom, leaving Wally and the other seven men out of the *Star Scout's* complement of twelve who were in total restraint. He was lightheaded from exhaustion; but a berserk something in him snarled like a cornered tiger and refused to break like Wally and the others.

When all's said and done, he thought half-crazily, there's worse ways to come to the end of it than a last charge, win or lose, alone into the midst of all your enemies.

Going down the corridor, the sight of another figure jolted him a little back toward common sense. Ben Akham, the drive engineer, came trudging back from the air-lock corridor with a flame thrower on his back. Soot etched darkly the lines on his once-round face.

"Get the hull cleared?" asked Jerry. Ben nodded exhaustedly.

"There's more jungle on her every morning," he grunted. "Now those big thistles are starting to drip a corrosive liquid. The hull needs an anti-acid washing. I can't do it. I'm worn out."

"We all are," said Jerry. His own five-eleven frame was down to a hundred and thirty-eight pounds. There was plenty of food—it was just that the four men left on their feet had no time to prepare it; and little enough time to eat it, prepared or not.

Exploration Team Five-Twenty-Nine, thought Jerry, had finally bitten off more than it could chew, here on the second planet of Star 83476. It was nobody's fault. It had been a gamble for Milt Johnson, the Team Captain, either way—to land or not to land. He had landed; and it had turned out bad.

By such small things was the scale toward tragedy tipped. A communication problem with the natives, a native jungle evidently determined to digest the spaceship, and eight of twelve men down with something like suicidal delirium tremens—any two of these things the Team could probably have handled.

But not all three at once.

Jerry and Ben reached the entrance of the Control Room together and peered in, looking for Milt Johnson.

"Must be ootside, talking to that native again," said Jerry.

"Ootside?—*Oot*-side!" exploded Ben, with a sudden snapping of frayed nerves. "Can't you say 'out-side'?—'*Out*-side,' like everybody else?"

The berserk something in Jerry lunged to be free, but he caught it and hauled it back.

"Get hold of yourself!" he snapped.

"Well . . . I wouldn't mind you sounding like a blasted

Scotchman all the time!" growled Ben, getting himself, nevertheless, somewhat under control. "It's just you always do it
when I don't expect it!"

"If the Lord wanted us all to sound alike, he'd have propped
up the Tower of Babel," said Jerry wickedly. He was not
particularly religious himself, but he knew Ben to be a table-
thumping atheist. He had the satisfaction now of watching
the other man bite his lips and control himself in his turn.

Academically, however, Jerry thought as they both headed
out through the ship to find Milt, he could not really blame
Ben. For Jerry, like many Scot-Canadians, appeared to speak
a very middle-western American sort of English most of the
time. But only as long as he avoided such vocabulary items as
"house" and "out"; which popped off Jerry's tongue as
"hoose" and "oot." However, every man aboard had his
personal peculiarities. You had to get used to them. That was
part of spaceship—in fact, part of human—life.

They emerged from the lock, rounded the nose of the
spaceship, and found themselves in the neat little clearing on
one side of the ship where the jungle paradoxically refused to
grow. In this clearing stood the broad-shouldered figure of
Milt Johnson, his whitish-blond hair glinting in the yellow-
white sunlight.

Facing Milt was the thin, naked, and saddle-colored, hu-
manoid figure of one of the natives from the village, or whatever it was, about twenty minutes away by jungle trail. Between Milt and the native was the glittering metal console of
the translator machine.

". . . Let's try it once more," they heard Milt saying as
they came up and stopped behind him.

The native gabbled agreeably.

"Yes, yes. Try it again," translated the voice of the console.

"I am Captain Milton Johnson. I am in authority over the
crew of the ship you see before me."

"Gladly would I not see it," replied the console on translation of the native's gabblings. "However—I am Communicator, messenger to you sick ones."

"I will call you Communicator, then," began Milt.

"Of course. What else could you call me?"

"Please," said Milt, wearily. "To get back to it—I also am a Communicator."

"No, no," said the native. "You are not a Communicator. It is the sickness that makes you talk this way."

"But," said Milt, and Jerry saw the big, white-haired captain swallow in an attempt to keep his temper. "You will notice, I am communicating with you."

"No, no."

"I see," said Milt patiently, "You mean, we aren't communicating in the sense that we aren't understanding each other. We're talking, but you don't understand me—"

"No, no. I understand you perfectly."

"Well," said Milt, exhaustedly. "I don't understand you."

"That is because you are sick."

Milt blew out a deep breath and wiped his brow.

"Forget that part of it, then," he said. "Many of my crew are upset by nightmares we all have been having. They *are* sick. But there are still four of us who are well—"

"No, no. You are all sick," said Communicator earnestly. "But you should love what you call nightmares. All people love them."

"Including you and your people?"

"Of course. Love your nightmares. They will make you well. They will make the little bit of proper life in you grow, and heal you."

Ben snorted beside Jerry. Jerry could sympathize with the other man. The nightmares he had been having during his scant hours of sleep, the past two weeks, came back to his mind, with the indescribably alien, terrifying sensation of drifting in a sort of environmental soup with identifiable things changing shape and identity constantly around him. Even pumped full of tranquilizers, he thought—which reminded Jerry.

He had not taken his tranquilizers lately.

When had he taken some last? Not since he woke up, in any case. Not since . . . yesterday, sometime. Though that was now hard to believe.

"Let's forget that, too, then." Milt was saying. "Now, the jungle is growing all over our ship, in spite of all we can do. You tell me your people can make the jungle do anything you want."

"Yes, yes," said Communicator, agreeably.

"Then, will you please stop it from growing all over our spaceship?"

"We understand. It is your sickness, the poison that makes you say this. Do not fear. We will never abandon you." Communicator looked almost ready to pat Milt consolingly on the head. "You are people, who are more important than any cost. Soon you will grow and cast off your poisoned part and come to us."

"But we can come to you right now!" said Milt, between his teeth. "In fact—we've come to your village a dozen times."

"No, no." Communicator sounded distressed. "You approach, but you do not come. You have never come to us."

Milt wiped his forehead with the back of a wide hand. "I will come back to your village now, with you," he said. "Would you like that?" he asked.

"I would be so happy!" said Communicator. "But—you will not come. You say it, but you do not come."

"All right. Wait—" about to take a hand transceiver from the console, Milt saw the other two men. "Jerry," he said, "you go this time. Maybe he'll believe it if it's you who goes to the village with him."

"I've been there before. With you, the second time you went," objected Jerry. "And I've got to feed the men in restraint, pretty soon," he added.

"Try going again. That's all we can do—try things. Ben and I'll feed the men," said Milt. Jerry, about to argue further, felt the pressure of a sudden wordless, exhausted appeal from Milt. Milt's basic berserkedness must be just about ready to break loose, too, he realized.

"All right," said Jerry.

"Good," said Milt, looking grateful. "We have to keep trying. I should have lifted ship while I still had five well men to lift it with. Come on, Ben—you and I better go feed those men now, before we fall asleep on our feet."

II

They went away around the nose of the ship. Jerry unhooked the little black-and-white transceiver, that would radio-relay his conversations with Communicator back to the console of the translator for sense-making during the trip.

"Come on," he said to Communicator, and led off down the pleasantly wide jungle trail toward the native village.

They passed from under the little patch of open sky above the clearing and into green-roofed stillness. All about them, massive limbs, branches, ferns and vines intertwined in a majestic maze of growing things. Small flying creatures, looking half-animal and half-insect, flittered among the branches overhead. Some larger, more animal-like, creatures sat on the heavier limbs and moaned off-key like abandoned puppies. Jerry's head spun with his weariness, and the green over his head seemed to close down on him like a net flung by some giant, crazy fisherman, to take him captive.

He was suddenly and bitterly reminded of the Team's high hopes, the day they had set down on this world. No other Team or Group had yet to turn up any kind of alien life much more intelligent than an anthropoid ape. Now they, Team 529, had not only uncovered an intelligent, evidently semi-cultured alien people, but an alien people eager to establish relations with the humans and communicate. Here, two weeks later, the natives were still apparently just as eager to communicate, but what they said made no sense.

Nor did it help that, with the greatest of patience and kindness, Communicator and his kind seemed to consider that it was the humans who were irrational and uncommunicative.

Nor that meanwhile, that the jungle seemed to be mounting a specifically directed attack on the human spaceship.

Nor that the nightmare afflicting the humans had already laid low eight of the twelve crew and were grinding the four left on their feet down to a choice between suicidal delirium or collapse from exhaustion.

It was a miracle, thought Jerry, lightheadedly trudging through the jungle, that the four of them had been able to survive as long as they had. A miracle based probably on some individual chance peculiarity of strength that the other eight men in straitjackets lacked. Although, thought Jerry now, that strength that was had so far defied analysis. Dizzily, like a man in a high fever, he considered their four surviving personalities in his mind's eye. They were, he thought, the four men of the team with what you might call the biggest mental crotchets.

—Or ornery streaks.

Take the fourth member of the group—the Medician, Arthyr Loy, who had barely stuck his nose out of the sick bay lab in the last forty-eight hours. Not only because he was the closest thing to an M.D. aboard the ship, was Art still determined to put the eight restrained men back on their feet again. It just happened, in addition, that Art considered himself the only true professional man aboard, and was not the kind to admit any inability to the lesser mortals about him.

And Milt Johnson—Milt made an excellent captain. He was a tower of strength, a great man for making decisions.

The only thing was, that having decided, Milt could hardly be brought to consider the remote possibility that anyone else might have wanted to decide differently.

Ben Akham was another matter. Ben hated religion and loved machinery—and the jungle surrounding was attacking *his* spaceship. In fact, Jerry was willing to bet that by the time he got back, Ben would be washing the hull with an acid-counteractant in spite of what he had told Jerry earlier.

And himself? Jerry? Jerry shook his head woozily. It was hard to be self-analytical after ten days of three and four hours sleep per twenty. He had what his grandmother had once described as the curse of the Gael—black stubbornness and red rages.

All of these traits, in all four of them, had normally been buried safely below the surfaces of their personalities and had only colored them as individuals. But now, the last two weeks had worn those surfaces down to basic personality bed-rock. Jerry shoved the thought out of his mind.

"Well," he said, turning to Communicator, "we're almost to your village now . . . You can't say someone didn't come with you, this time."

Communicator gabbled. The transceiver in Jerry's hand translated.

"Alas," the native said, "but you are not with me."

"Cut it out!" said Jerry wearily. "I'm right here beside you."

"No," said Communicator. "You accompany me, but you are not here. You are back with your dead things."

"You mean the ship and the rest of it?" asked Jerry.

"There is no ship," said Communicator. "A ship must have grown and been alive. Your thing has always been dead. But we will save you."

III

They came out of the path at last into a clearing dotted with whitish, pumpkin-like shells some ten feet in height above the brown earth in which they were half-buried. Wide cracks in the out-curving sides gave view of tangled roots and plants inside, among which other natives could be seen moving about, scratching, tasting and making holes in the vegetable surfaces.

"Well," said Jerry, making an effort to speak cheerfully, "here I am."

"You are not here."

The berserk tigerishness in Jerry leaped up unawares and took him by the inner throat. For a long second he looked at Communicator through a red haze. Communicator gazed back patiently, evidently unaware how close he was to having his neck broken by a pair of human hands.

"Look—" said Jerry, slowly, between his teeth, getting himself under control, "if you will just tell me what to do to join you and your people, here, I will do it."

"That is good!"

"Then," said Jerry, still with both hands on the inner fury that fought to tear loose inside him, "what do I do?"

"But you know—" The enthusiasm that had come into Communicator a moment before, wavered visibly. "You must get rid of the dead things, and set yourself free to grow, inside. Then, after you have grown, your unsick self will bring you here to join us!"

Jerry stared back. Patience, he said harshly to himself.

"Grow? How? In what way?"

"But you have a little bit of proper life in you," explained Communicator. "Not much, of course . . . but if you will rid yourself of dead things and concentrate on what you call nightmares, it will grow and force out the poison of the dead life in you. The proper life and the nightmares are the hope for you—"

"Wait a minute!" Jerry's exhaustion-fogged brain cleared suddenly and nearly miraculously at the sudden surge of excitement into his bloodstream. "This proper life you talk about—does it have something to do with the nightmares?"

"Of course. How could you have what you call nightmares

without a little proper life in you to give them to you? As the proper life grows, you will cease to fight so against the 'nightmares' . . ."

Communicator continued to talk earnestly. But Jerry's spinning brain was flying off on a new tangent. What was it he had been thinking earlier about tranquilizers—that he had not taken any himself for some time? Then, what about the nightmares in his last four hours of sleep?

He must have had them—he remembered now that he *had* had them. But evidently they had not bothered him as much as before—at least, not enough to send him scrambling for tranquilizers to dull the dreams' weird impact on him.

"Communicator!" Jerry grabbed at the thin, leathery-skinned arm of the native. "Have I been chang—growing?"

"I do not know, of course," said the native, courteously. "I profoundly hope so. Have you?"

"Excuse me—" gulped Jerry. "I've got to get oot of here—back to th' ship!"

He turned, and raced back up the trail. Some twenty minutes later, he burst into the clearing before the ship to find an ominous silence hanging over everything. Only the faint rustle and hissing from the ever-growing jungle swallowing up the ship sounded on his eardrums.

"Milt—Ben!" he shouted, plunging into the ship. "Art!"

A hail from farther down the main corridor reassured him, and he followed it up to find all three unrestrained members of the crew in the sickbay. But—Jerry brought himself up short, his throat closing on him—there was a figure on the table.

"Who . . ." began Jerry. Milt Johnson turned around to face him. The captain's big body mercifully hid most of the silent form on the table.

"Wally Blake," said Milt emptily. "He managed to strangle himself after all. Got twisted up in his restraint jacket. Ben and I heard him thumping around in there, but by the time we got to him, it was too late. Art's doing an autopsy."

"Not exactly an autopsy," came the soft, Virginia voice of the Medician from beyond Milt. "Just looking for something I suspected . . . and here it is!"

Milt spun about and Jerry pushed between the big captain and Ben. He found himself looking at the back of a human head from which a portion of the skull had been removed. What he saw before him was a small expanse of whitish, soft, inner tissue that was the brainstem; and fastened to it almost like a grape growing there, was a small, purplish mass.

Art indicated the purple shape with the tip of a sharp, surgical instrument.

"There," he said. "And I bet we've each got one."

"What is it?" asked Ben's voice, hushed and a little nauseated.

"I don't know," said Art harshly. "How the devil would I be able to tell? But I found organisms in the bloodstreams of those of us I've taken blood samples from—organisms like spores, that look like this, only smaller, microscopic in size."

"You didn't tell me that!" said Milt, turning quickly to face him.

"What was the point?" Art turned toward the Team Captain. Jerry saw that the Medician's long face was almost bloodless. "I didn't know what they were. I thought if I kept looking, I might know more. Then I could have something positive to tell you, as well as the bad news. But—it's no use now."

"Why do you say that?" snapped Milt.

"Because it's the truth." Art's face seemed to slide apart, go loose and waxy with defeat. "As long as it was something non-physical we were fighting, there was some hope we could throw it off. But—you see what's going on inside us. We're being changed physically. That's where the nightmares come from. You can't overcome a physical change with an effort of will!"

"What about the Grotto at Lourdes?" asked Jerry. His head was whirling strangely with a mass of ideas. His own great-grandfather—the family story came back to mind—had been judged by his physician in eighteen ninety-six to have advanced pulmonary tuberculosis. Going home from the doctor's office, Simon Fraser McWhin had decided that he could not afford to have tuberculosis at this time. That he would not, therefore, have tuberculosis at all. And he had dismissed the matter fully from his mind.

One year later, examined by the same physician, he had no signs of tuberculosis whatsoever.

But in this present moment, Art, curling up in his chair at the end of the table, seemed not to have heard Jerry's question. And Jerry was suddenly reminded of the question that had brought him pelting back from the native village.

"Is it growing—I mean was it growing when Wally strangled himself—that growth on his brain?" he asked.

Art roused himself.

"Growing?" he repeated dully. He climbed to his feet and picked up an instrument. He investigated the purple mass for a moment.

"No," he said, dropping the instrument wearily and falling back into his chair. "Looks like its outer layer has died and started to be reabsorbed—I think." He put his head in his hands. "I'm not qualified to answer such questions. I'm not trained . . ."

"Who is?" demanded Milt, grimly, looming over the table and the rest of them. "And we're reaching the limit of our strength as well as the limits of what we know—"

"We're done for," muttered Ben. His eyes were glazed, looking at the dissected body on the table. "It's not my fault—"

"Catch him! Catch Art!" shouted Jerry, leaping forward.

But he was too late. The Medician had been gradually curling up in his chair since he had sat down in it again. Now, he slipped out of it to the floor, rolled in a ball, and lay still.

"Leave him alone." Milt's large hand caught Jerry and held him back. "He may as well lie there as someplace else." He got to his feet. "Ben's right. We're done for."

"Done for?" Jerry stared at the big man. The words he had just heard were words he would never have imagined hearing from Milt.

"Yes," said Milt. He seemed somehow to be speaking from a long distance off.

"Listen—" said Jerry. The tigerishness inside him had woken at Milt's words. It tugged and snarled against the words of defeat from the captain's lips. "We're winning. We aren't losing!"

"Quit it, Jerry," said Ben dully, from the far end of the room.

"Quit it—?" Jerry swung on the engineer. "You lost your temper with me before I went down to the village, about the way I said 'oot'! How could you lose your temper if you were full of tranquilizers? I haven't been taking any myself, and I feel better because of it. Don't tell me you've been taking yours! —And that means we're getting stronger than the nightmares."

"The tranquilizer've been making me sick, if you must know! That's why I haven't been taking them—" Ben broke off, his face graying. He pointed a shaking finger at the purplish mass. "I'm being changed, that's why they made me sick! I'm changing already!" His voice rose toward a scream. "Don't you see, it's changing me—" He broke off, suddenly screaming and leaping at Milt with clawing fingers. "We're all changing! And it's your fault for bringing the ship down here. You did it—"

Milt's huge fist slammed into the side of the smaller man's jaw, driving him to the floor beside the still shape of the Medician, where he lay quivering and sobbing.

Slowly Milt lifted his gaze from the fallen man and faced Jerry. It was the standard seventy-two degrees Centigrade in the room, but Jerry saw perspiration standing out on Milt's calm face as if he had just stepped out of a steam bath.

"But he may be right," said Milt, emotionlessly. His voice seemed to come from the far end of some lightless tunnel. "We may be changing under the influence of those growths right now—each of us."

"Milt!" said Jerry, sharply. But Milt's face never changed. It was large, and calm, and pale—and drenched with sweat. "Now's the last time we ought to give up! We're starting to understand it now. I tell you, the thing is to meet Communicator and the other natives head on! Head to head we can crack them wide open. One of us has to go down to that village."

"No. I'm the captain," said Milt, his voice unchanged. "I'm responsible, and I'll decide. We can't lift ship with less than five men and there's only two of us—you and I—actually left. I can't risk one of us coming under the influence of the growth in him, and going over to the alien side."

"Going over?" Jerry stared at him.

"That's what all this has been for—the jungle, the natives, the nightmare. They want to take us over." Sweat ran down Milt's cheeks and dripped off his chin, while he continued to talk tonelessly and gaze straight ahead. "They'll send us— what's left of us—back against our own people. I can't let that happen. We'll have to destroy ourselves so there's nothing for them to use."

"Milt—" said Jerry.

"No." Milt swayed faintly on his feet like a tall tree under a wind too high to be felt on the ground at its base. "We can't risk leaving ship or crew. We'll blow the ship up with ourselves in it—"

"*Blow up my ship!*"

It was a wild-animal scream from the floor at their feet; and Ben Akham rose from almost under the table like a demented wildcat, aiming for Milt's jugular vein. So unexpected and powerful was the attack that the big captain tottered and fell. With a noise like worrying dogs, they rolled together under the table.

The chained tiger inside Jerry broke its bonds and flung free.

He turned and ducked through the door into the corridor. It was a heavy pressure door with a wheel lock, activating metal dogs to seal it shut in case of a hull blowout and sudden loss of air. Jerry slammed the door shut, and spun the wheel.

The dogs snicked home. Snatching down the portable fire extinguisher hanging on the wall alongside, Jerry dropped the foam container on the floor and jammed the metal nozzle of its hose between a spoke of the locking wheel and the unlocking stop on the door beneath it.

He paused. There was silence inside the sickbay lab. Then the wheel jerked against the nozzle and the door tried to open.

"What's going on?" demanded the voice of Milt. There was a pause. "Jerry, what's going on out there? Open up!"

A wild, crazy impulse to hysterical laughter rose inside Jerry without warning. It took all his will power to choke it back.

"You're locked in, Milt," he said.

"Jerry!" The wheel spoke clicked against the jamming metal nozzle, in a futile effort to turn. "Open up! That's an order!"

"Sorry, Milt," said Jerry softly and lightheadedly. "I'm not ready yet to burn the hoose about my ears. This business of you wanting to blow up the ship's the same sort of impulse to suicide that got Wally and the rest. I'm off to face the natives now and let them have their way with me. I'll be back later, to let you oot."

"Jerry!"

Jerry heard Milt's voice behind him as he went off down the corridor.

"Jerry!" There was a fusillade of pounding fists against the door, growing fainter as Jerry moved away. "Don't you see?—

That growth in you is finally getting you! Jerry, come back!
Don't let them take over one of us! Jerry . . ."

Jerry left the noise and the ship together behind him as he
stepped out of the airlock. The jungle, he saw, was covering
the ship's hull again, already hiding it for the most part. He
went on out to the translator console and began taking off
his clothes. When he was completely undressed, he unhooked
the transceiver he had brought back from the native village,
slung it on a loop of his belt, and hung the belt around his
neck.

He headed off down the trail toward the village, wincing
a little as the soles of his shoeless feet came into contact
with pebbles along the way.

When he got to the village clearing, a naked shape he recognized as that of Communicator tossed up its arms in joy
and came running to him.

"Well," said Jerry. "I've grown. I've got rid of the poison of
dead things and the sickness. Here I am to join you!"

"At last!" gabbled Communicator. Other natives were running up. "Throw away the dead thing around your neck!"

"I still need it to understand you," said Jerry. "I guess I
need a little help to join you all the way."

"Help? We will help!" cried Communicator. "But you must
throw that away. You have rid yourself of the dead things
that you kept wrapped around your limbs and body," gabbled
Communicator. "Now rid yourself of the dead thing hanging
about your neck."

"But I tell you, if I do that," objected Jerry, "I won't be
able to understand you when you talk, or make you understand me!"

"Throw it away. It is poisoning you! Throw it away!" said
Communicator. By this time three or four more natives had
come up and others were headed for the gathering. "Shortly
you will understand all, and all will understand you. Throw
it away!"

"Throw it away!" chorused the other natives.

"Well . . ." said Jerry. Reluctantly, he took off the belt with the transceiver, and dropped it. Communicator gabbled unintelligibly.

". . . come with me . . ." translated the transceiver like a faint and tinny echo from the ground where it had landed. Communicator took hold of Jerry's hand and drew him toward the nearest whitish structure. Jerry swallowed unobtrusively. It was one thing to make up his mind to do this; it was something else again to actually do it. But he let himself be led to and in through a crack in the structure.

Inside, the place smelled rather like a mixture of a root cellar and a hayloft—earthy and fragrant at the same time. Communicator drew him in among the waist high tangle of roots rising and reentering the packed earth floor. The other natives swarmed after them. Close to the center of the floor they reached a point where the roots were too thick to allow them to pick their way any further. The roots rose and tangled into a mat, the irregular surface of which was about three feet off the ground. Communicator patted the root surface and gabbled agreeably.

"You want me to get up there?" Jerry swallowed again, then gritted his teeth as the chained fury in him turned suddenly upon himself. There was nothing worse, he snarled at himself, than a man who was long on planning a course of action, but short on carrying it out.

Awkwardly, he clambered up on to the matted surface of the roots. They gave irregularly under him and their rough surfaces scraped his knees and hands. The natives gabbled, and he felt leather hands urging him to stretch out and lie down on his back.

He did so. The root scored and poked the tender skin of his back. It was exquisitely uncomfortable.

"Now what—?" he gasped. He turned his head to look at the natives and saw that green tendrils, growing rapidly from

the root mass, were winding about and garlanding the arms
and legs of Communicator and several other of the natives
standing by. A sudden pricking at his left wrist made him
look down.

Green garlands were twining around his own wrists and
ankles, sending wire-thin tendrils into his skin. In unconscious
reflex of panic he tried to heave upward, but the green bonds
held him fast.

"*Gabble-gabble-gabble . . .*" warbled Communicator, reas-
suringly.

With sudden alarm, Jerry realized that the green tendrils
were growing right into the arms and legs of the natives as
well. He was abruptly conscious of further prickings in his
own arms and legs.

"What's going on—" he started to say, but found his tongue
had gone unnaturally thick and unmanageable. A wave of
dizziness swept over him as if a powerful general anesthetic
was taking hold. The interior of the structure seemed to
darken; and he felt as if he was swooping away toward its
ceiling on the long swing of some monster pendulum . . .

It swung him on into darkness. And nightmare.

It was the same old nightmare, but more so. It was nightmare experienced *awake* instead of asleep; and the difference
was that he had no doubt about the fact that he was experiencing what he was experiencing, nor any tucked-away certainty that waking would bring him out of it.

Once more he floated through a changing soup of uncer-
tainty, himself a changing part of it. It was not painful, it
was not even terrifying. But it was hideous—it was an affront
to nature. He was not himself. He was a thing, a part of the
whole—and he must reconcile himself to being so. He must
accept it.

Reconcile himself to it—no! It was not possible for the unbending, solitary, individualistic part that was *him* to do so.
But accept it—maybe.

Jerry set a jaw that was no longer a jaw and felt the determination in him to blast through, to comprehend this incomprehensible thing, become hard and undeniable as a sword-point of tungsten steel. He drove through—

And abruptly the soup fell into order. It slid into focus like a blurred scene before the gaze of a badly myopic man who finally gets his spectacles before his eyes. Suddenly, Jerry was aware that what he observed was a scene not just before his eyes, but before his total awareness. And it was not the interior of the structure where he lay on a bed of roots, but the whole planet.

It was a landscape of factories. Countless factories, interconnected, intersupplying, integrated. It lacked only that he find his own working place among them.

Now, said this scene. *This is the sane universe, the way it really is. Reconcile yourself to it.*

The hell I will!

It was the furious unbending, solitary, individualistic part that was essentially *him*, speaking again. Not just speaking. Roaring—snarling its defiance, like a tiger on a hillside.

And the scene went—*pop.*

Jerry opened his eyes. He sat up. The green shoots around and in his wrists and ankles pulled prickingly at him. But they were already dying and not able to hold him. He swung his legs over the edge of the mat of roots and stood down. Communicator and the others, who were standing there, backed fearfully away from him, gabbling.

He understood their gabbling no better than before, but now he could read the emotional overtones in it. And those overtones were now of horror and disgust, overlying a wild, atavistic panic and terror. He walked forward. They scuttled away before him, gabbling, and he walked through the nearest crack in the wall of the structure and out into the sunlight, toward the transceiver and the belt where he had dropped them.

"Monster!" screamed the transceiver tinnily, faithfully translating the gabbling of the Communicator, who was following a few steps behind like a small dog barking behind a larger. "Brute! Savage! Unclean . . ." it kept up a steady denunciation.

Jerry turned to face Communicator, and the native tensed for flight.

"You know what I'm waiting for," said Jerry, almost smiling, hearing the transceiver translate his words into gabbling —though it was not necessary. As he had said, Communicator knew what he was waiting for.

Communicator cursed a little longer in his own tongue, then went off into one of the structures, and returned with a handful of what looked like lengths of green vine. He dropped them on the ground before Jerry and backed away, cautiously, gabbling.

"Now will you go? And never come back! Never . . ."

"We'll see," said Jerry. He picked up the lengths of green vine and turned away up the path to the ship.

The natives he passed on his way out of the clearing huddled away from him and gabbled as he went.

When he stepped back into the clearing before the ship, he saw that most of the vegetation touching or close to the ship was already brown and dying. He went on into the ship, carefully avoiding the locked sickbay door, and wound lengths of the green vine around the wrists of each of the men in restraints.

Then he sat down to await results. He had never been so tired in his life. The minute he touched the chair, his eyes started to close. He struggled to his feet and forced himself to pace the floor until the green vines, which had already sent hair-thin tendrils into the ulnar arteries of the arms around which they were wrapped, pumped certain inhibitory chemicals into the bloodstreams of the seven men.

When the men started to blink their eyes and look about sensibly, he went to work to unfasten the homemade strait-

jackets that had held them prisoner. When he had released
the last one, he managed to get out his final message before
collapsing.

"Take the ship up," croaked Jerry. "Then, let yourself into
the sickbay and wrap a vine piece around the wrists of Milt,
and Art, and Ben. Ship up first—then when you're safely in
space, take care of them, in the sickbay. Do it the other way
and you'll never see Earth again."

They crowded around him with questions. He waved them
off, slumping into one of the abandoned bunks.

"Ship up—" he croaked. "Then release and fix the others.
Ask me later. Later—"

. . . And that was all he remembered, then.

IV

At some indefinite time later, not quite sure whether he had
woken by himself, or whether someone else had wakened him,
Jerry swam back up to consciousness. He was vaguely aware
that he had been sleeping a long time; and his body felt sane
again, but weak as the body of a man after a long illness.

He blinked and saw the large face of Milt Johnson, partly
obscured by a cup of something. Milt was seated in a chair
by the side of the bunk Jerry lay in, and the Team Captain
was offering the cup of steaming black liquid to Jerry. Slowly,
Jerry understood that this was coffee and he struggled up on
one elbow to take the cup.

He drank from it slowly for a little while, while Milt
watched and waited.

"Do you realize," said Milt at last, when Jerry finally put
down the three-quarters empty cup on the nightstand by the
bunk, "that what you did in locking me in the sickbay was
mutiny?"

Jerry swallowed. Even his vocal chords seemed drained of
strength and limp.

"You realize," he croaked, "what would have happened if
I hadn't?"

"You took a chance. You followed a wild hunch—"

"No hunch," said Jerry. He cleared his throat. "Art found that growth on Wally's brain had quit growing before Wally killed himself. And I'd been getting along without tranquilizers—handling the nightmares better than I had with them."

"It could have been the growth in your own brain," said Milt, "taking over and running you—working better on you than it had on Wally."

"Working better—talk sense!" said Jerry, weakly, too pared down by the past two weeks to care whether school kept or not, in the matter of service courtesy to a superior. "The nightmares had broken Wally down to where we had to wrap him in a straitjacket. They hadn't even knocked me off my feet. If Wally's physiological processes had fought the alien invasion to a standstill, then I, you, Art, and Ben—all of us—had to be doing even better. Besides—I'd figured out what the aliens were after."

"What were they after?" Milt looked strangely at him.

"Curing us—of something we didn't have when we landed, but they thought we had."

"And what was that?"

"Insanity," said Jerry, grimly.

Milt's blond eyebrows went up. He opened his mouth as if to say something disbelieving—then closed it again. When he did speak, it was quite calmly and humbly.

"They thought," he asked, "Communicator's people thought that we were insane, and they could cure us?"

Jerry laughed; not cheerfully, but grimly.

"You saw that jungle around us back there?" he asked. "That was a factory complex—an infinitely complex factory complex. You saw their village with those tangles of roots inside the big whitish shells?— That was a highly diversified laboratory."

Milt's blue eyes slowly widened, as Jerry watched.

"You don't mean that—seriously?" said Milt, at last.

"That's right." Jerry drained the cup and set it aside. "Their technology is based on organic chemistry, the way ours is on the physical sciences. By our standards, they're chemical wizards. How'd you like to try changing the mind of an alien organism by managing to grow an extra part on to his brain —the way they tried to do to us humans? To them, it was the simplest way of convincing us."

Milt stared again. Finally, he shook his head.

"Why?" he said. "Why would they want to change our minds?"

"Because their philosophy, their picture of life and the universe around them grew out of a chemically oriented science." answered Jerry. "The result is, they see all life as part of a closed, intra-acting chemical circuit with no loose ends; with every living thing, intelligent or not, a part of the whole. Well, you saw it for yourself in your nightmare. That's the cosmos as they see it—and to them it's beautiful."

"But why did they want us to see it the way they did?"

"Out of sheer kindness," said Jerry and laughed barkingly. "According to their cosmology, there's no such thing as an alien. Therefore we weren't alien—just sick in the head. Poisoned by the lumps of metal like the ship and the translator, we claimed were so important. And our clothes and everything else we had. The kind thing was to cure and rescue us."

"Now, wait a minute," said Milt. "They saw those things of ours *work*—"

"What's the fact they worked got to do with it? What you don't understand, Milt," said Jerry, lying back gratefully on the bunk, "is that Communicator's peoples' minds were *closed*. Not just unconvinced, not just refusing to see—but *closed!* Sealed, and welded shut from prehistoric beginnings right down to the present. The fact our translator worked meant nothing to them. According to their cosmology, it shouldn't work, so it didn't. Any stray phenomena tending to prove it did were simply the product of diseased minds."

Jerry paused to emphasize the statement and his eyes drifted shut. The next thing he knew Milt was shaking him.

". . . Wake up!" Milt was shouting at him. "You can dope off after you've explained. I'm not going to have my crew back in straitjackets again, just because you were too sleepy to warn me they'd revert!"

". . . Won't revert," said Jerry, thickly. He roused himself. "Those lengths of vine released chemicals into their blood-streams to destroy what was left of the growths. I wouldn't leave until I got them from Communicator." Jerry struggled up on one elbow again. "And after a short walk in a human brain—mine—he and his people couldn't get us out of sight and forgotten fast enough."

"Why?" Milt shook him again as Jerry's eyelids sagged. "Why should getting their minds hooked in with yours shake them up so?"

". . . Bust—bust their cosmology open. Quit shaking . . . I'm awake."

"Why did it bust them wide open?"

"Remember—how it was for you with the nightmares?" said Jerry. "The other way around? Think back, about when you slept. There you were, a lone atom of humanity, caught up in a nightmare like one piece of stew meat in a vat stewing all life together—just one single chemical bit with no inde-pendent existence, and no existence at all except as part of the whole. Remember?"

He saw Milt shiver slightly.

"It was like being swallowed up by a soft machine," said the Team Captain in a small voice. "I remember."

"All right," said Jerry. "That's how it was for you in Com-municator's cosmos. But remember something about that cosmos? It was warm, and safe. It was all-embracing, all-settling, like a great, big, soft, woolly comforter."

"It was too much like a woolly comforter," said Milt, shuddering. "It was unbearable."

"To you. Right," said Jerry. "But to Communicator, it was

ideal. And if that was ideal, think what it was like when he had to step into a human mind—mine."

Milt stared at him.

"Why?" Milt asked.

"Because," said Jerry. "He found himself *alone* there!"

Milt's eyes widened.

"Think about it, Milt," said Jerry. "From the time we're born, we're individuals. From the moment we open our eyes on the world, inside we're alone in the universe. All the emotional and intellectual resources that Communicator draws from his identity with the stewing vat of his cosmos, each one of us has to dig up for and out of himself!"

Jerry stopped to give Milt a chance to say something. But Milt was evidently not in possession of something to say at the moment.

"That's why Communicator and the others couldn't take it, when they hooked into my human mind," Jerry went on. "And that's why, when they found out what we were like inside, they couldn't wait to get rid of us. So they gave me the vines and kicked us out. That's the whole story." He lay back on the bunk.

Milt cleared his throat.

"All right," he said.

Jerry's heavy eyes closed. Then the other man's voice spoke, still close by his ear.

"But," said Milt, "I still think you took a chance, going down to butt heads with the natives that way. What if Communicator and the rest had been able to stand exposure to your mind. You'd locked me in and the other men were in restraint. Our whole team would have been part of that stewing vat."

"Not a chance," said Jerry.

"You can't be sure of that."

"Yes I can." Jerry heard his own voice sounding harshly beyond the darkness of his closed eyelids. "It wasn't just that

I knew my cosmological view was too tough for them. It was the fact that their minds were closed—in the vat they had no freedom to change and adapt themselves to anything new."

"What's that got to do with it?" demanded the voice of Milt.

"Everything," said Jerry. "Their point of view only made us very uncomfortable—but our point of view, being individually adaptable, and open, threatened to destroy the very laws of existence as they saw them. An open mind can always stand a closed one, if it has to—by making room for it in the general picture. But a closed mind can't stand it near an open one without risking immediate and complete destruction in its own terms. In a closed mind, there's no more room."

He stopped speaking and slowly exhaled a weary breath.

"Now," he said, without opening his eyes, "will you finally get oot of here and let me sleep?"

For a long second more, there was silence. Then, he heard a chair scrape softly, and the muted steps of Milt tiptoeing away.

With another sigh, at last Jerry relaxed and let consciousness slip from him.

He slept.

—As sleep the boar upon the plain, the hawk upon the crag, and the tiger on the hill . . .

The Friendly Man

Mark Toren was very surprised to find someone waiting for him.

The awaiter was a young, pleasant-looking man wearing an open-throated sport shirt with a pipe in his mouth. He took the pipe from his mouth to wave cheerfully and pointed through a doorway into what seemed a rather pleasant living room.

"Come in," he said. "Come in, and make yourself at home."

Wondering, Mark followed him in. This was not according to what he had conceived as regulations. Did they have a reception room for all visitors from time?

He looked around the room wonderingly as he took a chair. It looked like any ordinary room, comfortably furnished in the style of his own century.

"You look puzzled," said the young man, who had taken a seat across from him—a deep leather armchair in which he lounged comfortably. Mark eyed him narrowly, noting the style of his clothes, which was the same as that of Mark's own.

"I am," he said, dryly. "You don't expect to go fifty thousand years into the future and find the present."

The young man chuckled. "You'd be surprised," he said. "Civilization has a way of coming full circle . . . oh, by the way, my name's Merkl: and yours is—?"

"Mark Toren," said Mark. "What do you mean by full circle?"

"Ups and downs," replied the young man, airily. "Dark Ages—a period of scientific advance—another Dark Age—another period of scientific advance—and so on."

Mark frowned. "That's odd," he said. "The cycle seemed that way in my time, surely. But according to my own prognostications, it should have leveled out to a steady uphill climb for the human race by at least twenty thousand years after my time. As a matter of fact, that's why I chose to go this far into the future; simply because that time seemed so remote that no one of my time could imagine what the human race would be like—" He interrupted himself suddenly, "If you don't mind, I'd like to ask a few questions about your present time."

"Shoot!" said the young man, blowing a cloud of smoke toward the ceiling.

"You speak my language," asked Mark, bluntly, "you're dressed as I am. How come?"

"Oh, that," said Merkl. "We have instruments that allow us to look a little distance along the time line in either direction. We saw you coming and got things fixed up to receive you."

"That much trouble for one visitor?" asked Mark.

"It wasn't much trouble," Merkl shrugged, "with our technology."

"Then," said Mark, "I take it that your world is very different from what I see here."

"Some," said Merkl. "We have a higher technological level, of course. At the same time, as I said, culturally, our civilization is at pretty much the same cyclic point that yours was at."

"At the same time," Mark said, his eyes taking on for a second, the fugitive gleam of the researcher, "it's going to be interesting for me." He paused, and when the other made no immediate response, continued. "You don't have any objection to my seeing it, do you?" he asked.

"Oh, none. None at all," replied the young man hurriedly. "Of course, you understand, we're going to have to give you and your temporal vehicle a bit of an examination, just to make sure there's nothing about either of you that might possibly be harmful to us."

"I assure you—" Mark was beginning stiffly, when the young man interrupted with an apologetic air.

"Oh, we realize that you have no intention of doing any harm, but you might, for example, be harboring disease germs to which we are no longer immune. Your ship might possess some latent energy which would react violently if it were inadvertently exposed to some of our technology. I assure you that there won't be anything to the examination. As a matter of fact, you can speed up the business considerably just by answering a few questions for me."

Mark grimaced wryly.

"I'd hoped the shoe would be on the other foot," he said. "I'm bursting with curiosity. However, go ahead."

"First," said Merkl, "just to confirm the findings of our instruments, suppose you tell me from what time you come?"

"Twenty-one Ninety A.D.," said Mark.

Merkl nodded.

"And what type of civilization did you have, then?"

"Well," said Mark, "we considered ourselves fairly well advanced. Our rockets had reached as far as the moons of Jupiter and we had fairly well established colonies on Mars and Venus. We were making fairly wide use of atomic power, although the installations were still so expensive as to restrict their use considerably—" he broke off, somewhat embarrassed.

"I suppose this all sounds awfully primitive and childlike to you," he said.

"Not at all," answered Merkl, quickly. "Not at all. Go on."

"Well—sociologically we were, I suppose, pretty primitive. Equality among the sexes was firmly established, of course. There was still some suppression of minorities, but not much.

The old Earth governments were still in force, although the
real power was wielded by the large business and labor or-
ganizations."

"I see," interjected Merkl. "Still the type of society where
a strong man could hack his way to power."

"Why, yes—" said Mark, and stopped abruptly. "Why do
you ask that?"

"Oh, for no particular reason," replied Merkl, easily. "The
situation is merely typical of such cyclic conditions as you've
been describing. Tell me more about the extent to which
planetary exploration had gone. No farther than Jupiter,
you say?"

"Not that I know of," answered Mark. "And I imagine I
would have heard of any further advances."

"Interesting," said Merkl. "Very interesting." He rose suddenly to his feet.

"I'll leave you now," he said. "The machines are ready to
scan you and your machine. The process will take several
days, but I assure you, will not cause you the slightest dis-
comfort. Make yourself comfortable here. This building is
yours, although I must warn you about stepping outside of it
until you are told it is safe to do so."

"Of course," said Mark. "But there are a few more things
I'd like to ask you—" He broke off, for Merkl had already
passed through the door and was gone.

After the young man left, Mark sat for a while in thought.
The reception he had been accorded was not what he had
expected—but then he chided himself for expecting it to con-
form to any preconceived notions.

He was not the first explorer in time to leave from the
period of the Twenty-second Century; but if he returned, he
would be the first to do that. The risk was a calculated one,
and he took it with no mental reservations. It was, however,
with some idea of playing safe that he had set his destination
at five thousand years in the future. Briefly, Mark had been
hoping to get beyond the cyclic ups and down to which Merkl

① 50 thousand.

had referred. Inevitably, he had thought, reverses and re-re-verses of history must come to an end eventually as man grew in mental maturity.

How far can the human race go in fifty thousand years, considering its progress during the past five thousand years of known history? Mark had asked himself that question and answered it with the obvious reply that it was impossible to imagine the answer. The most he could guess was that by then man would be a new creature entirely, bearing only the remotest resemblance to his ancestor of the Twenty-second Century. The least Mark had imagined was that man, fifty thousand years from then, would have passed into a completely new era.

And now, here was Merkl to tell him that, aside from a greatly improved technology, man was still on the same merry-go-round of history that he had been on in Mark's time. Mark shook his head over the information. Merkl's answer was plausible, even reasonable, but it did not *feel* right.

Mark shook the notion from his head and rose to explore the building where he was being temporarily held a prisoner. It consisted of three rooms and all the appurtenances of the normal Twenty-second Century bungalow. The only difference was a stairway that led up to the open roof, which gave him a view of the surrounding country.

The countryside was grassy and rolling; the air astoundingly fresh and clear, so that the few isolated groups of buildings he could see in the distance stood out sharply, like meticulously executed miniatures. He was struck by the isolated position of his bungalow, and had halfway resolved to ask Merkl about it, when it struck him that possibly they were playing extra-safe in the matter of possible contagion. Still, that was odd, when Merkl had not seemed at all shy about coming into quite close proximity to him. Of course, the scientific worker sometimes took long chances— He shrugged his shoulders and went back down the stairs. I'll just check

the time machine, he thought, and then get some sleep. As
soon as the examination period is over there'll no doubt be
plenty to do.

But when he came to the spot of his arrival, the time machine was gone.

Two days later, Merkl returned. Mark did not hear him
enter, but there he was, suddenly, in the entrance to the room
where they had had their first interview.

"Hello," said Merkl, with a friendly smile. "How are things
going?"

Mark jumped out of his seat.

"You've taken my machine!" he snapped.

"Why, yes," said Merkl. "It was easier to take it to the
machines which would scan it, than to bring the machines
here. I imagine you'll have it back in a day or so."

"Oh," Mark answered, somewhat mollified. Merkl came
on into the room, followed by an older, thinner man, who
nodded pleasantly to Mark.

"Mark," said Merkl, "I'd like to have you meet Termi, one
of our archaeologists. He's one of the group who's been
studying that machine of yours; and he's found it interesting. So interesting, in fact, that he wanted me to ask you if
you wouldn't mind chatting with him about it."

Mark could not help feeling slightly flattered. The thin
line of his mouth relaxed.

"Of course," he said. "Anything you would like to know."

"Thank you, sir," responded Termi. "Shall we sit down?"

All three took chairs, and Mark leaned forward, grasping
his knees with his hands, in an attitude of attentiveness.
Termi's smooth voice flowed over him.

"I must begin by an admission," said the archaeologist.
"Our records of time machines are very incomplete, Mark,
very. The most primitive ones of which we have any record
belong to a date some fifteen thousand years later than your
time. We assume that probably there was, following your

time, a period of scientific retrogression, in which the basic knowledge necessary to the construction of such a machine, was lost. So that your machine stands alone in our experience without any means available to tie it to later developments. It is not even readily apparent to us how you operated it; and I thought, just to save us the time and effort of experimentation, that you might not mind explaining the process to us."

"Not at all," answered Mark. "You must, of course, understand that there were others working on the subject of time travel during my period and that my machine is by no means typical. But they were all founded on the same principles.

"Briefly, it was the development of psychomechanics that allowed real research on the subject of time travel to begin. Psychomechanics found that there was a definite connection between the human body's perception of time and its *experience* of time. That is, the body tended to react to what it perceived as a speeded-up time flow by speeding up itself. The Mackenwald distorter was the first instrument to exploit this reaction by accelerating a subject's perception of time as much as three times normal; and, quite by accident, it was discovered that inanimate objects in close proximity to the body also tended to be affected by the speed-up process.

"From the matter of distorting the body relative to time, it was a short step to the problem of distorting time relative to the body. And from the research done in that direction finally was evolved the technique of putting the body in suspension relative to time—that is, into a timeless state.

"It's a little difficult to explain what I mean without demonstrating the processes as they occurred step by step. But, it should be easy to understand how, once it was possible to put a living person into a timeless state, all that was necessary for time travel, was to find a means of moving that body along the time stream to the point at which it wished to re-enter the time stream. Psychomechanics solved that difficulty by training the human mind to the point of using it as a propulsive unit in the timeless state. This, of course, was possible since it takes, even in practice, almost no energy to move a body relative to the time stream."

Termi leaned back in his chair and laughed.

"No wonder," he said. "That's a good joke on us. No wonder we couldn't find any evidence of a propulsive unit on your machine, when the propulsive unit was in your head, instead."

"Well," said Mark, a trifle embarrassed. "It's something like that."

"Well, well," said Termi, standing up, "thank you for being so kind as to explain it to me, Mark. Sometime later I'll have to drop back and have another chat with you. There are a lot of aspects of your time on which I'd be glad to have some firsthand information."

He turned toward the door. Merkl also rose to go, but Mark put out a hand to detain him.

"Look here, Merkl," he said, "aren't you through with investigating me, now? I'd like to get out of here and see firsthand what this world of yours is like."

Merkl stuffed his pipe thoughtfully.

"As a matter of fact," he said, "you seem to be turning out to be a more complex character than we had expected, Mark, and we're not quite done, yet. I imagine that in a week more, you can get out and around."

"A week!"

"Possibly a week," answered Merkl. "Possibly less. And now I really must go." And, wrenching his arm from Mark's grasp, he turned and was through the door before Mark could think of anything more to say.

Mark jumped to the door behind him, and flung it open. But there was nothing to be seen except a small sort of flying ship rising from the grass just outside the building. Defeated, Mark returned to the interior of the bungalow.

The week passed, leaving Mark with food for thought. The

bungalow was supplied with books of the Twenty-second Century type, but, on close inspection, Mark was unable to find one that he had not read before. So he spent his time mostly on the roof of the building, enjoying the sunlight and pondering the reception that he was receiving in this world of the future.

It was not until the week was nearly over that he was able to put his finger on the oddness of his situation—the feeling that had been bothering him ever since his arrival.

It had to do with the reactions exhibited by Merkl, Termi, and the race they represented. Subconsciously, Mark had expected these men of the future to be, if anything, supremely sure of themselves and their actions. And it was a lack of this sureness that he seemed to notice in the two men he had met so far.

He had assumed from the completeness of the building in which he found himself and the casual attitude of Merkl that they had been completely prepared for his arrival. Consequently, he had reasoned that there would be little fuss and bother about the investigation to which they insisted on submitting him. Instead, there seemed to be a great deal. It was puzzling.

Consequently, when Merkl next returned, at the end of the week, Mark was determined to pin him down on the matter of his further seclusion.

"Look here, Merkl," he said, "I'm not questioning your right to take adequate defensive measures against whatever inimical hosts my mind or body may be harboring, but you can't keep me shut up like this with nothing to do. I'll go crazy. Man, I'm human, too."

For some reason Mark's words seemed to catch the other completely off balance. He continued to stand facing the visitor from time, with his usual smile and puffing with his usual serenity on his pipe. But otherwise it was exactly as if a switch in his mind had been clicked off. He stood, staring at Mark for such a long time that Mark grew alarmed, thinking that the man had been struck by some sudden strange paralysis. Then, just as suddenly, he came out of it.

"You must stay here," he said. "It is impossible for you to go out right now."

"But—" cried Mark.

"I'm sorry," said Merkl, and, turning on his heels, fairly ran out the door to his waiting flier.

Mark, puzzled and angry, paced the bungalow after Merkl had left. He had no longer any doubt that he was being deliberately cut off from the world of the future. Why, he wondered. What on earth could be so wrong with him that he was not allowed even a close-up glimpse of the cities he could see from the roof? And out of his frustration, and the temper-wearing pressure of nearly two weeks enforced idleness, he formed a plan.

That night he crept up on the roof, being careful to allow no light to show. A half-insane plan had formed in his head. They had warned him against going out of the building, but the front door was unlocked. He assumed that if they expected him to leave against orders, they would not expect him to go to the trouble of dropping off one side of the roof, rather than walking directly out the door. At any rate, he would chance it.

He slithered over the roof's low railing, hung by his hands for a second, and then released his grip. He fell, but not hard, and, after rolling over a couple of times in the soft grass, lay still and waited.

There was no alarm. After a while, he got to his feet and moved softly off through the night to where the nearest city gleamed against the night sky.

He had estimated that the city was some eight or ten miles away, but after trudging for three or four minutes, he was surprised to see that the glow of its lights was considerably stronger, so that it appeared to light up half of the sky. Cautiously he slowed his pace, but the glow increased with

such rapidity that he finally had to drop into the grass for
fear of being seen outlined against the sky.

He crept forward. There was a small hillock in his way,
and for a moment this blacked out sight of the city. Then,
he reached the top of it, and looked over. The glare hit him
full in the face and he gave a sudden cry of animal fear.

For the city was only a model.

For a second, he lay staring at it. And then he had jumped
to his feet and was running down upon it. Its miniature
buildings towered to his chest, and the tiny streets were just
wide enough for him to walk through. Unbelievingly, he ran
his fingers over the structures. They were complete in every
detail; little masterpieces of imitation. But it was not just
that that set his mind reeling.

It was the fact that every one was a model of some building
in his home town. Each one was a replica of a structure he
had seen and known. Not one was unfamiliar.

Trembling, he lifted his eyes from the city. Beyond it
trembled a shimmering haze on which his eyes refused to
focus. Wonderingly, he moved toward it.

It hung, like a curtain of mist, just beyond the farther
limits of the city. He strode up to it, stood in front of it,
and cautiously extended his hands out and into it.

It gave without resistance and his hands plunged through,
disappearing from sight. With a wordless cry, he jerked them
back and looked at them in the reflected light of the city.
They were whole and good. He stood for a second more,
gathering his nerve, and then, taking a deep breath, walked
through the curtain.

His feet passed from soft turf to solid surface, the mist
thinned before his eyes. He brushed the last of it away with
one hand and saw—desolation.

He stood on a street where giants might have walked.
And on either side towered buildings. Not miniatures, these,
but mighty edifices that towered up until they were lost to

sight in the night sky. But there was no light here, and no movement. The fact was written on the dust of the street, in the blank and staring windows of the buildings.

The city was deserted.

Fear returned to Mark Toren with redoubled force. He felt lost and insignificant, like an insect upon the windowpane of eternity, about to be squashed by the thumb of a god. And he burst into wild, unreasoning flight down the street.

After some distance, he obeyed the impulse to hide, and darted into the open doorway of one of the buildings.

"Greetings!" boomed a deep voice.

He leaped backward in sheer panic to the street outside. The voice ceased. He turned and darted wildly for another doorway and slipped inside.

"Greetings!" boomed a voice, again.

He took a step backward, but this time curiosity in part conquered fear, so that he stayed where he was, flattened against a wall, in the shadows.

And the voice went on talking. Only this time he realized that the words were not impacts of sound on his ear, but welled up unbidden, within his mind.

"Greetings, visitor," came the words. "From wherever you have come, no matter what far-flung starborn world may be your home, greetings. You stand at the birthplace of the human race.

"This was our breeding place—this earth. Here we lifted our heads from the earth. Here we stood upright and walked. Here we grew and reached out to the stars. And here we have left our memorial of the last men to be planet-bound. Look about you and see. The heritage of the human race is here.

"Now we, the last men to be planet-bound, have finished our memorial and go to join our brothers between the stars. We do not go to some home, for we will have no other home. We have passed beyond the need of home, and all the reaches of stellar space are the same to us.

"For it was never ordained that man should cling to the small bodies of planets when the endless regions of the ether are his to wander in, as a bird might wander in the sky, winged and armored by the power of his mind.

"So, to you, visitor, greetings. Look on the works of man; his buildings, his machines, and the creatures of his machines. All this he has left, as you will one day leave your works and all that your hands have wrought for the greater freedom that comes between the stars."

The voice ceased, and Mark turned from the doorway, into the moonlit street again—and stopped. Waiting for him, rank on silent rank were Merkl and Termi, and others like them, although the others glinted, gaunt and bright in the moonlight without the kindness of artificial flesh to cover their metal bones. They said nothing, and their eyes glittered on him. And Mark knew that he should feel frightened, but the voice inside of the building had drained fear from him and he felt only pity for the ones before him.

"So," he said, finally, "you are the creatures of the machines."

"Yes," the answer came like a sighing wind from the crowd.

"And I am a man," said Mark. The pity inside him welled up and he asked gently: "What were you trying to do? What did you hope to learn from me?"

"We were trying to learn life," answered Merkl for them all. "We are Earthbound because, while we can think, we have no imagination. Man's imagination has taken him between the stars. We thought if we could learn to go back to the time when Man was still learning, we could learn, too."

"But," said Mark, "you could not use my machine unless you had imagination. The use of psychomechanics requires it." They did not answer.

"But why didn't you just come out directly and ask me?" asked Mark. "And why did you hide all this"—and his arm swept out to indicate the buildings—"from me?"

"Because we hate you," said Merkl unemotionally. "You are something we can never be and so we hate you."

"But you haven't harmed me—" began Mark, bewildered.

And then the realization struck him. "You cannot harm me," he said.

"We cannot harm you," said Merkl. "Therefore we hate you."

There was a long silence.

"I'm sorry," whispered Mark, "but I can't do anything for you."

"No," said Merkl, "you can do nothing for us. And we can learn nothing from you. The building in which you stayed was a gigantic scanner. We have analyzed you. We have read you like a book and we do not understand you. We have taken your machine to pieces—down to its component atoms—and put it back together again. But we cannot operate it. Now, we only want you to leave." He lifted his hand, the crowd parted, and Mark saw his time machine standing in the midst of them.

"We cannot travel in time," continued Merkl, "but there are machines here which can block off time from our period to yours. We will use them when you are gone. We have learned from your visit that it is not a good thing for your kind to meet ours. Now, go."

Mark stepped forward as if in a dream and walked to his machine down the waiting corridor of the friendly men. Without a word, he stepped inside it and lifted his hand to the controls. Then, some inexplicable emotion made him turn, and he looked once more at Merkl, who was standing beside him. Beneath his feet, the generators began to warm up with a humming sound.

"Robot," said Mark, almost wonderingly, staring at Merkl.

The mists of a vanishing time began to swirl up between them. Through the haze he saw the plastic face of the other strangely distorted.

"Don't curse me so!" cried the friendly man.

Love Me True

On the way to the colonel's office, Ted Homan asked the MP to take him around by the laboratories so he could get a look at Pogey.

"You think I'm nuts?" said the MP. "I can't do that. Anyway we haven't got time. And anyway, they wouldn't let you in there. All we could do is look in through the door."

"All right. I can see him through the door, anyway," said Ted. The MP hesitated. He was a lean, dark young kid from Colorado; and he looked older than Ted, who was a tow-headed, opened-faced young blond soldier of the type who never looks quite grown up. But Ted had been to Arcturus IV and back; while the MP had never been farther than Washington, D.C.

So they went to the laboratories; and the MP stood to one side while Ted peered through the wire and glass of the small window set high in the door to the experimental section. Inside were cages with white rats, and rabbits, some rhesus monkeys and a small, white-haired, terrier-looking bitch. The speaker grill above the door brought to Ted's ears the rustling sound of the creatures in their cages.

"I can't see him," said Ted.

"In the corner," said the MP.

Ted pressed closer to the door and caught sight of a cage in the corner containing what looked like some woman's silver fox fur neckpiece, including the black button nose and the bead-eyes. It was all curled up.

"Pogey!" said Ted. *"Pogey!"*

"He can't hear you," said the MP. "That speaker's one way, so the night guards can check, in the labs."

A white-coated man came into the room from a far door, carrying a white enamel tray with fluffy cotton and three hypodermic syringes lying in it. The little bitch and Pogey were instantly alert and pressing their nose to the bars of their cages. The bitch wagged her stub tail and whined.

"Love me?" said Pogey. "Love me?"

The white-coated man paid no attention. He left his tray and went out again. The bitch whined after him. Pogey drooped. Ted's hands curled into fists against the slick metal face of the door.

"He could've said something!" said Ted. "He could've spoke!"

"He was busy," said the MP nervously. "Come on—we got to get going."

They went on over to the colonel's office. When they came to the door of the outer office, the MP slid his gun around on his belt so it was out of sight under his jacket. Then they went in. A small girl with startlingly beautiful green eyes in a blue summer-weight suit, a civilian, was seated on one of the hard wooden benches outside the wooden railing, waiting. She looked closely at Ted as he and the MP came through the railing.

"He's waiting for you. Go on in," said the lieutenant behind the railing. They passed on, through a brown door and closed it behind them, into a rectangular office with a good-looking dark wood desk, a carpet and a couple of leather chairs this side of the desk.

"You can wait outside, Corporal," said the colonel, from behind the desk. The MP went out again, leaving Ted standing stiff and facing the desk. "You fool, Ted!" said the colonel.

"He's mine," said Ted.

"You just get that notion out of your head," said the colonel. "Get it out right now." He was a dark little man with a nervous mustache.

"I want him back."

"You're getting nothing back. It's tough enough as it is. All right, we all went to Arcturus together, and we're the first outfit to do something like that and so we're not going to let one of our own boys get slapped by regulations when we can handle it among ourselves. But you just get it straight you aren't getting that antipod back."

Ted said nothing.

"You listen to me good now," said the colonel. "Do you know what they can do to your for striking a commissioned officer? Instead of getting out, today, you could be starting fifteen years hard labor. Plus what you'd get for smuggling the antipod back."

Ted still said nothing.

"Well, you're lucky," said the colonel. "You're just plain lucky. The whole outfit went to bat for you. We got the necessary papers faked up to make the antipod an experimental animal the outfit brought back—not you, the outfit. And Curry—*Lieutenant* Curwen, Ted, you might remember —is going to pretend you didn't try to half-kill him when he came to take the antipod away from you. I was going to make you go over and apologize to him; but he said no, he didn't blame you. You're just lucky."

He stopped and looked at Ted.

"Well?" he said.

"You don't understand," said Ted. "They die if they don't have somebody to love them. I was at that weather observation point all by myself for six months. I know. Pogey'll die."

"Look . . . oh, go out and get drunk, or something!" exploded the colonel. "I tell you we've done the best we can. Everybody's done the best they can; and you're lucky to be walking out of here with a clean record." He picked up the phone on his desk and began punching out a number. "Get out."

Ted went out. Nobody stopped him. He went to the temporary barracks the expedition had been assigned to, changed into civilian clothes and left the base. He was in about his fifth bar that evening when a woman sat down on the stool next to him.

"Hi there, Ted," she said.

He turned around and looked at her. Her eyes were as green as a well-watered lawn at sunset, her hair was somewhere between brunet and blond and she wore a tailored blue suit. Then he recognized her as the girl in the colonel's outer office. With her face only a foot or so away she looked older than she had in the office; and she saw he saw this, for she leaned back a little from him.

"I'm June Malyneux," she said, "from *The Recorder*. I'm a newspaperwoman." Ted considered this, looking at her.

"You want a drink, or something?" he said.

"That'd be wonderful," she said. "I'd like a Tom Collins."

He bought her a Tom Collins; and they sat there side by side in the dim bar looking at each other and drinking.

"Well," she said, "what did you miss most when you were twenty-three and a half quadrillion miles from home?"

"Grass," said Ted. "That is, at first. After a while I got used to the sand and the creepers. And I didn't miss it so much any more."

"Did you miss getting drunk?"

"No," said Ted.

"Then why are you doing it?"

He stopped drinking to look at her.

"I just feel like it, that's all," he said. She reached out and laid a hand on his arm.

"Don't be mad," she said. "I know about it. It's pretty hard to keep secrets from newspaper people. What are you going to do about it?"

He pulled his arm out from under her hand and had another swallow from his glass.

"I don't know," he said. "I don't know what to do."

"How'd you happen to get the . . . the—"

"Antipod. When they hunch their back to walk it looks like the front pair of legs're working against the back pair."

"Antipod. How'd you make a pet of it in the first place?"

"I was alone at this weather observation point for a long time." Ted was turning his glass around and around, and watching the rim revolve like a hoop of light. "After a while Pogey took to me."

"Did any of the other men make pets out of them?"

"Nobody I know of. They'll come up to you; but they're real shy. They scare off easy. Then after that they won't have anything to do with you."

"Did you scare any off?" June said.

"I must have," he shrugged, "—at first. I didn't pay any attention to them for a long time. Then I began to notice how they'd sit and watch me and my shack and the equipment. Finally Pogey got to know me."

"How did you do it?" she asked.

He shrugged again.

"Just patient, I guess," he said.

The bar was filling up around them. A band had started up in the supper club attached, and it was getting noisy.

"Come on," June said. "I know a quieter place where we can hear ourselves talk." She got up; and he got up and followed her out.

They took a taxi and went down to a place on the beach called Digger's Inn. It had a back porch overlooking the surf which was washing upon the sand, some fifteen feet below. The porch had a thatched roof; and the small round tables on it were lit by candles and the moonlight coming in across the waves. They had switched to rum drinks and Ted was getting quite drunk. It annoyed him; because he was trying to tell June what it had been like and his thickened tongue made talking clumsy.

". . . The farther away you get," he was saying. "I mean—the farther you go, the smaller you get. You understand?" She sat, waiting for him to tell her. "I mean . . . suppose you were born and grew up and never went more than a block from home. You'd be real big. You know what I mean? Put you and that block side by side, like on a table, and both of you'd show." He drew a circle and a dot with his forefinger on the dampness of the table between them to illustrate. "But suppose you traveled all over the city, then you'd look *this* big, side by side with it. Or the world, or the solar system—"

"Yes," she said.

". . . But you go some place like Alpha Centauri, you go twenty-three quadrillion, four hundred trillion miles from home, and"—he held up thumb and forefinger nails pinched together—"you're all alone out there for months, what's left of you then?" He shook the thumb and forefinger before her eyes. "You're that small. You're nothing."

She glanced from his pinched fingers to his face without moving anything but her eyes. His elbow was on the table, his thumb and forefinger inches before her face. She reached up and put her own hand gently over his fingers.

"No, listen—" he insisted, shaking his hand loose. "What's left when you're that small? What's left?"

"You are," she said.

He shook his head, hard.

"No!" he said. "I'm not. Only what I can do? But what can I do when I'm that high?" He closed his hand earnestly around her arm. "I'm little and I do little things. Everything I do is too little to count—"

"Please," she was softly prying at his fingers with her other hand, "you're hurting—"

". . . I can love," he said. "I can give my love."

Her fingers stilled. They stopped trying to loosen his. She

looked up at him and he looked drunkenly down at her. Her eyes searched his face almost desperately.

"How old are you?" she whispered.

"Twenty-five," he said.

"You don't look that old. You look—younger than I am," she said.

"Doesn't matter how old I am," said Ted. "It just matters what I can do."

"Please," she said. "You're squeezing too hard. My arm—"

He let go of her.

"Sorry," he said. He went back to his drinking.

"No, tell me," she said. Her right hand massaged the arm he had squeezed. "How did you get him out?"

"Pogey?" he said. "We practiced. I wrapped him around my waist, under my shirt and jacket."

"And he didn't show? And you got him on the ship that way when you came back."

"They weighed us on," said Ted, dully. "But I'd thought of that. I'd taken off twelve pounds. And exercised so I wouldn't look gaunted down. Pogey weighs just about eleven."

"And they didn't know it until you got here?"

"Sneak inspection. To beat the government teams to it, so nobody'd be embarrassed. Colonel ordered it; but Curry pulled it—Lieutenant Curwen—and he found him, and—" Ted ran down staring at his glass.

"What would you have done?" June said. "With—Pogey, I mean?"

He looked over at her, surprised.

"I would have kept him. With me. I would have taken care of him." He looked at her. "Don't you understand? Pogey *needs* me."

"I understand," she said. "I do." She moved a little toward him, so that her shoulder rubbed against the sleeve of his arm. "I'll help you get him out."

"You?" he said.

"Oh, yes!" she said, quickly. "Yes, I can!"

"How?" he said. And then—"Why? We've been talking here all this time; and now all of a sudden you want to help Pogey and me. Why? It isn't that newspaper of yours—"

"No, no!" she said. "I didn't really care at first, that was it. I mean it was a good story, that was all. Just that. And then, something about the way you talk about him . . . I don't know. But I changed sides, all of a sudden. Ted, you believe me, don't you?"

"I don't know," he said thickly.

"Ted," she said. "Ted." She moved close to him, her head was tilted back, her eyes half-closed. He stared stupidly down at her for a moment; then, clumsily, he put his arms around her and bent his own head and kissed her. He felt her tremble in his arms.

He let her go at last. She drew back a little from him and wiped the corners of her eyes, with her forefinger.

"Now," she said shakily, "do you believe me?"

"Yes," he said. He watched her for a second as she got out handkerchief, lipstick and compact. "But how're we going to do it? They've got him."

"There're ways," she said, sliding the lipstick around her upper lip carefully. She rolled her upper lip against the lower, and blinked a little, examining the result in the mirror. "I'm quite good, you know," she said to the compact. "I can manage all sorts of things. And I . . . I want to manage this for you."

"How?" he said.

"You have to know what's going on." She folded the compact and put it away with a sharp snap. "That expedition of yours to Alpha Centauri cost forty billion dollars."

"I know," he said. "But what's that got to do—"

"The military's sold on the idea of further stellar exploration and expansion. They want a program of three more expeditions of increasing size; one that would cost a hundred and fifty billion during the next twenty years." She glanced at him the way a schoolteacher might. "That's a lot of money. But now's the ideal time to ask for it. All of you have just got back. Popular interest is high . . . so on."

"Sure," he said. "But what's that got to do with Pogey?"

"They don't want a fuss. No scandal. Nothing that'll start an argument at this stage in the game. Now tell me," she turned to face him, "you're released from service now, aren't you?"

"Yes." Ted nodded, frowning at her, "they signed me out today before they took me to see the colonel. I'm a civilian."

"All right. Fine," she said. "And you know where Pogey is. Can you go get him and get him outside the base?"

"Yeah," he said. "Yeah, I thought of that. But I was saving it for last—if I couldn't think of a better way where they couldn't come after us."

"They won't. You leave that part of it to me. Pogey was your pet; and his kind was listed harmless by the expedition when they were on Alpha Centauri. There's enough of a case there to make good weepy newspaper copy. I'll have a little talk with your colonel and some others."

"But what good'll that do if they just take him back anyway?"

"They won't. Legally, they're got you, Ted. But they'll let you get away with it rather than risk the publicity. Wait and see."

"You think so?" he said, his face lighting up. "You really think they will?"

"I promise," she answered, watching him. He surged to his feet. The little round table before them rocked. "I'll go get him right now."

"You better have some coffee first."

"No. No. I'm sober." He took a deep breath and straightened up; and the fuzziness from the liquor seemed to burn out of his head.

"You'll need some place to bring him," she said. "I've got an apartment—" He shook his head.

"I'll call you," he said. "We may just move around. I'll call you tomorrow. When'll you be seeing the colonel?" He was already backing away from her.

"First thing in the morning." She got up hurriedly and came after him. "But wait—I'm coming."

"No . . . no!" he said. "I don't want you mixed up in it. I'll call you. Where'll I call you?"

"Parketon 5-45-8321—the office," she called after him. And then he was gone, through the entrance to the interior bar of the Inn. She reached the entrance herself just in time to see his tow head and square shoulders moving beyond the drinkers at the bar and out the front door of the place.

Outside, Holman called a cab.

"Richardson Space Base," he told the driver. His permanent pass was good to the end of the week; and they passed through the gates of the base, when they reached them, with only a nod and a yawn from the guard.

He left the cab outside the laboratories and stepped off into the shadows. He followed along paths of darkness until he came to the section where Pogey was being kept. A night guard came out of the door just before he reached it, swinging his arm with the machine pistol clipped to one wrist, and looking ahead down the corridor with the sleepy young face of a new recruit. Ted stood still in the shadows until the door of the next section had swung to behind the guard, then went inside.

He found the door he had looked through earlier. A light burned inside the room and most of the animals in the cages were curled up with their heads tucked away from the glare of it. The door was locked, but there was an emergency handle under glass above it. Ted broke the glass, turned the handle and went in; and the animals woke at the noise and looked at him wonderingly.

He opened the door to Pogey's cage.

"Pogey. . . . Pogey. . . ." he said; and the antipod leaped up and came into his arms like a child and clung there. Together they went out into the night. When he got back into the cab, Ted bulged a little around the waist under his shirt; but that was all.

The sky was paling into dawn as they got back into the city. Ted paid off the cab and took the public tubes. Wedged into a corner seat, he drowsed against the soft cushions, feeling Pogey stir warmly now and again around his waist; until, waking with a start he looked at the watch on his wrist and saw that it was after eleven a.m. He had been shuttling back and forth beneath the city for seven hours.

He got stiffly off the tubes and phoned the number June had given him. She was not in, they told him at the other end, but she should be back shortly. He hung up and found a restaurant and had breakfast. When he called for the second time, he heard her voice answer him over the phone.

"It's all right," she said. "But you better stay out of sight for a while anyway. Where can I meet you."

He thought.

"I'm going to get a hotel room," he said. "I'll register under the name of—William Wright. Where's a good hotel where they have individual entrances and lobbies for the room groups?"

"The Byngton," she said. "One hundred and eighty-seventh and Chire Street—fourth level. I'll meet you there in half an hour."

"All right," he said, and hung up.

He went to the Byngton and registered. He had just gone up to his room and let Pogey out on the bed, when the talker over the door to the room told him he had a visitor.

"There she is—" he said to Pogey; and went out alone, closing the door of the room carefully behind him. June was waiting for him in the bright sunlight of the little glassed-in lobby a dozen yards from his door; and she ran to him as he appeared. He found himself holding her.

"We did it! We did it!" She clung to him tightly. Awkwardly, but a little gently, he disengaged her arms so that he could see her face.

"What happened?" he said.

"I phoned ahead—before I went out at nine this morning," she said, laughing up at him. "When I got there, your colonel was there, and General Daton—and some other general from the United Services. I told them you'd taken Pogey—but they knew that; and I told them you were going to keep him. And I showed them some copy I'd written." She almost pirouetted with glee. "And oh, they were angry! I'd stay out of their way for a long time, Ted. But you can keep him. You can keep Pogey!"

She hugged him again. Once more he put her arms away.

"It sounds awful easy. You sure?" he said.

"You've got to keep him quiet. You've got to keep him out of sight," she said. "But if you don't bother them, they'll leave you alone. The power of the Fourth Estate—of course it helps if you're on the national board of the Guild."

"Guild?"

"Newspaperman's Guild," she said. "Didn't I tell you, darling? Of course, I didn't. But I've been northwestern sector representative to the Guild for fourteen"—she stumbled suddenly, caught herself on the word, and the animation of her face crumpled and fled—"years," she finished, barely above a whisper, her eyes wide and palely watching upon his face.

But he only frowned impatiently.

"Then it's set for sure," he said. "I mean—from now on they'll leave us alone?"

"Oh, yes!" she said. "Yes! You and Pogey are safe, from now on."

He sighed so deeply and heavily that his shoulders heaved.

"Pogey's safe then," he murmured. Then he looked back at

her. He took her hand in his. "I . . . don't know how to thank you," he said.

She stared at him, pale-faced, wide-eyed.

"Thank me!" she said.

"You did an awful lot," he said. "If it hadn't been for you . . . but we had to have faith somebody'd come through." He shook her hand, which went lifelessly up and down in his. "I just can't thank you enough. If there's ever anything I can do to pay you back." He let go of her hand and stepped backward. "I'll write you," he said. "I'll let you know how we make out." He took another step backward and turned toward the door of his room. "Well, so long—and thanks again."

"Ted!" Her voice thrust at him like an icepick, sharply, bringing him back around to face her. "Aren't you," she moved her lips stiffly with the words, "going to invite me in?"

He rubbed the back of his neck with one hand, clumsily.

"Well," he said. "I was up all night; and I had all those drinks . . . and Pogey is pretty shy with strangers—" He turned a hand palm out toward her. "I mean, I know he'd like you; but some other time, huh?" He smiled at her wooden face. "Give me a call tomorrow, maybe? I tell you, I'm out on my feet right now. Thanks again."

He turned and opened the door to his room and went in, closing it behind him, leaving her there. Once on the inside he set the door on lock and punched the DO NOT DIS-TURB sign. Then he turned to the bed. Pogey was still curled up on it, and at the sight of the antipod Ted's face softened. He knelt down by the side of the bed and put his face down on a level with Pogey's. The antipod humped like an otter playing and shoved its own nose and bead-eyes close to his.

"Love me?" said Pogey.

"Love you," breathed Ted. "We're all right now, Pogey, just like we knew we'd be, aren't we?" He put his face down sideways on the coverlet of the bed and closed his eyes. "Love Pogey," he whispered. "Love Pogey."

Pogey put out a small pink tongue and stroked Ted's fore-head with it.

"What now?" murmured Ted, sleepily.

Pogey's bead-eyes glowed like two small flames of jet.

"Now," Pogey said, "we go to Washington—for more like you."

Our First Death

Juny Vewlan died about 400 hours of the morning and we
buried her that same day before noon at 1100 hours, because
we had no means of keeping the body. She had not wanted
to be cremated; and because she was our first and because
some of her young horror at the thought of being done away
with entirely had seeped into the rest of us during her illness
(if you could call it illness—at any rate, as she lay dying), an
exception was made in her case and we decided in full assembly to bury her.

As for the subsidiary reasons for this decision of ours, they
were not actually clear to us at the time, nor yet indeed for a
long time afterward. Certainly the fatherless, motherless girl
had touched our hearts toward the end. Certainly the old
man—her grandfather Gothrud Vewlan, who with his wife,
Van Meyer and Kurt Meklin made up our four Leaders—
caught us all up in the heartache of his own sorrow, as he
stood feebly forth on the platform to ask of us this last favor
for his dead grandchild. And certainly Kurt Meklin murmured
against it, which was enough to dispose some of the more
stiff-necked of us in its favor.

However—we buried her. It was a cold hard day, for winter
had already set in on Our Planet. We carried her out over the
unyielding ground, under the white and different sky, and
lowered her down into the grave some of our men had dug for
her. Beneath the transparent lid of her coffin, she looked
younger than sixteen years—younger, in fact, than she had
looked in a long time, with her dark hair combed back from

around the small pointed face and her eyes closed. Her hands were folded in front of her. She had, Gothrud told us, also wished some flowers to hold in them; and none of us could imagine where she had got such an idea until one of the younger children came forward with an illustration from our library's *Snow White and the Seven Dwarfs*, showing Snow White in *her* coffin with a bunch of flowers that never faded clasped in her hands. It was clear then, to some of us at least, that Juny had not been free from the dream of herself as a sort of captive—now sleeping—princess, merely putting in her time until the Prince her lover should arrive and carry her off.

But we had, of course, no flowers.

After she had been lowered into the grave and all of us had come up to look at her, Lydia Vewlan, Gothrud's wife and colony doctor as well as one of the Leaders, read some sort of service over her. Then, when all was finished, a cloth was laid over the transparent face of the plastic coffin and the earth was shoveled back. It had been dug out in chunks—a chunk to a spadeful; and the chunks had frozen in the bitter air, so that it was like piling angular rocks back upon the coffin, heavy purple rocks with the marblings of white shapes that were the embryos of strange plants frozen in hibernation. Because of their hard awkward shapes, they made quite a pile above the grave when they were all put back; and in fact it was not until the following summer was completely gone that the top of the grave was level again with the surrounding earth. By that time we had a small fence of white plastic pickets all around it; and it was part of the duty of the children in the colony to keep them scrubbed clean and free of the gray mold.

After the burial we all went back to the mess building for our noon meal. Outside, as we took our places at the tables, the midday wind sprang up and whistled around our metal huts and the stripped skeleton of the ship, standing apart at its distance on the landing spot and looking lonely and neglected in the bleak light from the white sky.

The Leaders of our colony sat at the head of the file of tables that stretched the length of the mess hut. Their table was just large enough for the four of them and was set a little apart from the rest so that they could discuss important matters in relative privacy. The other, larger tables stretched away in order, with the ones at the far end with the small chairs and the low tops for the very young children—those who were just barely able to eat by themselves without supervision. These, the children, had as a group been unusually silent and solemn during the burial procedures, impressed by the emotions of their elders. But now, as they started to eat, their natural energy and exuberance began to break free of this restraint and show itself all the more noticeably for having been held down this long. In fact they began to pose quite a small disciplinary problem, and this necessitating the attentions of their elders, a diversion was created, which together with the warmth and the good effect of the hot food, bred a lightening of spirits among us adults as well. Our natural mood of optimism, which the Colonial Office had required in selecting us for a place on the immigration rosters, pressed down before by the awareness of death in our midst, began to rise again. And it continued to rise, like a warm tide throughout the length of the hut, until finally it reached the four who sat at the head table. But here it lapped unavailingly against the occupied minds of those who, twenty-four hours a day, breathed the constant atmosphere of responsibility for us all.

To talk and not be heard, they must lower their voices and lean their heads together. And this, while a perfectly natural action, had a tendency to impart an air of tenseness to their discussions. So they sat now, following the burial, in such an atmosphere of tenseness; and although the rest of us did not discover what they were then saying until long afterward—

indeed until Maria Warna told us about it months later—
there were those among us at the long tables who, glancing
upward, noticed something perhaps graver than usual about
their talking at that meal.

In particular, it had been Kurt Meklin—Kurt, with his old
lined face thrust forward above his plate like some gray guard-
ian of ancient privilege, who had been urging some point upon
the other three all through the meal. But what it was, he
had avoided stating openly, talking instead in half-hints, and
obscure ambiguities, his black hard eyes sliding over to glance
at Lydia, and then away again, and then back again. Until,
finally, when the last plates had been removed and the coffee
served, Lydia rose at last to the challenge and spoke out
unequivocally.

"All right, Kurt!" she said—she, the strong old woman,
meeting the clever old man eye to eye. "You've been hinting
and hawing around ever since we got back from the burying.
Now, what's wrong with it?"

"Well, now that you ask me, Lydia," said Kurt. "It's a
question—a question of what she died of."

Gothrud, who had sat the whole meal with his head hanging and eating almost nothing, now suddenly raised his eyes
and looked across at Kurt.

"What kind of a question's that?" demanded Lydia. "You
saw me enter it on the records—death from natural causes."

"I'll tell you what she really died of," said Gothrud, suddenly.

"Well now," said Kurt, interrupting Gothrud, and with
another of his side-glances at Lydia. "Do you think that's
sufficient?"

"Sufficient? Why shouldn't it be sufficient?"

"Well now, of course, Lydia . . ." said Kurt. "I know
nothing of doctoring myself, and we all know that the
Colonial Office experts gave Our Planet a clean bill of health
before they shipped our little colony out here. But I should
think—just for the record, if nothing else—you'd have wanted

to make an examination to determine the cause of death."

"I did."

"Naturally—but just a surface examination. Of course with the colony in a sentimental mood about the girl—eh, Van?"

Van Meyer, the youngest of them all, was turning his coffee cup around and around between his thick fingers and staring at it. His heavy cheeks were slablike on either side of his mouth.

"Leave me out of it," he said, without looking up.

Lydia sniffed at him, and turned back to Kurt.

"Stop talking gibberish!" she commanded.

"Gibberish . . . sorry, Lydia," said Kurt. "I don't have the advantages of your medical education. A pharmacist really knows so little. But—it's just that I think you've left the record rather vague. *Natural causes* really doesn't tell us exactly what she died of."

"What she died of!" broke in Gothrud with sudden, low-voiced violence. "She died of a broken heart."

"Don't be a fool, Gothrud," said his wife, without looking at him. "And keep your voice down, you, Kurt. Do you want the whole colony to hear? Now, out with it. You sat with us and agreed to bury her. If you had any questions, you should have come out with them then."

"But I had to bend to the sentimentality of the colony," said Kurt. "It was best to let it go then. Later, I thought, later we can . . ." He fell silent, making a small, expressive gesture with his hand.

"Later we can do *what?*" grated Lydia.

"Why, I should think that naturally—as a matter of record —that in a case like this you'd want to do an autopsy on her."

"Autopsy!" The word jolted a little from Lydia's lips.

"Why, certainly," said Kurt, spreading his hands. "This way is much simpler than insisting on it in open Assembly. After curfew tonight, when everybody is in barracks—"

A low strangled cry from Gothrud interrupted him. From the moment in which the word *autopsy* had left Kurt's lips, he had been sitting in frozen horror. Now, it seemed, he managed at last to draw breath into his lungs to speak with.

"Autopsy!" he cried, in a thin, tearing, half-strangled whisper. "*Autopsy!* She didn't want to be touched! We agreed not to burn her; and now you'd— No—"

"Why, Gothrud—" said Kurt.

"Don't *why Gothrud* me!" said Gothrud, his deep sunk eyes at last flaming into violence. "A decision's been made by the colony. And none of you are going to set it aside."

"We are the Leaders," said Kurt.

"Leaders!" Gothrud laughed bitterly. "The ex-druggist— you, Kurt. The ex-nurse and—" he glanced at Van Meyer— "the ex-caterer's son, the ex-nothing."

Van Meyer held his cup and stared at it.

"And the ex-high school teacher," said Kurt, softly.

"Exactly!" said Gothrud, lifting his head to meet him stare for stare. "The ex-high school teacher. Me. As little an ex as the rest of you, Kurt, and as big a Leader right now. And a Leader that says you've got no right to touch Juny to settle your two-bit intriguing and feed your egos—" He choked.

"Gothrud—" said Kurt. "Gothrud, you're overwrought. You—"

Gothrud coughed raspingly and went on. "I tell you—" He choked again, and had to stop.

Lydia spoke swiftly to him, in low, furious German. "Shut up! Will you kill yourself, old man?"

"That's being done for me," Gothrud answered her in English, and faced up to Kurt again. "You hear me!" he said. "We're nothings. Leaders. Great executives. Only none of us has been five miles from the landing spot. Only none of us organized this colony. None of us flew the ship, or assigned the work, or built the huts, or planned the plantings. All we did was sign the roster back on Earth, and polite young experts with twice our brains did it all for us. By what right are we Leaders?"

"We were elected!" snapped Kurt.

"Fools elected by fools!" Gothrud's head was beginning to swim from the violence of his effort in the argument. Through a gathering mist, he seemed to see Kurt's face ripple as if it were under water, and rippling, sneer at him. With a great effort, he gripped the edge of the table and went on.

"I tell you," he rasped, "that people have rights. That you won't—that you can't—that—"

His tongue had suddenly gone stubborn and refused to obey him. It rattled unintelligibly in his mouth and around him the room was being obscured by the white mist. Gothrud felt a sudden constriction in his throat; and, gasping abruptly for breath, he pushed back his chair and tried to stand up, clawing at his collar to loosen it.

Through the black specks that swarmed suddenly before his eyes, he was conscious of Van Meyer rising beside him and of Lydia's voice ordering the younger man to catch him before he fell.

"Come on, Gothrud," said the voice of Van Meyer, close to his ear. "You've been under too much of a strain. You better lie down. Come on, I'll help you."

Through the haze he was conscious of being half-assisted, half-carried from the dining room. There was a short space of confusion, and then things cleared for him, to allow him to find himself lying on his bunk in the room he shared with Lydia. Van Meyer, alone with him, stood over the washstand, filling a hypodermic syringe from a small frosted bottle of minimal, his gross bulk hunched over concentratedly with a sort of awkward and pathetic kindness.

"Feeling better?" he asked Gothrud.

"I'm all right," Gothrud answered. But the words came out thick and unnaturally. "What are you doing?"

"I'm going to give you a shot to make you sleep," said Van.

"Van—" said Gothrud. "Van—" Talking was really a tremendous effort. He swallowed desperately and went on. "*You* understand about Juny—don't you?"

"Why, yes, Gothrud."

"She shouldn't have come, you see. We made her—because she had no other family, Lydia and I. She never wanted to come. We talked her into it. She was just coming out of being a child—"

"Don't talk, Gothrud," said Van, struggling with the delicate plunger of the hypodermic. "You need to rest."

"—She was the only one that age. All the rest of us, adults or young children; and her in between, all alone. A whole lost generation, Van, in one lonely little girl."

"Now, Gothrud—"

"I tell you," cried Gothrud, struggling up onto one elbow, "we robbed her of every reason to live. She should have had love and fun and the company of young people her own age back on Earth. And we brought her here—to this desolate outpost of a world—"

Van Meyer had finally got the syringe properly filled. He came over to the bed with it and reached for Gothrud's arm when the older man sank back.

"That's why we owe it to her to leave her untouched the way she wanted," said Gothrud, in a low, feverish voice, as the needle went in. "But it's not that so much, Van. If it were for some good purpose, I wouldn't object. But it isn't. It's for Lydia—and Kurt. Van—" He grasped the younger man's arm as he started to turn away from the bunk, and held him, compelling Van Meyer to turn back.

"Van—" he said. "Things are going wrong here. You know that. It's Lydia. Married all those years back on Earth, and I never let myself see it. I watched her drive our son and daughter from our house. I watched her bend Juny to her way and bring her here with us. And Van"—his voice sunk to a whisper—"I never let myself see it until I got here, that awful hunger in her. It's power, she wants, Van, power. That's what she's always wanted, and now she sees a chance of getting it. Listen to me, Van, watch out for her. She did for Juny. It'll be me next, and then Kurt, and then—"

"Now, Gothrud—now just relax—" said Van, pulling his arm at last free from the older man's grasp, which now began to weaken as the drug took hold.

"Promise me you'll watch. . . ." whispered Gothrud. "You must. I trust you, Van. You're weak, but there's nothing rotten in you. Kurt's no good. He's another like Lydia. Watch them. Promise—promise. . . ."

"I—I promise," said Van, and the minimal came in on Gothrud with a rush, like a great black wave that swept in and over him, burying him far beneath it, deep, and deep.

When Gothrud awoke, the room he shared with Lydia was in darkness; and through the single small, high window in the outer wall, with its reinforcing wire mesh patterning the glass, he saw the night sky—for a wonder momentarily free of clouds—and the bright stars of the Cluster. Van Meyer's shot of minimal must have been a light one, for he had awakened clear-headed and, he felt quite sure, long before it had been planned for him to awaken. He felt positive in his own mind that they would have planned for him to sleep until morning; and only the unpredictable clock of his old body, ticking erratically, now fast and now slowing, running down toward final silence, had tricked them.

The illuminated clock-face on his bedside table read 21:20 and curfew was at 2100 hours. He fumbled into his clothes, got up, went over to the window and peered out, craning his neck. Yes, the colony was now completely lost in darkness, except for the small, yellow-gleaming windows of the Office Hut. Feverishly he turned and began to climb into his weather suit, struggling hastily into the bulky, overall-like outfit, zipping it tight and pulling the hood over his head. At the last minute, as he was going out the door, he remembered the diary; and, going back, dug through the contents of his locker until his fingers closed over the cylindrical thickness of it. He lifted it out, a faint hint of clean, light, young-girl's perfume reaching him from it momentarily. Then he stuffed it through the slit of his weather suit to an inside pocket; and went out the door.

The most direct route to the Office Hut led across the open compound. But as he started across this, leaning against the wind, an obscure fear made his feet turn away from the direct bulk of his destination and veer in the direction of the new grave. He went, chiding himself for his foolishness all the way, for although he knew now that the other three Leaders had held him in secret contempt for a long time, he was equally sure that they would not dare go directly against his wishes in this matter without consulting him.

So it was that when he came finally to Juny's grave and saw it gaping black and open under the stars, he could not at first bring himself to believe it. But when he did, all the strength went out of him and he fell on his knees beside the open trench. For a wild moment as he knelt there, he felt that, like a figure out of the Old Testament, he should pray—for guidance, or for a divine vengeance upon the desecrators of the grave of his grandchild. But all that came out of him were the crying reproaches of an old man: "Oh, God, why didn't you make me stronger? Why didn't you make me young again when this whole business of immigration was started? I could take a gun and—"

But he knew he would not take a gun; and if he did, the others would simply walk up and take it away from him. Because he could not shoot anybody. Not even for Juny could he shoot anybody. And after a while he wiped his eyes and got to his feet and went on toward the Office Hut, hugging one arm to his side, so that he could feel the round shape of the diary through all his heavy suit insulation.

When he came to the Office Hut, the door was locked. But he had his key in his pocket as always. His heart pounded and the entryway of the Hut seemed full of a soft mist lurking

just at the edge of his vision. He leaned against the wall for a
moment to rest, then painfully struggled out of his weather
suit. When he had hung it up beside the others on the wall
hooks, he opened the inner door of the Hut and went in.

The three were clustered around the long conference table
at the far end of the office, Lydia with her dark old face
looking darker and older even than usual above the white
gown and gloves of surgery. They looked up at the sound of
the opening door; and Van Meyer moved swiftly to block
off Gothrud's vision of the table and came toward him.

"Gothrud!" he said. "What are you doing here?" And he
put his hands on Gothrud's arms.

Gothrud struggled feebly to release himself and go around
the younger man to the table, but was not strong enough.

"Let me go. Let me go!" he cried. "What have you done to
her? Have you—"

"No, no," soothed Van Meyer. Still holding Gothrud's
arms, he steered the older man over to a chair at one of the
desks and sat him down in it. All the way across the room, he
stayed between Gothrud and the conference table and when
he had Gothrud in the chair, he pulled up another for himself
and sat down opposite, so that the table was still hidden. Kurt
and Lydia came over to stand behind him. All three looked at
Gothrud.

Lydia's face was hard and bitter as jagged ice. The absorbent
face mask around her neck, unfastened on one side and
hanging by a single thread, somehow made her look, to Gothrud's eyes, not like a member of the profession of healing,
but like some executioner, interrupted in the course of her
duty.

"You!" she said.

Gothrud stared up at her, feeling a helpless fascination.

"You—you mustn't—" he gasped.

"*Du!*" she broke out at him suddenly, in low voiced,
furious German. "You old fool! Couldn't you stay in bed and

keep out of trouble? Don't I have enough trouble on my hands with this one-time pill-peddler trying to undermine my authority, but I must suffer with you as well?"

"Lydia," he answered hoarsely, in the same language. "You can't do this thing. You mustn't let Kurt push you into it. It's a crime before God and man that you should even consider it."

"I consider—I consider the colony."

"No. You do not. You do not!" cried Gothrud in agony. "You think only of yourself. What harm will it do you if you tell the truth? It can't alter the facts. The colony will be upset for a little while, but then they will get over it. Isn't that better than living a lie and backing it up with an act of abomination?"

"Be silent!" snapped Lydia. "What I am doing, I am doing for the best of all concerned."

"I won't let you!" he cried. Changing swiftly into English, he swung away from her and appealed to the two men.

"Listen," he said. "Listen: you know there's no need for this—this autopsy. Colonial Office experts, men who *know*, certified this planet as clean. So it can't be any disease. And what would it benefit you to discover some physical frailty?"

"Ah? She was frail?" asked Kurt. "Something in the family?"

"No, she was not!" Lydia almost shouted. "Stop playing the goose, Kurt." Suddenly regaining control of herself, she dropped her voice all at once to normal level again. "I'm surprised at you, Kurt, letting yourself be misled by a sick old man who never was able to look on the girl dispassionately."

"Dispassionately!" cried Gothrud, straining forward against Van Meyer's prisoning hands. "Did you look at Juny dispassionately? Did you bring her along to die out here, dispassionately, taking her away from everything that she longed for? I tell you—I tell you, she died of a broken heart! God—" He choked suddenly. "God forgive me for being so soft, so weak and flabby-soft that I let you have your way about her coming. Better an orphanage back on Earth, for her. Better the worst possible life, alive, back there, than this—to have her dead, so young, and wasted—wasted—"

He sobbed suddenly.

"Van," commanded Lydia, evenly, "take him back to Quarters."

"No!" shouted Gothrud, coming suddenly to his feet and with surprising strength pushing the younger man aside, so that he half-toppled in his chair and caught at a desk to keep from falling. Gothrud took two quick strides across to a recorder that perched on a nearby desk. Pulling the diary from his pocket, he snapped it onto the spindle and turned the playback on.

"She died of a broken heart—for all she wanted and couldn't have," cried Gothrud. "And here's your proof. Listen!"

"What are you doing?" snapped Kurt.

Gothrud turned blazing eyes upon him.

"This was her diary," he said. "Listen. . . ."

The speaker had begun to murmur words in the voice of a young girl. Gothrud reached out and turned up the volume. The sweet clear tones grew into words in the still air of the grim rectangular office, all plastic and metal about the four who listened.

"*. . . and after that we flew out over Lake Michigan. The lake was all dark, but you could see the moon lighting a path on the water, all white and wonderful. And the lights went up the shore for miles. I just put my head on Davy's shoulder . . .*"

"Shut it off!" snapped Kurt, suddenly. "What are you trying to do, Gothrud?"

"Listen to her heart breaking," said Gothrud, his head a little on one side, attentively. "Listen and try to think of her dispassionately."

"You're out of your head, Gothrud!" said Lydia. "What odds is it, what the girl recorded back on Earth?"

"On Earth? On Earth?" echoed Gothrud. "She recorded it here, night by night, in her own room."

Before them the diary fell silent for a second and then took up with a new entry.

"*. . . Month eight, fourth day: Today Walter took me to the Embassy ball. I wore my new formal all made out of yards of real night-mist lace. It was like walking in the center of a pink cloud. Walter has the high emotional index typical of such intense characters; and he was very jealous of me. He was afraid that I might take it into my head to turn around and go back to Our Planet and the colony. I let him worry for a little while, before I explained that I can never, never go back because of a clause the studio put in my contract that says I am not allowed to leave the Earth without studio permission which they will never give. And since I'm signed up with them for years and years . . .*"

Lydia's hand came down like a chopping knife on the cut-off, killing Juny's voice in mid-sentence.

"That's enough of that," she said. "Van, take him out."

"You heard," said Gothrud, staring at the two men. Van hesitated.

"Go on, Van!" snapped Lydia. Reluctantly, Van moved forward.

"Kurt—" cried Gothrud.

"It's up to Lydia," replied the druggist, tonelessly.

"Then we'll go ahead," said Lydia decisively, turning away.

"No, by heaven, you won't!" shouted Gothrud, fending off Van and taking a step forward. At the motion, the sudden familiar wave of dizziness swept over him, so that he staggered and was forced to cling to a nearby chair for support.

"All right," he said, fighting to clear his head. "If you won't stop—if you really won't stop—then I'll tell you. Lydia has no right. Lydia—"

"Be silent!" shouted Lydia in German, suddenly halting and wheeling about, her face deadly.

"No," said Gothrud in English. "No. Not any more. Listen,

Kurt—and you too, Van. You know what kind of doctor Lydia is. A fourteen-day wonder. She was a registered nurse and the Colonial Office sent her to school for two weeks and gave her a medical diploma." He looked straight at Lydia, who stood frozen, her mouth half-open in an angry gape and her hands fisted by her side. "What you don't know, and what I've kept to myself all this time is that the diploma means nothing. Nothing."

"What's this?" said Kurt.

Gothrud laughed, chokingly.

"As if you haven't suspected, Kurt. Don't think I don't know why you suggested this autopsy. But all you had were suspicions. I know. I was at the school with her."

"I suspected nothing—"

Gothrud laughed, hoarsely.

"Then you're a fool, Kurt. Who believes that a doctor can be made in two weeks when it takes eight years back on Earth? A two-week doctor would be prosecuted on Earth. But we little people who go out to colonize take what we can bring along with us. Us with our nurse-doctors, our druggist-Leaders, our handyman-engineers. Yes. Do you know what they taught us in those two weeks, Kurt—except that I didn't get a diploma for my part in it? Lydia learned how to attempt a forceps delivery, an appendectomy, and a tonsillectomy. They taught her the rudiments of setting broken bones and the proper methods for prescribing some two hundred common drugs."

He was still looking at Lydia as he spoke. She still had not moved, and her hands were still clenched, but her face had taken on an expression of complete serenity.

"This," said Gothrud, staring at her. "This woman who has never held a scalpel in her hand in her life before is the trained specialist that you are expecting to make a professional examination of Juny's body."

Kurt turned to face Lydia.

"Lydia," he said. "Lydia, is this true?"

"Don't be ridiculous, Kurt," replied Lydia, calmly. "He's lying of course."

"How do we know it's not you who are lying?"

"Because I'm in complete control of my faculties. Gothrud's senile."

"Senile?" said Van.

"Of course. The first signs showed up in him some time back. I was hoping it would come on more slowly; but you've all noticed these fainting fits of his, and how he gets wrought up over every little thing. Poor Gothrud," she said, looking at him.

He stared back at her, so aghast at the depths of her perfidy that he could not even bring himself to speak.

"He's made this all up, of course," she went on. "The method by which I was trained was naturally top secret. I've been sworn to silence, of course, but I can tell you that the required information is fed directly to the brain. It's such a new and revolutionary method that it's being restricted to highly important Government Service, such as training key colonists like myself. That explains why the ordinary medical colleges don't know about it yet."

"Lydia," said Kurt. "You say this is true? You swear it's true? How can you prove it?"

"Proof?" she said airly. "Watch me do the autopsy."

Kurt's old eyelids closed down over his eyes until he seemed to look out through a narrow slit.

"All right, Lydia," he said. "That's just what we'll do."

A wordless cry broke from the lips of Gothrud. He snatched up a chair and took one step toward Lydia. Instantly Van Meyer jumped forward and caught him. Frantically, the old man struggled, his breath coming in short terrible gasps.

"Hold him, Van, while I give him a sedative!" cried Lydia—but before she could reach the hypodermic kit on the table across the room, Gothrud suddenly stopped struggling and stiffened. His eyes rolled upward until only the whites showed, for just a second before the lids dropped down over them. He sagged bonelessly. And Van Meyer, lowering him into a chair, snatched back his hands in horror, as if they had suddenly become covered with blood. But Lydia brusquely came across the room, pushed him aside, and bent over the motionless figure.

She took its pulse and rolled one eyelid back momentarily.

"That's all right," she said, stepping back. "Leave him alone. It's easier this way. Come on back to the table with me, both of you, I'll need your assistance."

But for a second, yet, she herself did not move; instead, standing, she stared down at the man she had lived with for more than 50 years. There was a particular glitter in her eye.

"Poor Gothrud," she said softly.

She turned away crisply and led the way back to the conference table, re-tying her face mask as she went.

"Stand over there, Kurt," she said. "You, Van, hand me that scalpel. That one, there." Her eyes jumped at him, as he hesitated. "Move, man! It's only a body."

They went to work. When Lydia was about half through, Gothrud came to himself a little in the chair and called out in a dazed voice to ask what they were doing.

"Don't answer," muttered Lydia, bent above her work. "Pay no attention to him."

They did not answer Gothrud. After a little while he called out again. And when they did not answer this time, either, he subsided in his chair and sat talking to himself and crying a little.

It was an unpleasant job. Van Meyer felt sick; but Kurt went about his duties without emotion, and Lydia was industriously and almost cheerfully busy about her part of it.

"Well," she said, at last. "Just as I suspected—nothing."

She untied her mask and frankly wiped a face upon which perspiration gleamed.

"Wrap her up," she said. "And then you can take her back out again." She glanced over to where her husband was. He had stopped talking to himself and was sitting up, staring at them with bright eyes. "Well, how are you, Gothrud?"

Gothrud did not answer, although he looked directly at her; and Van Meyer, standing beside her, stirred uncomfortably. Kurt sat down on a desk opposite her and mopped his face with a tissue. He produced one of the colony's few remaining cigarets and lighted it.

"And you didn't find anything?" he said sharply to Lydia.

She transferred her gaze from Gothrud to him.

"Not a thing," she said.

Kurt blinked his eyes and turned his head away. But Van Meyer continued to stare at her, uneasily and curiously.

"Lydia," he asked.

"What, Van?"

"What was it, then?"

"What was what?"

"I mean," he said. "Now that you've . . . seen her, what was it that made her die?"

"Nothing made her die," replied Lydia. "She just died. If I'm to write a more extensive report, I'll put down that death was due to heart failure—with general debility as a contributing factor."

In the silence that fell between them, the single word came sharp and clear from the old man seated across the room.

"Heart," said Gothrud.

"Yes," said Lydia, turning once more to face him. "If it makes you feel any better, Gothrud, it was her heart that killed her."

"Yes," repeated Gothrud. "Yes, her poor heart. Her heart that none of you understood. Lydia—"

"What?" she demanded sharply.

He stretched out his arms to her, his wrinkled fingers cupped and trembling.

"Her heart," he said. "Lydia. Give me the broken pieces."

The next day Gothrud was very weak and could not leave his bed. For three days Lydia looked after him alone; but it turned out to take too much of her time from the duties required of her by her colony positions, and on the fourth day they brought in Maria Warna from the unmarried women's barracks to stay with him and take care of him. And during the next few weeks he rambled a good deal in his talk, so that, one way or another, he told Maria everything. And eventually, later, she told it to the rest of us. But that was a long time after when things were different.

Gothrud lingered for a few days more than three weeks and finally died. He was cremated, as was everyone else who died after that. That was the same week that the last of the tobacco and cigarets were used up; and those of us who smoked had a hard time getting used to doing without them.

In the Bone

I

Personally, his name was Harry Brennan.

Officially, he was the *John Paul Jones*, which consisted of four billion dollars worth of irresistible equipment—the latest and best of human science—designed to spread its four-thousand-odd components out through some fifteen cubic meters of space under ordinary conditions—designed also to stretch across light-years under extraordinary conditions (such as sending an emergency messenger-component home) or to clump into a single magnetic unit in order to shift through space and explore the galaxy. Both officially and personally—but most of all personally—he represents a case in point.

The case is one having to do with the relative importance of the made thing and its maker.

It was, as we know, the armored horseman who dominated the early wars of the Middle Ages in Europe. But, knowing this, it is still wise to remember that it was not the iron shell that made the combination of man and metal terrible to the enemy—but rather the essentially naked man inside the shell. Later, French knights depending on their armor went down before the cloth-yard shafts of unarmored footmen with bows, at Crécy and Poitiers.

And what holds true for armor holds true for the latest developments of our science as well. It is not the spacecraft or the laser on which we will find ourselves depending when a time of ultimate decision comes, but the naked men within and behind these things. When that time comes, those who

rank the made thing before its maker will die as the French
knights died at Crécy and Poitiers. This is a law of nature as
wide as the universe, which Harry Brennan, totally unsus-
pecting, was to discover once more for us, in his personal
capacity.

Personally, he was in his mid-twenties, unremarkable except
for two years of special training with the *John Paul Jones*
and his superb physical condition. He was five-eleven, a hundred seventy-two pounds, with a round, cheerful face under
his brown crew-cut hair. I was Public Relations Director of
the Project that sent him out; and I was there with the rest
to slap him on the back the day he left.

"Don't get lost, now," said someone. Harry grinned.

"The way you guys built this thing," he answered, "if I
got lost the galaxy would just have to shift itself around to get
me back on plot."

There was an unconscious arrogance hidden in that answer,
but no one marked it at the time. It was not the hour of
suspicions.

He climbed into the twelve-foot-tall control-suit that with
his separate living tank were the main components of the
John Paul Jones and took off. Up in orbit, he spent some
thirty-two hours testing to make sure all the several thousand
other component parts were responding properly. Then he
left the solar system.

He clumped together his components, made his first shift
to orbit Procyon—and from there commenced his explorations
of the stars. In the next nine weeks, he accumulated literally
amazing amounts of new information about the nearby stars
and their solar systems. And—this is an even better index of
his success—located four new worlds on which men could
step with never a spacesuit or even a water canteen to sustain
them. Worlds so like Earth in gravity, atmosphere and even
flora and fauna, that they could be colonized tomorrow.

Those were his first four worlds. On the fifth he encountered his fate—a fate for which he was unconsciously ripe.

The fact was the medical men and psychologists had overlooked a factor—a factor having to do with the effect of Harry's official *John Paul Jones* self upon his entirely human personal self. And over nine weeks this effect changed Harry without his ever having suspected it.

You see, nothing seemed barred to him. He could cross light-years by touching a few buttons. He could send a sensing element into the core of the hottest star, into the most poisonous planetary atmospheres or crushing gravities, to look around as if he were down there in person. From orbit, he could crack open a mountain, burn off a forest or vaporize a section of icecap in search of information just by tapping the energy of a nearby sun. And so, subtly, the unconscious arrogance born during two years of training, that should have been noted in him at take-off from Earth, emerged and took him over—until he felt that there was nothing he could not do; that all things must give way to him; that he was, in effect, master of the universe.

The day may come when a man like Harry Brennan may hold such a belief and be justified. But not yet. On the fifth Earthlike world he discovered—World 1242 in his records—Harry encountered the proof that his belief was unjustified.

II

The world was one which, from orbit, seemed to be the best of all the planets which he had discovered were suitable for human settlement; and he was about to go down to its surface personally in the control-suit, when his instruments picked out something already down there.

It was a squat, metallic pyramid about the size of a fourplex apartment building; and it was radiating on a number of interesting frequencies. Around its base there was mechanical movement and an area of cleared ground. Further out, in the native forest, were treaded vehicles taking samples of the soil, rock and vegetation.

Harry had been trained for all conceivable situations, including an encounter with other intelligent, space-going life. Automatically, he struck a specific button, and immediately a small torpedo-shape leaped away to shift through alternate space and back to Earth with the information so far obtained. And a pale, thin beam reached up and out from the pyramid below. Harry's emergency messenger component ceased to exist.

Shaken, but not yet really worried, Harry struck back instantly with all the power his official self could draw from the GO-type sun, nearby.

The power was funneled by some action below, directly into the pyramid itself; and it vanished there as indifferently as the single glance of a sunbeam upon a leaf.

Harry's mind woke suddenly to some understanding of what he had encountered. He reached for the controls to send the *John Paul Jones* shifting into the alternate universe and away.

His hands never touched the controls. From the pyramid below, a blue lance of light reached up to paralyze him, select the control-suit from among the other components and send it tumbling to the planetary surface below like a swatted insect.

But the suit had been designed to protect its occupant, whether he himself was operative or not. At fifteen hundred feet, the drag chute broke free, looking like a silver cloth candle-snuffer in the sunlight; and at five hundred feet the retro-rockets cut in. The suit tumbled to earth among some trees two kilometers from the pyramid, with Harry inside bruised, but released from his paralysis.

From the pyramid, a jagged arm of something like white lightning lashed the ground as far as the suit, and the suit's outer surface glowed cherry-red. Inside, the temperature suddenly shot up fifty degrees; instinctively Harry hit the panic button available to him inside the suit.

The suit split down the center like an overcooked frankfurter and spat Harry out; he rolled among the brush and fernlike ground cover, six or seven meters from the suit.

From the distant pyramid, the lightning lashed the suit, breaking it up. The headpiece rolled drunkenly aside, turning the dark gape of its interior toward Harry like the hollow of an empty skull. In the dimness of that hollow Harry saw the twinkle of his control buttons.

The lightning vanished. A yellow lightness filled the air about Harry and the dismembered suit. There was a strange quivering to the yellowness; and Harry half-smelled, half-tasted the sudden, flatbite of ozone. In the headpiece a button clicked without being touched; and the suit speaker, still radio-connected with the recording tank in orbit, spoke aloud in Harry's voice.

"Orbit . . ." it said. ". . . into . . . going . . ."

These were, in reverse order, the last three words Harry had recorded before sighting the pyramid. Now, swiftly gaining speed, the speaker began to recite backwards, word for word, everything Harry had said into it in nine weeks. Faster it went, and faster until it mounted to a chatter, a gabble, and finally a whine pushing against the upper limits of Harry's auditory register.

Suddenly, it stopped.

The little clearing about Harry was full of silence. Only the odd and distant creaking of something that might have been a rubbing branch or an alien insect, came to Harry's ears. Then the speaker spoke once more.

"Animal . . ." it said flatly in Harry's calm, recorded voice and went on to pick further words from the recordings, ". . . beast. You . . . were an animal . . . wrapped in . . . made clothing. I have stripped you back to . . . animal again. Live, beast . . ."

Then the yellowness went out of the air and the taste of ozone with it. The headpiece of the dismembered suit grinned, empty as old bones in the sunlight. Harry scrambled to his feet and ran wildly away through the trees and brush. He ran in panic and utter fear, his lungs gasping, his feet pounding the alien earth, until the earth, the trees, the sky itself swam about him from exhaustion; and he fell tumbling to earth and away into the dark haven of unconsciousness.

When he woke, it was night, and he could not quite remember where he was or why. His thoughts seemed numb and unimportant. But he was cold, so he blundered about until he found the standing half-trunk of a lightning-blasted tree and crept into the burned hollow of its interior, raking frill-edged, alien leaves about him out of some half-forgotten instinct, until his own body-warmth in the leaves formed a cocoon of comfort about him; and he slept.

From then on began a period in which nothing was very clear. It was as if his mind had huddled itself away somehow like a wounded animal and refused to think. There was no past or future, only the endless now. If now was warm, it had always been warm; if dark—it had always been dark. He learned to smell water from a distance and go to it when he was thirsty. He put small things in his mouth to taste them. If they tasted good he ate them. If he got sick afterwards, he did not eat them again.

Gradually, blindly, the world about him began to take on a certain order. He came to know where there were plants with portions he could eat, where there were small creatures he could catch and pull apart and eat and where there was water.

He did not know how lucky he was in the sheer chance of finding flora and fauna on an alien world that was edible— let alone nourishing. He did not realize that he had come down on a plateau in the tropical highlands, with little variation in day and night temperature and no large native predators which might have attacked him.

None of this, he knew. Nor would it have made any difference to him if he had, for the intellectual center of his brain had gone on vacation, so to speak, and refused to be called back. He was, in fact, a victim of severe psychological shock. The shock of someone who had come to feel himself absolute master of a universe and who then, in a few short seconds, had been cast down from that high estate by something or someone inconceivably greater, into the state of a beast of the field.

But still, he could not be a true beast of the field, in spite of the fact his intellectual processes had momentarily abdicated. His perceptive abilities still worked. His eyes could not help noting, even if incuriously, the progressive drying of the vegetation, the day-by-day shifting in the points of setting and rising of the sun. Slowly, instinctively, the eternal moment that held him stretched and lengthened until he began to perceive divisions within it—a difference between *now* and *was*, between *now* and *will be*.

III

The day came at last when he saw himself.

A hundred times he had crouched by the water to drink and, lowering his lips to its surface, seen color and shape rising to meet him. The hundredth and something time, he checked, a few inches above the liquid plane, staring at what he saw.

For several long seconds it made no sense to him. Then, at first slowly, then with a rush like pain flooding back on someone rousing from the anesthesia of unconsciousness, he recognized what he saw.

Those were eyes at which he stared, sunken and dark-circled under a dirty tangle of hair. That was a nose jutting between gaunt and sunken cheeks above a mouth, and there was a chin naked only because once an ultrafine laser had burned

out the thousand and one roots of the beard that grew on it.
That was a man he saw—*himself.*

He jerked back like someone who has come face-to-face
with the devil. But he returned eventually, because he was
thirsty, to drink and see himself again. And so, gradually, he
got used to the sight of himself.

So it was that memory started to return to him. But it did
not come back quickly or all at once. It returned instead by
jerks and sudden, partial revelations—until finally the whole
memory of what had happened was back in his conscious
mind again.

But he was really not a man again.

He was still essentially what the operator of the pyramid
had broken him down into. He was still an animal. Only the
memory and imaginings of a man had returned to live like a
prisoner in a body that went on reacting and surviving in
the bestial way it had come to regard as natural.

But his animal peace was broken. For his imprisoned mind
worked now. With the control-suit broken up—he had returned to the spot of its destruction many times, to gaze
beastlike at the rusting parts—his mind knew he was a prisoner, alone on this alien world until he died. To know that
was not so bad, but remembering this much meant remembering also the existence of the someone or something that had
made him a prisoner here.

The whoever it was who was in the pyramid.

That the pyramid might have been an automated, mechanical device never entered his mind for a moment. There
had been a personal, directed, living viciousness behind the
announcement that had condemned him to live as a beast.
No, in that blank-walled, metallic structure, whose treaded
mechanical servants still prospected through the woods, there
was something alive—something that could treat the awesome
power of a solar tap as a human treated the attack of a mosquito—but something *living.* Some being. Some Other, who
lived in the pyramid, moving breathing, eating and gloating—

or worse yet, entirely forgetful of what he had done to Harry
Brennan.

And now that he knew that the Other was there, Harry
began to dream of him nightly. At first, in his dreams, Harry
whimpered with fear each time the dark shape he pursued
seemed about to turn and show its face. But slowly, hatred
came to grow inside and then outside his fear. Unbearable
that Harry should never know the face of his destroyer. Lying curled in his nest of leaves under the moonless, star-
brilliant sky, he snarled, thinking of his deprivation.

Then hate came to strengthen him in the daylight also.
From the beginning he had avoided the pyramid, as a wild
coyote avoids the farmyard where he was once shot by the
farmer. But now, day after day, Harry circled closer to the
alien shape. From the beginning he had run and hidden
from the treaded prospecting machines. But now, slowly, he
grew bolder, standing close enough at last to touch them
as they passed. And he found that they paid no attention to
him. No attention at all.

He came to ignore them in turn, and day by day he ventured closer to the pyramid. Until the morning came when
he lay, silently snarling, behind a bush, looking out across
the tread-trampled space that separated him from the nearest copper-colored face of the pyramid.

The space was roughly circular, thirty meters across,
broken only by a small stream which had been diverted to
loop inwards toward the pyramid before returning to its
original channel. In the bight of the loop a machine like a
stork straddled the artificial four-foot-wide channel, dipping
a pair of long necks with tentacle-clustered heads into the
water at intervals. Sometimes Harry could see nothing in
the tentacles when they came up. Occasionally they carried
some small water creature which they deposited in a tank.

Making a perfect circle about the tramped area, so that

the storklike machine was guarded within them, was an open fence of slender wands set upright in the earth, far enough apart for any of the machines that came and went to the forest to pass between any two of them. There seemed to be nothing connecting the wands, and nothing happened to the prospecting machines as they passed through—but the very purposelessness of the wands filled Harry with uneasiness.

It was not until after several days of watching that he had a chance to see a small native animal, frightened by something in the woods behind it, attempt to bolt across a corner of the clearing.

As it passed between two of the wands there was a waveriness in the air between them. The small animal leaped high, came down and lay still. It did not move after that, and later in the day, Harry saw the indifferent treads of one of the prospecting machines bury it in the trampled earth in passing.

That evening, Harry brought several captive, small animals bound with grass up to the wand line and thrust them through, one by one at different spots. All died.

The next night he tried pushing a captive through a small trench scooped out so that the creature passed the killing line below ground level. But this one died also. For several days he was baffled. Then he tried running behind a slow-moving machine as it returned and tying a small animal to it with grass.

For a moment as the front of the machine passed through, he thought the little animal would live. But then, as the back of the machine passed the line, it, too, died.

Snarling, Harry paced around outside the circle in the brush until the sun set and stars filled the moonless sky.

In the days that followed, he probed every gap in the wand-fence, but found no safe way through it. Finally, he came to concentrate on the two points at which the diverted stream entered and left the circle to flow beneath the storklike machine.

He studied this without really knowing what he was seeking. He did not even put his studying into words. Vaguely, he knew that the water went in and the water came out again unchanged; and he also wished to enter and come out safely. Then, one day, studying the stream and the machine, he noticed that a small creature plucked from the water by the storklike neck's mass of tentacles was still wriggling.

That evening, at twilight, while there was still light to see, he waded up the two-foot depth of the stream to the point where the killing line cut across its watery surface and pushed some more of his little animals toward the line underwater.

Two of the three surfaced immediately, twitched and floated on limply, to be plucked from the water and cast aside on the ground by the storklike machine. But the third swam on several strokes before surfacing and came up living to scramble ashore, race for the forest and be killed by wands further around the circle.

Harry investigated the channel below the killing line. There was water there up to his mid-thigh, plenty to cover him completely. He crouched down in the water and took a deep breath.

Ducking below the surface, he pulled himself along with his fingertips, holding himself close to the bottom. He moved in as far as the tentacled ends. These grabbed at him, but could not reach far enough back to touch him. He saw that they came within a few inches of the gravel bottom.

He began to need air. He backed carefully out and rose above the water, gasping. After a while his hard breathing stopped, and he sat staring at the water for a long while. When it was dark, he left.

The next day he came and crept underwater to the grabbing area of the storklike machine again. He scooped out several handfuls of the gravel from under the place where the

arms grabbed, before he felt a desperate need for air and had
to withdraw. But that day began his labors.

IV

Four days later the bottom under the grasping tentacles
was scooped out to an additional two feet of depth. And the
fifth twilight after that, he pulled himself, dripping and
triumphant, up out of the bend of the diverted stream inside
the circle of the killing wands.

He rested and then went to the pyramid, approaching it
cautiously and sidelong like a suspicious animal. There was a
door in the side he approached through which he had seen
the prospecting machines trundle in and out. In the dimness
he could not see it; and when he touched the metallic side
of the structure, his fingers, grimed and toughened from
scrabbling in the dirt, told him little. But his nose, beast-
sensitive now, located and traced the outline of the almost
invisible crack around the door panel by its reek of earth and
lubricant.

He settled down to wait. An hour later, one of the machines came back. He jumped up, ready to follow it in; but
the door opened just before it and closed the minute it was
inside—nor was there any room to squeeze in beside it. He
hunkered down, disappointed, snarling a little to himself.

He stayed until dawn and watched several more machines
enter and leave. But there was no room to squeeze inside,
even with the smallest of them.

During the next week or so he watched the machines enter
and leave nightly. He tied one of his small animals to an
entering machine and saw it pass through the entrance alive
and scamper out again with the next machine that left. And
every night his rage increased. Then, wordlessly, one daytime after he had seen a machine deep in the woods lurch
and tilt as its tread passed over a rock, inspiration took him.

That night he carried through the water with him several
cantaloupe-sized stones. When the first machine came back

to the pyramid, in the moment in which the door opened before it, he pushed one of the rocks before the right-hand tread. The machine, unable to stop, mounted the rock with its right tread, tilted to the left and struck against that side of the entrance.

It checked, backed off and put out an arm with the grasping end to remove the rock. Then it entered the opening. But Harry was already before it, having slipped through while the door was still up and the machine, busy pulling the stone aside.

He plunged into a corridor of darkness, full of clankings and smells. A little light from the opening behind him showed him a further, larger chamber where other machines stood parked. He ran toward them.

Long before he reached them, the door closed behind him, and he was in pitch darkness. But the clanking of the incoming machine was close behind him, and the adrenalinized memory of a wild beast did not fail him. He ran, hands outstretched, directly into the side of the parked machine at which he had aimed and clambered up on it. The machine entering behind him clanked harmlessly past him and stopped moving.

He climbed cautiously down in the impenetrable darkness. He could see nothing; but the new, animal sensitivity of his nose offered a substitute for vision. He moved like a hunting dog around the chamber, sniffing and touching; and slowly a clear picture of it and its treaded occupants built up in his mind.

He was still at this when suddenly a door he had not seen opened almost in his face. He had just time to leap backwards as a smaller machine with a boxlike body and a number of upward-thrusting arms entered, trundled to the machine that had just come back and began to relieve the prospecting machine of its sample box, replacing it with the one it carried itself.

This much, in the dim light from the open door, Harry

was able to see. But then, the smaller machine turned back toward the doorway; and Harry, waking to his opportunity, ducked through ahead of it.

He found himself in a corridor dimly lit by a luminescent strip down the center of its ceiling. The corridor was wide enough for the box-collecting machine to pass him; and, in fact, it rolled out around him as he shrank back against one metal wall. It went on down the corridor, and he followed it into a larger room with a number of machines, some mobile, some not, under a ceiling lit as the corridor had been with a crossing translucent strip.

In this area all the machines avoided each other—and him. They were busy with each other and at other incomprehensible duties. Hunched and tense, hair erect on the back of his neck and nostrils spread wide, Harry moved through them to explore other rooms and corridors that opened off this one. It took him some little time; but he discovered that they were all on a level, and there was nothing but machines in any of them. He found two more doors with shallow steps leading up to them, but these would not open for him; and though he watched by one for some time, no machine went up the steps and through it.

He began to be conscious of thirst and hunger. He made his way back to the door leading to the chamber where the prospecting machines were parked. To his surprise, it opened as he approached it. He slipped through into darkness.

Immediately, the door closed behind him; and sudden panic grabbed him, when he found he could not open it from this side. Then, self-possession returned to him.

By touch, smell and memory, he made his way among the parked machines and down the corridor to the outside door. To his gratification, this also opened when he came close. He slipped through into cool, fresh outer air and a sky already graying with dawn. A few moments later, wet but free, he was back in the woods again.

From then on, each night he returned. He found it was not necessary to do more than put any sizeable object before a returning machine. It would stop to clear the path, and he could enter ahead of it. Then, shortly after he was inside, a box-collecting machine would open the inner door.

Gradually, his fear of the machines faded. He came to hold them in a certain contempt. They always did the same thing in the same situation, and it was easy to trick or out-maneuver them.

But the two inner doors of the machine area with the steps would not open to him; and he knew the upper parts of the pyramid were still unexplored by him. He sniffed at the cracks of these door, and a scent came through—not of lubri-cating medium and metal alone, but of a different musky odor that raised the hairs on the back of his neck again. He snarled at the doors.

He went back to exploring minutely the machine level. The sample boxes from the prospecting machines, he found, were put on conveyorbelt-like strips that floated up on thin air through openings in the ceiling—but the openings were too small for him to pass through. But he discovered some-thing else. One day he came upon one of the machines tak-ing a grille off the face of one of the immobile devices. It carried the grille away, and he explored the opening that had been revealed. It was the entrance to a tunnel or duct lead-ing upward; and it was large enough to let him enter it. Air blew silently from it; and the air was heavy with the musky odor he had smelled around the doors that did not open.

The duct tempted him, but fear held him back. The ma-chine came back and replaced the grille; and he noticed that it fitted into place with a little pressure from the outside, top and bottom. After the machine had left he pressed, and the grille fell out into his hands.

After a long wait, he ventured timorously into the tube— but a sudden sound like heavy breathing mixed with a wave of a strong, musky odor came at him. He backed out in panic, fled the pyramid and did not come back for two days.

When he came back, the grille was again neatly in place. He removed it and sat a long time getting his courage up. Finally, he put the grille up high out of reach of the machine which had originally removed it and crawled into the duct.

He crept up the tube at an angle into darkness. His eyes were useless, but the musky odor came strongly at him. Soon, he heard sounds.

There was an occasional ticking, then a thumping or shuffling sound. Finally, after he had crawled a long way up through the tube, there was a sound like a heavy puffing or hoarse breathing. It was the sound that had accompanied the strengthening of the musky odor once before; and this time the scent came strong again.

He lay, almost paralyzed with terror in the tube, as the odor grew in his nostrils. He could not move until sound and scent had retreated. As soon as they had, he wormed his way backward down to the lower level and freedom, replaced the grille and fled for the outside air, once again.

But once more, in time, he came back. Eventually returned to explore the whole network of tubes to which the one he had entered connected. Many of the branching tubes were too small for him to enter, and the biggest tube he could find led to another grille from which the musky-smelling air was blasted with force.

Clearly it was the prime mover for the circulation of air through the exhaust half of the pyramid's ventilating system. Harry did not reason it out to himself in those intellectual terms, but he grasped the concept wordlessly and went back to exploring those smaller tubes that he could crawl into.

These, he found, terminated in grilles set in their floors through which he could look down and catch a glimpse of some chamber or other. What he saw was mainly incomprehensible. There were a number of corridors, a number of what could be rooms containing fixed or movable objects of various sizes and shapes. Some of them could be the equivalent of chairs or beds—but if so, they were scaled for a being plainly larger than himself. The lighting was invariably the low-key illumination he had encountered in the lower, machine level of the pyramid, supplied by the single translucent strip running across the ceiling.

Occasionally, from one grille or another, he heard in the distance the heavy sound of breathing, among other sounds, and smelled more strongly the musky odor. But for more than a week of surreptitious visits to the pyramid, he watched through various grilles without seeing anything living.

V

However, a day finally came when he was crouched, staring down into a circular room containing what might be a bed shape, several chair shapes and a number of other fixed shapes with variously spaced and depthed indentations in their surfaces. In a far edge of the circular room was a narrow alcove, the walls of which were filled with ranked indentations, among which several lights of different colors winked and glowed.

Suddenly, the dim illumination of the room began to brighten. The illumination increased rapidly, so that Harry cringed back from the grille, lifting a palm to protect his dimness-accustomed eyes. At the same moment, he heard approaching the sound of heavy breathing and sniffed a sudden increase in the musky odor.

He froze. Motionless above the grille, he stopped even his breathing. He would have stopped his heart if he could, but it raced, shaking his whole body and sounding its rapid beat in his ears until he felt the noise of it must be booming through the pyramid like a drum. But there was no sign from below that this was so.

Then, sliding into sight below him, came a massive figure on a small platform that seemed to drift without support into the room.

The aperture of the grille was small. Harry's viewpoint

was cramped and limited, looking down directly from over-head. He found himself looking down onto thick, hairless brown-skinned shoulders, a thick neck with the skin creased at the back and a forward-sloping, hairless brown head, egg-shaped in outline from above, with the point forward.

Foreshortened below the head and shoulders was a bulging chinline with something like a tusk showing; it had a squat, heavy, hairless, brown body and thick short forearms with stubby claws at the end of four-fingered hands. There was something walruslike about the tusks and the hunching; —and the musky odor rose sickeningly into Harry's human nostrils.

The platform slid level with the alcove, which was too narrow for it to enter. Breathing hoarsely, the heavy figure on it heaved itself suddenly off the platform into the alcove, and the stubby hands moved over the pattern of indentations. Then, it turned and heaved itself out of the alcove, onto the flat, bed surface adjoining. Just as Harry's gaze began to get a full-length picture of it, the illumination below went out.

Harry was left, staring dazzled into darkness, while the heavy breathing and the sound of the figure readjusting itself on the bed surface came up to his ears. After a while, there was no noise but the breathing. But Harry did not dare move. For a long time he held his cramped posture, hardly breathing himself. Finally, cautiously, inch-by-inch, he retreated down the tube, which was too small to let him turn around. When he reached the larger tubes, he fled for the outside and the safety of the forest.

The next day, he did not go near the pyramid. Or the next. Every time he thought of the heavy, brown figure entering the room below the grille, he became soaked with the clammy sweat of a deep, emotional terror. He could understand how the Other had not heard him or seen him up behind the grille. But he could not understand how the alien had not *smelled* him.

Slowly, however, he came to accept the fact that the Other

had not. Possibly the Other did not have a sense of smell.
Possibly . . . there was no end to the possibilities. The fact
was that the Other had not smelled Harry—or heard him—
or seen him. Harry was like a rat in the walls—unknown
because he was unsuspected.

At the end of the week, Harry was once more prowling
around back by the pyramid. He had not intended to come
back, but his hatred drew him like the need of a drug addict
for the drug of his addiction. He had to see the Other again,
to feed his hate more surely. He had to look at the Other,
while hating the alien, and feel the wild black current of
his emotions running toward the brown and hairless shape.
At night, buried in his nest of leaves, Harry tossed and
snarled in his sleep, dreaming of the small stream backing
up to flood the interior of the pyramid, and the Other drowning—of lightning striking the pyramid and fire racing through
it—of the Other burning. His dreams became so full of rage
and so terrible that he woke, twisting and with the few rags
of clothing that still managed to cling unnoticed to him,
soaked with sweat.
  In the end, he went back into the pyramid.
  Daily he went back. And gradually, it came to the point
where he was no longer fearful of seeing the Other. Instead,
he could barely endure the search and the waiting at the
grilles until the Other came into sight. Meanwhile, outside
the pyramid in the forest, the frill-edged leaves began to dry
and wither and drop. The little stream sank in its bed—only
a few inches, but enough so that Harry had to dig out the
bottom of the streambed under the killing barrier in order to
pass safely underwater into the pyramid area.
  One day he noticed that there were hardly any of the
treaded machines out taking samples in the woods any more.
  He was on his way to the pyramid through the woods,
when the realization struck him. He stopped dead, freezing
in midstride like a hunting dog. Immediately, there flooded

into his mind the memory of how the parking chamber for
the treaded machines, inside the base of the pyramid, had
been full of unmoving vehicles during his last few visits.

Immediately, also, he realized the significance of the drying leaves, the dropping of the water level of the stream.
And something with the urgency of a great gong began to ring
and ring inside him like the pealing of an alarm over a
drowning city.

Time had been, when there had been no pyramid here.
Time was now, with the year fading and the work of the
collecting machines almost done. Time would be, when the
pyramid might leave.

Taking with it the Other.

He began to run, instinctively, toward the pyramid. But,
when he came within sight of it, he stopped. For a moment
he was torn with indecision, an emotional maelstrom of
fear and hatred all whirling together. Then, he went on.

He emerged a moment later, dripping, a fist-sized rock in
each hand, to stand before the closed door that gave the
machines entrance to the pyramid. He stood staring at it, in
broad daylight. He had never come here before in full daylight,
but his head now was full of madness. Fury seethed in him,
but there was no machine to open the door for him. It was
then that the fury and madness in him might have driven
him to pound wildly on the door with his stones or to wrench
off one of the necks of the storklike machine at the stream
and try to pry the door open. Any of these insane things he
might have done and so have attracted discovery and the
awesome power of the machinery and killing weapons at the
command of the Other. Any such thing he might have done
if he was simply a man out of his head with rage—but he was
no longer a man.

He was what the Other had made him, an animal, although with a man locked inside him. And like an animal,
he did not rave or rant, any more than does the cat at the

mousehole, or the wolf waiting for the shepherd to turn in for the night. Instead, without further question, the human beast that had been Harry Brennan—that still called himself Harry Brennan, in a little, locked-away, back corner of its mind—dropped on his haunches beside the door and hunkered there, panting lightly in the sunlight and waiting.

Four hours later, as the sun was dropping close to the treetops, a single machine came trundling out of the woods. Harry tricked it with one of his stones and, still carrying the other, ran into the pyramid.

He waited patiently for the small collecting machine to come and empty out the machine returned from outside, then dodged ahead of it, when it came, into the interior, lower level of the pyramid. He made his way calmly to the grille that gave him entrance to the ventilating system, took out the grille and entered the tube. Once in the system, he crawled through the maze of ductwork, until he came at last to the grille overlooking the room with the alcove and the rows of indentations on the alcove walls.

When he looked down through the grille, it was completely dark below. He could hear the hoarse breathing and smell the musky odor of the Other, resting or perhaps asleep, on the bed surface. Harry lay there for a number of slow minutes, smelling and listening. Then he lifted the second rock and banged with it upon the grille.

For a second there was nothing but the echoing clang of the beaten metal in the darkness. Then the room suddenly blazed with light, and Harry, blinking his blinded eyes against the glare, finally made out the figure of the Other rising upright upon the bed surface. Great, round, yellow eyes in a puglike face with a thick upper lip wrinkled over two tusks stared up through the grille at Harry.

The lip lifted, and a bubbling roar burst from the heavy fat-looking shape of the Other. He heaved his round body off the bed surface and rolled, waddling across the floor to just below the grille.

Reaching up with one blunt-clawed hand, he touched the grille, and it fell to the floor at his feet. Left unguarded in the darkness of the ductwork, Harry shrank back. But the Other straightened up to his full near six-and-a-half feet of height and reached up into the ductwork. His blunt clawed hand fastened on Harry and jerked. Off balance, Harry came tumbling to the floor of the chamber.

A completely human man probably would have stiffened up and broken both arms, if not his neck, in such a fall. Harry, animal-like, attempted to cling to the shape of the Other as he fell, and so broke the impact of his landing. On the floor, he let go of the Other and huddled away from the heavy shape, whimpering.

The Other looked down, and his round, yellow eyes focused on the stone Harry had clung to even through his fall. The Other reached down and grasped it, and Harry gave it up like a child releasing something he has been told many times not to handle. The Other made another, lower-toned, bubbling roar deep in his chest, examining the rock. Then he laid it carefully aside on a low table surface and turned back to stare down at Harry.

Harry cringed away from the alien stare and huddled into himself, as the blunt fingers reached down to feel some of the rags of a shirt that still clung about his shoulders.

The Other rumbled interrogatively at Harry. Harry hid his head. When he looked up again, the Other had moved over to a wall at the right of the alcove and was feeling about in some indentations there. He bubbled at the wall, and a second later Harry's voice sounded eerily in the room.

". . . You are . . . the one I . . . made a beast . . ."

Harry whimpered, hiding his head again.

"You can't . . ." said Harry's voice, ". . . even speak now. Is . . . that so . . ."

Harry ventured to peek upward out of his folded arms, but ducked his head again at the sight of the cold, yellow eyes staring down at him.

". . . I thought . . . you would be . . . dead by now," said the disembodied voice of Harry, hanging in the air of the chamber. ". . . Amazing . . . survival completely without . . . equipment. Must keep you now . . ." The eyes, yellow as topaz, considered Harry, huddled abjectly on the floor, ". . . cage . . . collector's item . . ."

The alien revolved back to the indentations of the wall a little way from the alcove. The broad, fleshy back turned contemptuously on Harry, who stared up at it.

The pitiful expression of fear on Harry's face faded suddenly into a soundless snarl. Silently, he uncoiled, snatched up the rock the Other had so easily taken from him, and sprang with it onto the broad back.

As he caught and clung there, one arm wrapped around a thick neck, the stone striking down on the hairless skull, his silent snarl burst out at last into the sound of a scream of triumph.

The Other screamed too—a bubbling roar—as he clumsily turned, trying to reach around himself with his thick short arms and pluck Harry loose. His claws raked Harry's throat-encircling arm, and blood streamed from the arm; but it might have been so much stage make-up for the effect it had in loosening Harry's hold. Screaming, Harry continued to pound crushingly on the Other's skull. With a furious spasm, the alien tore Harry loose, and they both fell on the floor.

The Other was first up; and for a second he loomed like a giant over Harry, as Harry was scrambling to his own feet and retrieving the fallen rock. But instead of attacking, the Other flung away, lunging for the alcove and the control indentations there.

Harry reached the alcove entrance before him. The alien dodged away from the striking rock. Roaring and bubbling, he fled waddling from his human pursuer, trying to circle around the room and get back to the alcove. Half a head taller than Harry and twice Harry's weight, he was refusing personal battle and putting all his efforts into reaching the alcove with its rows of indented controls. Twice Harry headed him off; and then by sheer mass and desperation, the Other turned and burst past into the alcove, thick hands outstretched and grasping at its walls. Harry leaped in pursuit, landing and clinging to the broad, fleshy back.

The other stumbled under the added weight, and fell, face down. Triumphantly yelling, Harry rode the heavy body to the floor, striking at the hairless head . . . and striking . . . and striking . . .

VI

Sometime later, Harry came wearily to his senses and dropped a rock he no longer had the strength to lift. He blinked around himself like a man waking from a dream, becoming aware of a brilliantly lit room full of strange shapes —and of a small alcove, the walls of which were covered with rows of indentations, in which something large and dead lay with its head smashed into ruin. A deep, clawing thirst rose to take Harry by the throat, and he staggered to his feet.

He looked longingly up at the dark opening of the ventilator over his head; but he was too exhausted to jump up, cling to its edge and pull himself back into the ductwork, from which he could return to the stream outside the pyramid and to the flowing water there. He turned and stumbled from the chamber into unfamiliar rooms and corridors.

A brilliant light illuminated everything around him as he went. He sniffed and thought he scented, through the musky reek that filled the air about him, the clear odor of water. Gradually, the scent grew stronger and led him at last to a room where a bright stream leaped from a wall into a basin where it pooled brightly before draining away. He drank deeply and rested.

Finally, satiated, he turned away from the basin and came

face-to-face with a wall that was all-reflecting surface; and he stopped dead, staring at himself, like Adam before the Fall.

It was only then, with the upwelling of his returning humanness, that he realized his condition. And words spoken aloud for the first time in months broke harshly and rustily from his lips like the sounds of a machine unused for years.

"My God!" he said, croakingly. "I've got no clothes left!"

And he began to laugh. Cackling, cackling rasping more unnaturally even than his speech, his laughter lifted and echoed hideously through the silent, alien rooms. But it was laughter all the same—the one sound that distinguishes man from the animal.

He was six months after that learning to be a complete human being again and finding out how to control the pyramid. If it had not been for the highly sophisticated safety devices built into the alien machine, he would never have lived to complete that bit of self-education.

But finally he mastered the controls and got the pyramid into orbit, where he collected the rest of his official self and shifted back through the alternate universe to Earth.

He messaged ahead before he landed; and everybody who could be there was on hand to meet him as he landed the pyramid. Some of the hands that had slapped his back on leaving were raised to slap him again when at last he stepped forth among them.

But, not very surprisingly, when his gaunt figure in a spare coverall now too big for it, with shoulder-length hair and burning eyes, stepped into their midst, not one hand finished its gesture. No one in his right senses slaps an unchained wolf on the back; and no one, after one look, wished to risk slapping the man who seemed to have taken the place of Harry.

Of course, he was still the same man they had sent out—of *course* he was. But at the same time he was also the man who had returned from a world numbered 1242 and from a duel to the death there with a representative of a race a hundred times more advanced than his own. And in the process he had been pared down to something very basic in his human blood and bone, something dating back to before the first crude wheel or chipped flint knife.

And what was that? Go down into the valley of the shades and demand your answer of a dead alien with his head crushed in, who once treated the utmost powers of modern human science as a man treats the annoyance of a buzzing mosquito.

Or, if that once-mighty traveler in spacegoing pyramids is disinclined to talk, turn and inquire of other ghosts you will find there—those of the aurochs, the great cave bear and the woolly mammoth.

They, too, can testify to the effectiveness of naked men.

The Bleak and Barren Land

I

Kent Harmon stepped out into the pitchy blackness of the night and the soft, warm, sulphur-smelling rain of the lowlands on Modor. The darkness wrapped him like some gently odorous cloak as he squelched over the yielding ground to the light of the communications shack and stepped inside.

Tom Schneider, the operator, looked up as Kent banged the door behind him. The by-pass channel direct to Earth was occupying his attention at the moment, but he grinned sympathetically at Kent, and fishing around in the message basket before him with his one free hand, dug out a flimsy from Central Headquarters and handed it up.

"This what you called me about?" asked Kent, taking it. Tom turned his homely pale and boyish face briefly from the controls that were occupying his attention and nodded briefly. A monitor hum squealed suddenly up to the limits of human audibility, and disappeared. Tom relaxed.

"On channel," he said, into the transmitter plate, "receiving. Go ahead, Earth."

The message tape began to click out and Kent looked down at the flimsy. It was an official communication to him from the Central Headquarters Colonial Office. Kent fingered the little black mustache that had once been his pride and joy— back in government circles on Earth where there was someone to see it—and let his mind spell out the single line of code:

CH to Col Rep Modor—Xmas Alert 500
40T 23:76W & 49:40N

The message tape stopped clicking. Tom switched off and stretched in his chair, turning to Kent.

"Something new?" he asked, casually. Then, something odd and rigid in the sharp, almost too-handsome features of the Colonial Representative pricked up his interest. "Bad news?"

"They're letting a colony come in," answered Kent without thinking—and instantly regretted having said it. Tom jerked suddenly upright in his chair.

"You're crazy!" he burst out. Kent, on guard again, smoothed out his face. He shrugged and put the flimsy in his pocket, turning toward the door.

"Hold on, dammit!" Tom reached out a long, skinny arm and caught the sleeve of Kent's jacket, halting him. "A colony? Where?"

"About five hundred kilos west of here," said Kent, distastefully. There was nothing secret about the information, but he would have appreciated being able to think the matter over before releasing it. Now he was committed.

"But that's in the barren land," said Tom incredulously. "What'll the Modorians say? And how come they're letting colonists in anyway?"

"We're open for settlement," answered Kent, sharply, realizing with disgust as he said it that he sounded pompous and official. He jerked his sleeve out of the other's hand, forestalling Tom's flow of questions.

"I can't talk about it now, Tom," he said irritably. "And for God's sake keep as quiet about it yourself as you can. You know what a touchy subject colonists are with the prospectors and the adopted men." He strode to the door.

"But this is *it!*" cried Tom behind him, his high voice squeaking still higher in alarm and excitement. "The Modorians—"

Kent slammed the door of the message shack behind him, cutting off the flow of words.

It was a moment in which he wanted to be alone to think. Here, at the trading post, there would be no opportunity, now that Tom knew the news. The operator was probably broadcasting it now, and inside of an hour, there would be angry prospectors and adopted men—men who had formed working friendships with some Modorian or other—knocking on his door. Kent turned away from the small huddle of buildings and made for the landing field where his flyer stood.

The little machine was silent in the darkness. He crawled inside, set the controls, and bucketed upward into the night.

For several seconds, the flyer seemed to hang in the smoky blackness, then it burst through the overhanging cloud layer above the valley and rode high above in the white moonlight. Kent checked the controls and looked down.

The moon of Modor was close to Modor and the night was brilliant. Below him the valley brimmed with dark clouds, stretching away and down to the sea. To the west and north the hills began and the uplands, stony and bare and clear. He turned the nose of the flyer westward and fled away from the valley, out over the silent landscape.

The cabin of the little flyer was cold with the chill of high altitude. Kent turned on the heating system, locked the controls on the five hundred kilos distant area where the colonist ship was due to land, and sat back, lighting the pipe that he carried in his jacket pocket, and setting himself to consider the situation.

The fumes of the pipe rose comfortingly about him as he dragged the smoke deep into his lungs, and he grinned wryly, remembering how this, too, had been a subject of censure back at Colonial Office on Earth. Kent was a government career man, and a good one. The only trouble was that in appearance he was a little too good—he looked the part.

He was spare and darkly handsome. A little short, by

present day standards; but that did not show up unless you saw him standing alongside a taller man. What, in ancient times would have been called the empire-builder type of man, he was keen-minded, alert, impeccable as to dress and manner—and he smoked a pipe.

Kent chuckled a little sadly, remembering. It had been the pipe that sent him out here to Modor—the straw, in a manner of speaking that broke the camel's back.

It was the casual note nowadays in government circles. Diplomats and representatives, from the least to the greatest, strove to look like college kids—if they were young enough— or small businessmen—if they were too old for the first role. The last thing to look like was what you were. Kent, of course, had. Couldn't help himself, in fact. In consequence, he was looked on with suspicion by his fellows and immediate superiors. Here's someone trying to show us all up, they said; and when he began smoking the pipe, that was the final straw. The pipe was too perfect. It was archaic and ostentatious. The perfection of Kent Harmon was ridiculous alongside the careful cultivated lack of dignity of the Colonial Office. Result—assignment to Modor.

Well—damn them all—thought Kent, comfortably sucking in smoke. He enjoyed the pipe, and at least out here he could smoke to his heart's content.

But to get back to this business of colonists—he frowned. It looked as if the disapproval of the Colonial Office was still following him. Letting five hundred Earth-born humans into Modor to settle on the barren land was a fool's trick, and a flat outrage of a sort of unwritten agreement that had existed for over two hundred years between Modorians and humans, ever since the first ship had landed, in fact. Modorians were not the ordinary—by human standard—type of alien.

Kent glanced out through the window of his flyer. Down below, the ground was a tumbled wilderness of rock with only an occasional clump of spiny bush to break the monotony. It looked lifeless and deserted, but Kent knew that somewhere down there there was almost sure to be at least two or three scattered Modorians, sleeping, and probably even some humans, each with his Modorian, the Modorian that had "adopted" him and made it possible for him to roam the wilderness, prospecting or trapping.

No, the Modorians were not the ordinary alien. For one thing, they were the most intelligent race Man had yet discovered on the worlds he had taken over—some said even more intelligent than Man, himself; Kent, after five years on Modor, inclined to that view himself. But that was only the beginning of their uniqueness.

A female Modorian was about three feet high, nervous, suspicious and with about the apparent intelligence and characteristics of a chimpanzee. She resembled the male only in her thinness, the three opposed fingers of her hands, the large tarsier-like eyes and the covering of soft gray fur. She mated for life and rode her male pickaback as he roamed the stony face of his desert-like world.

But the male! Seven feet or more in height when he was fully grown, inhumanly strong and resourceful, indifferent to extremes of temperature that varied from a hundred and fifty degrees above zero to ninety below, of a different, stranger, steelier flesh than man's, he lived in comfort with nothing more than a steel spear and a few small hand tools on a world where a man without several tons of equipment would have frozen or starved in no time. The Modorians had never built cities because they did not need them—and for another reason.

And this was the strangest part of all. For the one great characteristic of the male Modorian was his utter independence. He needed nothing. He asked for nothing. He could be neither coerced, nor bribed, nor tricked, nor forced. He said and did only what he wished. He was a law unto himself and only to himself. What other living beings did was no concern of his, with the single exception of his own personal female —and, oddly enough, man.

For the Modorians, strangely, seemed to be fascinated by men. They neither needed them, nor objected to them; but they seemed to be eternally confounded by the fact that here were male creatures almost as intelligent as themselves, who could be dependent, and were. Almost anti-social where his own kind was concerned, a male Modorian often "adopted" a human man, watching over him with a sort of puzzled solicitude as the odd, weak creature toiled over the barren land, scrabbling in the burrows of little pack rat-like animals for the precious stones that to the Modorians were not worth a second glance.

Daily the Modorian rescued his prospector from landslide, blizzard, starvation and heat exhaustion, aided him in his search, and, on occasions when they met another of his own kind, discussed his charge gravely in the sonorous tones of the Modorian tongue. It was only through this that men had discovered that the Modorians, beneath the eternal calm and indifference of their exterior, were actually capable of deep and abiding affection and other emotions. And these men, eventually understanding, came to return the liking almost fiercely.

It was these humans, rather than the Modorians themselves, who would be Kent's ostensible problem, now that the news of the coming colonists was out. Central Headquarters on Earth had never made any kind of a colonization treaty with the Modorians. To do so would have required an individual agreement with each one of the males, which was impossible, even if every male had proved to be interested in such a treaty. But with an unusual wisdom, the Foreign Office had, until now, restricted any human settlement to the deep valleys, which because of the cloudiness and humidity, the Modorians did not care for.

But, the land area of these valleys was small, and the

human civilization was bursting under the pressure of over-population. The day when humans would come into the barren land with their rock pulverizers and fertilizers and farming equipment was inevitable. Sitting alone in his flyer, Kent shivered. The Modorians to date had really never been crossed by humans. What if that icy, infinitely capable mind, inhuman self-control and superhuman determination should be turned against man? What if the icy Modorian logic should decide that man was a pest, and dangerous, instead of an appealing pet? What could you do then against five millions of an enemy whose mind could be altered only by complete extermination?

True—Man, himself was counted now by quintillions—but —Kent shook his head—Central Headquarters had no real idea of how intelligent the Modorians actually were.

A bell on the instrument panel rang suddenly, sharply. Kent put out his hand to bring the flyer to a hovering halt, and looked down. The place where the colonists would land in less than forty hours lay below him, a shallow rocky bowl hemmed by low hills. He sat gazing at it for several minutes, then bit his lips, and turning the flyer, scooted for home. It would be up to him to stop trouble before it got started; and he could think of only one factor that would operate in his favor. The fact that each Modorian worked for himself and alone.

The one to stop, thought Kent grimly, would be the first Modorian who attempted to make trouble for the colony.

Stop the first Modorian—well, it was a good decision, thought Kent as he opened his eyes the following morning, his mind automatically taking up at exactly the point where it had left off the night before. But how? And how would he know when the first Modorian to start something, started something? The pale ghost of fear weaved for a moment through the back of his mind. Familiarity with the Modorians did not breed contempt. Quite the opposite. You were more likely to feel your own good opinion of yourself dwindling on prolonged contact. Maybe he should warn Earth? Ridiculous to expect anything really—he checked himself abruptly. Now with a night's sleep behind him, he was more than ever certain that the Colonial Office had granted the permit with an eye to putting him, personally, on the spot. There was no doubt a strong element that would have liked to get him out of the service completely.

For a moment the memory of green Earth plucked at him with nostalgic fingers. Home. What ninety per cent of the humans on Modor here would give their right arm for—passage back and security on the world of their forefathers, was his for the asking. All he had to do was bow politely out of the Colonial Office and accept a minor position elsewhere with some other governmental branch. Kent shook his head ruefully. Some odd little quirk within him kept him, and would always keep him, from buying on those terms.

He went into the office section of his quarters. On the instrument panel, the red lights for visiphone and doorbell were blinking furiously, and silently, their sound circuits disconnected. Kent grinned briefly at them. There would be angry prospectors and adopted men at the other ends of those circuits, clamoring for him. Well, let them. They had nothing to tell him about their attitude toward the present situation that he didn't know already. He would remain incommunicado until the colony ship came.

Leisurely, he drew a cup of coffee from the wall dispenser and sat down at his desk to draft a full report on the situation as it stood at the present time.

II

Forty hours, almost to the minute, after the original message had arrived, the ship bearing the colonists flashed radio signal it was entering the atmosphere. Kent rose to its summons and the second morning of his self-incarceration, dressed, and went out to his flyer.

In the dull, cloud-filtered light of day, the valley looked
gray and depressing. Water dripped steadily from everything;
and not even the careful landscaping with grass and trees and
bushes brought in from Earth, nor the carefully colored and
designed buildings of the trading station did much to relieve
the view. The place looked deserted, now, and probably was
—everyone having taken to the air at the first radio signal
from the incoming ship. They would be waiting for her—and
Kent—at the landing spot five hundred kilometers westward.

Kent climbed into the flyer and took off.

By the time he landed it was nearly mid-morning and the
temperature of the open area where the settlement was to be
was already shooting up. In the clear brilliant sunlight the
ship was down and the scene was a study in harsh beauty,
from the yellow dust of the hollow, where four great weather-
control pylons and individual shelters were already springing
up, to the looming hills, their crowns rust-red against the
molten sky. As Kent brought the flyer down he had already
spotted the signs of trouble, the prospectors held back from
the edge of the camp by armed colonists and milling in an angry group, while their Modorians stood apart, and scattered.
As he opened the door of the flyer, the prospectors made a
rush and surrounded him.

"Quiet down!" he said crisply, stepping down among them.
There was not a man that did not overtop him by two inches
or more, and his neatness threw him in dandified contrast to
their rough trail clothes. "There's nothing to be done right
now, anyhow."

"Listen, Harmon!" said one young giant, shoving his way
through his fellows. "You've got to contact Central Headquarters. Tell'm we don't want planters in here."

"I've done it," said Kent, dryly. "I expressed the attitude
of you men in the report I sent out yesterday."

"The hell you did!" flared the young giant.

"The hell I didn't, Simmons," said Kent, evenly. "The re-

port's gone in and all you can do is wait and hope that the
Colonial Office recommends moving this group."

"We won't wait for that," Simmons threatened. "We're
giving these planters twenty-four hours to get out."

The rest took up the cry. "That's right, Branch!" "You tell
him!" Kent waited until the clamor died down.

"So you're thinking of using force," he said.

"That's right," retorted Branch Simmons belligerently.
Kent snorted contemptuously.

"You're out of your head," he said, incisively. "I'll yank the
trading license of the first man that tries anything like that,
and blackball him for any attempt he ever makes at Earth
citizenship. Do any of you want to risk that?"

His black eyes challenged them, and they looked away.
There was not a man facing him who did not hope someday
to make a big enough gem find to buy his way back to Earth
citizenship.

"Besides," went on Kent. "You've got no grounds for com-
plaint. The only ones who can protest legally are the Modorians themselves."

"Our boys don't like it," grumbled one of the older prospectors.

"No?" said Kent, turning toward the scattered group of
friendly Modorians who stood a little way off. "Let them tell
me about it then."

He strode away from the humans and up to the group of
gray-furred natives.

"You know me," he said, speaking to all of them. "Have
any of you anything to say to me?"

Like lean and silent gods, they rested on their spears, towering over him, gazing down at him with large, inscrutable
eyes. Not one of them answered. Kent turned back to the
prospectors.

"I'm going down into the settlement," he said. "One of
you can go with me, if you like. Now, who's it going to be—
you, Branch?"

"Me," said Branch, hitching his gun belt around his waist. "I'll go."

"All right," said Kent, and led the way.

The prospectors waited in a little group apart from the others. Kent and Branch Simmons went down the slope until they reached the perimeter of the settlement area and were halted by two pink-cheeked youngsters, still in their light Earth-surface tunic and kilts, but carrying power-rifles.

"You can't go in," one of them informed Kent and the tall prospector in a high tenor.

"Oh, yes we can," said Kent. "I'm the Colonial Office Representative on this planet, and this man goes with me. I want to talk to your leader." The gun barrels wavered, and Kent strode forward, Branch following.

"Pretty little kids," said Branch contemptuously in Kent's ear. The young prospector was barely into his twenties, himself. Kent ignored him, searching the tangle of rising construction with his eyes.

Evidently the two sentries had orders to remain at their posts, for they did not follow them. The problem of locating the settlement leaders might have been a time-consuming one if their entrance had not attracted notice from the would-be colonists working nearby, and who started at once to yell back the word that outsiders had gotten past the perimeter. A few seconds of this produced a young man as large as Branch himself, and with the perfect muscles of a weight-lifter, and a lighter boy and girl of about the same age, all of whom approached at a run.

"Put your hands up!" roared the weight-lifter, waving a power-rifle at Branch and Kent as they came up.

"Don't point that thing at me, pretty-boy," said Branch, baring his teeth.

"Yes, put it away!" snapped Kent. "I'm the Colonial Office Representative and this man is with me."

"I don't care who—" began the weight-lifter.

"Well, you damn well will," barked Kent, his temper breaking forth, "when you find yourself in a forced labor draft bound for the Frontier Planets. Don't you know what Colonial Representative means? I'm the legal authority on this planet."

The other lowered his gun, but scowled.

"We've got a charter—" he growled.

"The settlement has," said Kent. "But the settlement may have to get along without you, if I decide to have you deported as a troublemaker. Now, put it up!"

Reluctantly, the young man laid his gun aside.

"That's more like it," said Kent, cooling off already and half-ashamed of his heat of a few seconds before. But then, it is never pleasant to look down the barrel of a gun when there is a chance it may be in the hands of a fool who will press the firing button. "You're in authority, here?"

"That's right," said the weight-lifter. "Hord Chalmers is my name."

"No you're not," the girl interrupted. "Dad is. You better wait for him, too."

Branch snorted under his breath and she looked at him unfavorably. She was a pretty little thing, black-haired and thin-featured, almost the twin of the slighter boy that made up the group.

"Then where is he?" asked Kent.

"Right here, sir, right here," said a new voice, somewhat out of breath, and they all turned to see a little, gray-haired, pot-bellied man with a kindly face trot up to the meeting. He came to a winded stop and threw a somewhat stern glance at Hord Chalmers.

"You take too much on yourself, Hord," he said.

"Somebody has to," said Hord, darkly.

"That's enough of that, boy," said the older man sharply. "You're my assistant and nothing more. Now don't you forget it! Sorry, sir—" he turned to Kent. "My name's Peter Lawrence, and these are my son, Bob, and my daughter,

Judy. Hord here's my nephew. Did I hear you say you were the Colonial Representative on Modor?"

"That's right," said Kent, dryly. "I'd like to see your charter and talk to you about a few things."

"I've got the charter here," said Peter Lawrence, pulling the little microfilm case from his pocket. "If you'd like to talk privately—"

"That won't be necessary," said Kent. He took the case, flipped up the magnifier, and scanned it. He handed it back. "You seem to be the only one in the whole bunch that's not twenty-one," he said. "Mind telling me about that?" Lawrence looked a little shy.

"Well," he said. "When they came of age, the kids had to leave Earth—you know how it is—" Kent nodded. Overcrowded Earth denied citizenship to even its native-born unless they had certified employment by the time they were twenty-one. "—and so I thought I might just as well come along with them and help them get a start."

Kent nodded, hiding the sympathy he felt. An older man like Lawrence could have stayed safe at home. It was a rare individual nowadays that would go adventuring on a raw new world for the sake of his children when he, himself, was middle-aged.

"They're a good bunch of kids," said Lawrence warmly.

Branch snorted, and Lawrence looked at him in some surprise.

"Oh, yes," said Kent wryly. "Let me introduce Branch Simmons, one of our prospectors, and adopted men. My name is Kent Harmon. Branch is one of the reasons I've come to talk to you."

"How do you do, son," said Peter Lawrence, holding out his hand. Branch ignored it, and after a second the older man let it fall to his side.

"Well!" said the girl.

"Hush, Judy," said Peter Lawrence, automatically. "What about him, Mr. Harmon?"

"Branch," said Kent, "is a representative of the prospectors and adopted men—you know about conditions here on Modor?"

"Yes," said Peter.

"The prospectors feel your settlement is a threat both to their way of life and that of the Modorians—and they've taken it on themselves to speak up for the Modorians."

"Those animals?" said Hord, incredulously.

"Shut your fat mouth," answered Branch, savagely.

"That's enough," said Kent looking at both of them. "For your information, Chalmers, the Modorians are held in rather deep affection by our prospectors—seeing that all of them have owed their lives to a Modorian at one time or another. I feel it my duty to inform you, Lawrence, that in accordance with the wishes of the prospectors, I've registered their protest against your settlement."

"But—why?" burst out the older man, bewilderedly. "There's millions of miles of empty land here. We're just taking up one tiny spot."

"I know the land looks empty—" began Kent, but the deep voice of Branch interrupted him.

"Let me explain this, Kent," he said, stepping forward. "Listen, Lawrence. If a bear came and pitched a tent in your living room would you be satisfied by his saying there were lots of other living rooms on the planet?" He reached out one long forefinger and prodded the older man on the chest. "You'd say, 'Hell, no!' You'd say, 'I don't care how much room there is, this place is mine.'"

"But look, son—" protested Peter.

"Don't 'son' me," growled Branch, "save that for these hot-house babies you brought along with you."

"—Mr. Simmons"—amended Peter. "Where else is there for us to go? Good God! You don't suppose we'd have picked this place if there was anything else available to us with the money we had? Look at it"—his pudgy arm gestured, widespread, at the rocky and empty land around them. "We've sunk everything we've got into equipment just to make this habitable. Pulverizers, fertilizers, plant food—weather control equipment, passage money. All we've got is here."

"That's your problem," said Branch.

"We can't go," said Peter. "We couldn't if we wanted to and I'm sure Central Headquarters isn't going to force us off Modor." He turned toward Kent. "You don't think they will, do you?"

"No," said Kent, "off the record, I don't think they will."

Hord Chalmers took a half-step forward.

"Anyway," he said to Branch, defiantly. "What business of yours is it, anyway? Let those natives talk for themselves if they want to."

"They won't talk," said Branch, more calmly than he had spoken so far. "They leave the talking up to us. If we can't make you leave, they will."

"Those—" said Chalmers.

"Yes, those!" interrupted Branch fiercely. "If they act, there won't be any more talking, by your or me, ever." And they glared at each other like two strange dogs about to clash.

"The Colonial Office gave me to understand there wouldn't be any trouble with the natives," cried Peter Lawrence a little wildly.

III

The next morning Kent woke in the shelter that had been assigned to him in the growing settlement. He rolled out of bed, dressed and ate. On the desk in the barren shelter that held his cot, and nothing else beside, there was a small pile of government dispatches that had been flown up early that morning. He lit a cigarette, perched on one corner of the desk, and tore open the envelopes.

Most were routine matters relating to trading and shipping. One was an acknowledgment of his report and an official refusal of the prospector's protest against the settlers. The last was a note from Tichi Marlowe, the daughter of one of his few close friends back on Earth. Tichi was adolescent and fiercely loyal. She had also had a crush on him. He smiled a little sadly and picked up her note.

Darling Kent:
   I wish you were coming back here. Everything is dead and double-dead around here since you shipped out. Daddy never brings anyone home any more but old men with indigestion—and I'm so sick of kids. Anyway, I think about you all the time. Daddy says to give you his best regards, and his wishes that you should come back soon, too. He says he bets you have your hands full with that new colony. I bet so, too. I've been hearing all about it, and I think the whole situation is real gummy.

Lots of love,

Tichi (PRSM .2:9 TKMarlowe, Wash.)

Kent whistled and smiled a little grimly. Tichi could be embarrassing, but she could also be useful, with her little girl manner and her childish slang. The words—"real gummy"—were intended to convey to Kent just what he had suspected earlier—that the landing of the colony had been a deliberate attempt by a certain clique in the Office to put him in a discrediting situation. Bless Tichi and her little ears alert to capital gossip!

However—he folded the letter and put it away—there was nothing he could do about it now. He could not quit right in the middle of this situation, even if he wanted to—and he didn't want to.

He went outside and looked up to the hills.

What he had expected was there. Singly and in small family groups, during the night they had been drifting in, silently, purposefully, from maybe as far as fifty or a hundred miles away—a Modorian alone could move at amazing speed for surprising lengths of time. And now the heights were scattered with them, lean, gray figures outlined against the horizon, leaning on their spears and looking down on the camp. The wild Modorians—those who had never struck up a partnership with any man, were coming in.

"Mr. Harmon—"

He turned, looking down. The little leader of the colonists was at his elbow, round face worried.

"Are they dangerous?" he asked.

"Yes," said Kent. "Yes, they're dangerous."

"Well, what should I do? Should I arm more of the boys and let the girls handle all the construction?"

"Don't arm anybody," said Kent.

"But what if they start something? They've got those spears. I know they're only savages—"

"Mr. Lawrence," Kent interrupted wearily. "They're not savages. If you and your bunch of youngsters would just get that through your heads, you'd be a lot safer." He pointed. "Those up there on the hills are Modorians who've never had more than an occasional contact with people. But you won't find one of them who can't talk your own language as well or better than you can, and doesn't know as much or more about the Universe and the human race as you do. They're not savages, and they're not fools. You're making the common mistake of most newcomers when you think that the intelligence of a race can be measured by its technology."

"But can't we do something?" cried Peter. "Maybe I can pay them for the land. We have a little money left."

"They've no use for money," said Kent. "This desert that is no good to you without a lot of work, is a Garden of Eden to them. The only thing they want from you is what you've taken from them—land."

"But they've got so much land!"

"They want it all," said Kent. "And why not—it was all theirs to start with."

"Well," said Peter hopelessly. "What can we do?"

"You can't do anything," said Kent. He took a step backward, reached in through the door of his shelter and picked up his jacket. He shrugged his arms into it. "But maybe I can. I don't know. Wait here and keep all your kids inside the limits of the settlement. I'm going up and see if any of them will talk to me."

"But—" cried Peter again. But Kent ignored him, walking away. The little man trotted behind him for a few steps, but, finding himself outdistanced, slowed down and gave up; and stood staring in doubt and indecision after the Colonial Representative's trim back as it dwindled away in the distance, climbing the hillside.

Kent walked along the crest of the encircling hills. For several hours he had been going, now, stopping in front of each Modorian in hope that the tall creature would speak to him. So far none had. Some ignored him. Some looked at him gravely, then looked away again, down into the hollow. A few were talking together like orators, declaiming in their own, sonorous incomprehensible tongue, and these he did not even bother to approach. The sun was climbing and its naked rays were coming down hot on the hillside when finally he found one who would talk.

The Modorian was tall and unusually gaunt. As with most Modorians, there was nothing about him to mark his age, but something about his pose as he leaned on the spear gave Kent an impression of great age. As Kent came up and stood before him, the other tilted his head downward and looked at the man with his large, dark, incurious eyes.

"Which man are you?" he said.

The voice was high-pitched, a tenor by human standard, but a certain monotonous and mechanical style of delivery kept it from the reediness that would have been apparent in a like human voice.

"Kent Harmon," said Kent. "Colonial Representative. Do you have a name I can call you by?"

The Modorian looked away from him and down at the settlement.

"Call me Maker," he said. For a moment he stood gazing in silence, then he turned his head back to Kent.

"This land," he said, "from pole to pole, from ocean to ocean, and across the ocean, is mine. Do you understand that, man?"

"I understand," said Kent.

"But they down there do not understand," said Maker.

"No," said Kent. There was another brief silence.

"To know and understand are two different things," went on Maker. "Do they know this?"

"They've been told," said Kent. "But they haven't any choice, Maker. There's no room on any other world for them so they have had to come here."

"Man," said Maker, "you lie to me. There are more worlds in the universe than men, and more than there will ever be of men, should each man be given a world to himself."

"But not liveable worlds."

"Yes, liveable worlds," said Maker. "There are more worlds on which men can live than men will ever occupy. If you do not know this, man, I tell you now."

Kent shrugged.

"I will tell you the truth, Kent Harmon, and you can deny it if you can. There is more than enough room for men. But men go where it is closest and easiest. Hear me. Those below come here because fear keeps them from other worlds unknown, where savage races live. They come here rather than go beyond what men call their Frontier in space. Is this true or not?"

Kent bowed his head.

"It is true," said Maker. "Fear is all they know. Let them fear me."

He turned his gaze back to the settlement below. Twice

more Kent spoke to him, without getting an answer. The Modorian had withdrawn into his own thoughts. Kent turned and went down the hill to the colonists.

"Well," he said grimly to Peter Lawrence, "at least I know which one the trouble is going to come from."

The second day there were more than a thousand Modorians on the hillsides. Maker had dug down through the loose rock to the solid granite bedrock and cleared a space there several yards in area. It would have been an inconceivable amount of work for a single man to perform in even a week, but the Modorian had done it easily in less than one day and a night.

Kent went back up to see him again.

"Maker," he said. "What you're doing is foolish. I and all of the men except the prospectors will combine to stop you if you create anything dangerous."

Maker looked up from the bottom of the pit where he stood.

"Look, man," he said. "It is to be settled here whether I will drive men from my land, or whether they will drive me from it. You may meet my blow, but not avoid it; or all others like me will say to themselves—'This is not settled' and try it for themselves."

"I don't understand," said Lawrence, puzzled, when Kent repeated this statement to him, Hord Chalmers and Peter's two youngsters.

"He was pointing out a fact," said Kent wryly. "If I wanted to risk the lives of half a dozen men, I could take him into custody. If I wanted to violate Colonial Office directives, I could shoot him, just on suspicion, although all I have against him so far is that he's dug a hole in the ground. But that wouldn't settle anything. Conceivably, what he's doing, any other male Modorian can do, and if I stopped him, they'd all be trying."

"A skinny native playing in the dirt and you all get the

wind up—" Hord Chalmers, who was standing by his uncle, burst into a sudden sarcastic laugh.

It was echoed suddenly by the deep-throated laughter of Branch. He was striding toward them, and the sound of his laughing was carefree on the thin air. He came up to them and stopped, grinning, his thumbs hooked into his gunbelt.

"Getting worried, eh?" he said.

"Who let you in here?" demanded Peter with a frown. But before Branch could answer, Hord had cut in.

"Worried!" he snorted. "Of that fleabag up on the hills? I thought he was just digging a hole to hide in."

But Branch's face did not lose its cheerfulness.

"You can't make me mad, today, Buster," he said. "Things are going too well."

"Branch—" interrupted Kent sharply. "If you know what Maker is planning to do, it's your duty to let us know." Branch sobered, but his eyes did not soften as he looked down at Kent.

"Harmon," he said. "I kind of like you, and most of the boys do, too. But I'll see you damned in hell before I'll tell you anything that might help these dirt-grubbers—besides, I don't know."

He looked stolidly at the Colonial Representative; but before Kent had a chance to answer, the big prospector was attacked from a quarter so unexpected that they were all taken by surprise. It was little Judy Lawrence who spoke up in sudden, furious anger, her delicate face, now burned and peeling from the merciless sun, taut with emotion.

"Do you know what's wrong with you?" she cried.

"Judy—" stammered Peter.

"Oh, leave me alone!" she cried. "None of you has guts enough to tell him what he really is—but I will." She turned like a small ferocious terrier on the tall young bulk of Branch, and Kent was suddenly, fleetingly reminded of Tichi as she tore into him. "I'll tell you what you are. You're a dog in the manger. You can't really do anything with this desert. You can't make it grow and turn green and beautiful, or build homes, or have children—and you don't want anybody else to have them either. You want them all to be just as miserable and just as ugly and savage as you are!" Branch's face whitened. For a moment the youth beneath his hard competent shell showed through and the rest could glimpse a boyish hurt and rage.

"You can talk!" he cried. "You can talk about homes—" he choked on his swelling emotion and took a sudden blind, half-step toward her. His round face lighting up, Hord moved suddenly between them. Wildly, Branch turned on him. There was an eye-blurring flash of movement, the thud of a blow, and the heavier, Earth-born human lay stretched on the ground. Branch faced them over the fallen man, half-crouched, his fists knotted, his face contorted, something mad about his twisted features.

"Get out!" said Peter, sharply. The little middle-aged man moved forward on the big prospector, and Kent saw Branch tense as the older man came within reach. Swiftly he reached forward and yanked him back.

"Come on," said Branch, wildly, his voice scaling up, "the whole fat, lousy, stinking crew of you!" Kent shoved Peter aside and confronted the staring young man himself.

"Branch," he said in a calm, steady voice. "Branch."

"Homes!" half-sobbed Branch, his voice shaking, "cute little—boxy little—"

"Branch!" snapped Kent. "Branch!"

Gradually, the young man began to relax, and the insane light died slowly from his eyes. The tenseness drained out of him and he straightened, his calmness regained, but somehow empty. He sighed and shivered. Kent felt hardness underneath his right hand, and, glancing down, saw his hand was cramped around his gun butt. He let go and flexed the aching fingers.

"You better go, Branch," he said.

Branch shook himself like a big dog coming out of water.

"I'll go," he said, emptily. "It doesn't matter. They won't be here long anyway."

"You—" began Judy, but Kent's hand clamped down sharply on her slim arm and the sudden pain made her gasp. Her twin brother spoke up.

"Never mind, Judy," said Bob. "It's all a bluff. Like Hord says, a dirty savage digging a hole in the ground."

Branch looked at him, but his eyes were withdrawn and his voice when he answered was remote and disinterested.

"Go ahead and dream," he said, turning away. "You'll learn. When a Modorian starts to throw his weight around— the earth moves."

They watched his slim figure shorten in the distance. Peter Lawrence spoke up.

"Bob!" he said sharply. "Look after Hord. And I want you to talk to the boys on guard and make sure that young man never gets in here again."

"Why he—he's insane!" said Judy, fascinatedly. Kent released her arm and looked at her somewhat sardonically. An evil genius impelled him to speak.

"You're probably right, Miss Lawrence," he said. "In fact, I wouldn't be a bit surprised if you were. You see, Branch is one of the Reclaimed—one of the kids that was recaptured from a raiding alien life-form when we cleaned them out of the Sagittarius section of our Frontier. He was just old enough to remember the raid that killed off his parents and he was a prisoner for nearly a dozen years. When you were going out on your first date back on Earth, Branch was living in a cage."

Judy's mouth fell open, and the hand with which she had been massaging her bruised arm stopped abruptly.

Kent smiled at her and turned away.

IV

There was not a great deal of technical help to be had on Modor, since the planet was primarily a trading station. But, such as it was, Kent corralled it from all the inhabited valleys, ordered it to the settlement site with all possible speed. On the third day after the landing of the colonists, men began to arrive, and Kent spent a weary day tramping up the hillside with geologists, mining engineers, weather station men and chemical engineers—all of whom looked at what Maker was doing, shook their heads, shrugged their shoulders, and left the Colonial Representative just as wise as he had been before.

Nor could he really blame them, thought Kent, moodily, standing on the edge of Maker's pit as the sunset lengthened, and a biting chill came in over the darkening land. Modor's creation looked like the fantastic building of some powerful, aberrant child.

By main strength, Modor had sunk the steel shaft of his twelve-foot spear half its length into the solid granite. Around this he had built a sort of crude framework of long narrow splinters of rock, gummed together with a sort of soft clay—and inside this framework he was creating a strange crystalline structure by the medium of dissolving certain minerals in water and pouring them along the rock splinters.

At first, progress had been slow, most of the mineral solution running off the splinters and being wasted. But as the little bit that remained dried, forming adhering crystals, the thing began to grow rapidly, until now a rough, globular mass appeared within the framework, covering and completely enclosing the exposed end of the steel spear-shaft.

Now that phase of the construction seemed to be finished. Maker had turned away from the crystal and stone and was seated off to one side and fashioning what appeared to be a very long, light bow, using wood from one of the stunted bushes and a tendon from one of the small burrowing animals he had killed. He had somehow stretched the tendon enormously over a fire, and now he was engaged in binding it to the wooden arc.

Kent went down the side of the pit with a rush and rattle of loose stones, and approached him.

"You've been working two days and nights straight, Maker," he said. "Don't you ever sleep?"

He had not really expected an answer, and he was surprised when the other replied.

"Sleep is death," said the Modorian, not looking up from what his hands were doing.

Above the mouth of the pit, the first breath of the evening wind moaned abruptly, sending a chill down Kent's back. He shivered.

"You don't really believe that, Maker," he said, half-jokingly to throw off the sudden feeling of depression.

"Man," said Maker, "you talk like a fool."

Kent got out his pipe and bit hard on the stem. His hands searched his pockets for tobacco, but found none. He stayed with the empty pipe clamped between his teeth, looking down at the squatting Modorian, who worked on in the gathering gloom without looking up.

"You know," volunteered Kent. "There's still time for me to send an official protest from you to Central Headquarters."

"Words are for men," said Maker. "I do not play with my mouth. Nor will I tell you, Harmon, what you want to know. What I am going to do, I will keep to myself."

Darkness thickened around them. Kent strained to see, while the larger pupils of the Modorian dilated easily to take advantage of the waning light.

"Tell me this, anyhow," said Kent. "Will what you have in mind involve the killing of people. If worse comes to worst, I would rather move them against orders than have anyone die."

"It is to the death," said Maker.

His last words were lost in blackness as the final rays of the sun fell behind the hill.

"Thanks, Maker," said Kent.

There was no answer from the obscurity. Kent turned and climbed his way back up to the edge of the pit. At the top he turned and looked down again. A spark leaped suddenly into being in the shadows and a little flame flared up, illuminating the pit. By its light Kent saw Maker rise to his feet and cross over to the crystalline mass, the now-completed bow in his hand. He reached out into the structure and with one slow, soft movement, drew the bowstring across the jagged glinting facets around the hidden spear-shaft.

An odd, discordant, musical note cried sharply out on the night air. It pierced Kent, seeming to shiver in his very bones; and he turned swiftly, going away down the hillside toward the settlement, while behind him the crystals cried, again and again, every time in a different note, like the devil tuning up his violin. Lonesome, questioning, the varied discordant notes of Maker laboring over his creation followed him as he walked among the houses, but dying, dying in the distance, until at last the slam of his door shut them from his ears entirely.

Kent lay awake in the dark, his tired mind searching. Like the sad montage of a dream, faces moved through his mind—the desperate young features of Branch, and Maker's inscrutable huge dark eyes. The serious, worried face of Peter, and Hord's beefy handsome countenance. In his mind's eye he saw them circling his bed, looking down at him, all of them waiting, looking to him for a solution, an answer.

They crowded around him. There was Bob's tense, thin features, and the delicate beauty of his sister Judy, her eyes frightened and haunting. By them they evoked the golden-haired image of Tichi, looking on and wondering, and all the host of peoples, human and alien alike, the knowledge of whose existence lived within his consciousness. To his tired mind the immediate problem swelled and grew enormously, until it blotted out all other problems in the Universe, until it was The Problem—the great question that must eventually be answered if any human and any alien were ever to exist permanently side by side.

And somehow, it was all up to him. Under the scourge of

his conscience, Kent's hard body twisted in the narrow bed.
He was the administrator, the trained executive. His was
the ethical and the moral responsibility. To stop Maker by
force meant blood on his hands. To let him go ahead with
the strange creation of his alien mind meant blood on Kent's
hands—the blood of the colonists. Why must it always end
in killing? Why must there always be no choice? Branch
had no choice but to stick by the Modorians. The colonists
had no place else to go. The Modorians, seeing the future
clearly—humans flooding in to take the land that was all in
all to them—had no choice but to resist. There must be an
answer—and there was no answer. The tension built up,
reached an unendurable pitch—and broke.

In the darkness Kent laughed in sudden bitter irony and
sat up, swinging his legs over the side of the bed. He lit the
lamp, reached for his pipe, filled and lit it. As always, at the
last minute, an odd, cold sense of humor came to save him
from himself—and this time it had been a wishful mental
picture of himself washing his hands. He laughed again, and
sighed deeply. It had been a mistake to let himself think—
his sphere was action.

In the end like goes to like, when a side must be chosen—
and Kent was human. For all his admiration for Modorians
in general and sympathy with Maker in particular, he realized
that he must protect and maintain the colony at the cost of
any native sacrifice. He pulled on the pipe and white smoke
streamed up around him, past his head and out the ventilator
above his bed. If necessary, he would call in the Space
Guard. Whatever Modor's instrument was capable of doing,
either above ground or below—

He caught himself suddenly, in midthought. Inspiration
had suddenly come to him.

Charlie Colworth did not like being gotten up in the
middle of the night; but when the Colonial Representative
pounds at your very door, which is halfway across the planet

from where you saw him last, you are forced to rise to the occasion. Cursing to himself, he pulled clothes onto his skinny body and wandered, yawning, into the front room of his quarters, where Kent was waiting.

Kent handed him a cup of his own coffee. "Here," he said. "You'll need it."

Charlie complied, and shuddered. The stuff was black, and he was a strong cream-and-sugar man.

"I suppose it's about that colony mess," he grumbled.

"That's right," said Kent.

"Well, now what?" said Charlie, dropping on the couch. "And what's it got to do with me?" Kent grinned.

"Sorry, Charlie," he said. "But you know that area best of any of the geologists we have here. I want to know what's under that granite Maker anchored his gadget in."

"More granite," said Charlie sourly, "now can I go back to bed?"

"I don't think so," said Kent. "What's under the more granite?"

"Hell," said Charlie. "It's a capstone. Magma, probably."

"By magma I take it you mean molten rock—lava?"

"It's only called lava after it comes out on the surface," said Charlie, grumpily.

"What would happen if the granite was split open?" asked Kent. "Would this magma rise up and flow over the surface?"

"If the pressure was—what in hell are you talking about?" said Charlie. "That's one of the most stable areas on this planet's surface. The K'tabi Shield. It's at least two miles thick and may be as much as fifty. Something like that doesn't split open."

"Charlie," said Kent, "what do you know about vibrations in rock?"

"As much as a well-brought-up earthquake," answered Charlie. "Now, are you going to tell me what all this is about, or do I go back to sleep?"

"I'll show you," said Kent. "Right now I want you to put

on some outer clothes, pick up detector equipment and come
out with me to find out what effect Maker's gadget is having
on the K'tabi Shield."

"Good God, is *that* it?" said Charlie.

They were climbing the hillside outside the settlement in
the early dawn, Charlie and Kent. With them was a man
loaded down with detector equipment, and the Wonder Boy,
as Karl Mencht, the ace troubleshooter for Modor's only
spaceship repair yard was called. What had drawn the ex-
clamation from Charlie's lips was the varying sound emanat-
ing from Maker's equipment as the sleepless Modorian continued to draw his bowstring across it.

"Interesting," said the Wonder Boy in his customary
clipped tones, cocking his boyish head on one side to listen.

"That's what you say," grunted Charlie. "It sends shivers
down my back."

"Subsonics," said the Wonder Boy.

"Go to hell," said Charlie. He stopped abruptly. "Here,"
he said, "if there's anything going on at all, we're plenty
close enough to pick it up, now. And there's an outcropping
of granite here I can tie into. Set it down."

Gently, the man carrying the equipment lowered it into
place and set it up. Charlie fiddled with the dials.

"Now we'll see," he said. "Just as I thought—nothing—
Holy Hannah!"

Coincidental with a squeak from Maker's distant bow, a
needle on one of the dials had jumped clear across the scale
and out of sight. It returned to rest in the same moment
that the sound died away.

"But he can't do that—" said Charlie, fascinated. They
watched the needle for a moment in which the squeaks
continued, then the needle jumped again.

"He just hits it by accident every so often," said Charlie,
in an awed voice. "But when he does—*wow!*"

"What's he doing, exactly?" asked Kent.

"He must be making this whole area of the shield vibrate," said Charlie. "And he can't do that. I must be seeing things."

"Nonsense," said the Wonder Boy. "You can vibrate anything."

"By rubbing a crystal on a rod just touching the surface of an area this size? You'd have to amplify—why you'd have to amplify—"

"Ever stop to think?" said the Wonder Boy. "Using area as sounding board. Don't know rocks myself, but makes sense."

" 'Makes sense'—you're nuts," said Charlie. The Wonder Boy shrugged.

"All right," said Kent, crisply. "Going on the assumption that my hunch was right and Maker can vibrate the rock underneath here enough to cause either a volcanic eruption or an earthquake—have either of you any ideas about how to stop him?"

"Smash his gadget," said Charlie.

"If I did that, what's to stop every other Modorian from trying it where I can't see him? Anyway that's not it. It's my belief that the rest of the Modorians—" he gestured to the ridge of the hills around them where the pink dawnlight was beginning to pick out the lean gray shapes that watched in silence—"are looking on this as sort of a test-case. If I beat Maker at his own game, they'll give up and leave the colony alone. If I don't, every single one of them will take his individual and particular swing at every settlement group that comes along after this."

"Ruin your career," said the Wonder Boy.

"Wonder Boy," said Charlie. "You've got a filthy mind. For half a credit I'd kick your pretty white teeth down your throat."

"Never mind that," said Kent. "Any ideas?"

Charlie shrugged.

"Interesting problems," said Wonder Boy. "Fight fire with fire, maybe."

"How?" asked Kent.

"Damp his vibration. Counter-vibrations. Could do it—got crews—equipment down at the repair yard. Engineering feat, be interesting. Very."

"The Modorian might beat you anyway. Embarrassing. Very," mocked Charlie.

"Try it," said the Wonder Boy, to Kent. "Up to you."

"Of course," said Kent. "You go ahead with it as fast as you can. Charlie, what actually is liable to happen if Maker cracks the shield?"

"Possibly the lava flow you were worried about," said Charlie. "But more probably a landslip."

"Either way, the settlement is in danger of being destroyed?"

Charlie grimaced.

"I'd use the word 'obliterated,' " he said.

"Then I've got to get those people out of there. Charlie, you help Karl here as much as you can; and Karl—rush it."

"Course!" said the Wonder Boy; and "Hell, yes!" said Charlie. Kent turned and went plunging off down the hillside toward the camp.

V

He went down the hill in a blind rush—so intent on what he was doing, in fact, that he had run on Branch and Judy Lawrence almost before he realized they were in his way. He skidded to a halt to avoid bumping into them and for a second the three of them looked at each other in not-too-friendly surprise. Kent was the first to recover his tongue.

"Good Lord," he said, "what are you doing out here?" She looked at him a little defiantly.

"I came out to apologize to Branch," she said.

"Oh?" said Kent, and looked from her to the tall young prospector, who colored slightly. "Well, don't let me interrupt you," Kent said, stepping around them.

Judy reached out a hand and caught at his arm.

"Oh, Mr. Harmon—"

"What?" demanded Kent, wheeling to face her with a touch of exasperation at being delayed.

"We're all through talking. I wonder if we could go back to the settlement with you?"

"Why not?" said Kent, turning away again. But then a hint of something odd struck him. "But, come to think of it, why?"

She still met his eyes somewhat defiantly.

"Well you see," she said. "I went out looking for Branch last evening. And night comes down so quickly, here. Well —we got lost."

"Lost?" said Kent, incredulously, looking at Branch.

"That's right," said the young man with dogged belligerence. "We got lost. She hasn't been home since last night."

They both stared at him. And suddenly understanding struck him, bringing a rich sense of humor in its wake. Here was their personal world about to blow up and all these two babies could find time to worry about—

"All right," said Kent, the hint of a grin twisting his lips in spite of himself. "Come on, both of you, and I'll see if I can't put in a good word for you with your father, Judy. I take it you have the instincts of an honest man, Branch?"

"What?" said Branch, uneasily.

"Never mind," said Kent. "Come on—and hurry!"

Kent did not speak on the walk back.

"Judy!" cried Peter Lawrence, when he first caught sight of them. And—"What are you doing here, Simmons? I gave orders—"

"I brought him, Daddy," said Judy, putting her arm through his.

"You might as well reconcile yourself, Lawrence," said Kent. "These things happen quickly on the Outer Worlds."

"What?"

"Yes," said Kent abruptly, without any excess courtesy. "And now that that's settled, I've got something important to talk to you about. We've found out what Maker's doing—and it's dangerous. I'm rushing equipment up here to try and save the settlement, but it may not get here in time; and I want you to evacuate all your people."

"Evacuate?" cried Peter, spinning to face Kent. "Why?"

"Because," snapped Kent, "I say so. We may have anything from an earthquake to an active volcano taking place here within the next minute. Get your kids out. You can have reasons later."

"Why, this is some kind of a trick—" cried Peter, his face purpling.

"Don't be a fool," said Kent.

"I won't move until I know just what you mean by this high-handed order."

"Give me that," said Kent, exasperatingly, reaching out and yanking off the button mike that was fastened to Peter's tunic. He thumbed the switch, and loudspeakers all over the settlement bellowed his voice.

"All right," they boomed. "This is the Colonial Representative speaking. Everybody come to the Headquarters Building. Everybody. That means everybody, sick and well alike. As fast as you can. No loitering."

Kent cut off the mike. Peter made an unsuccessful grab for it. Kent fended him off and put it in his pocket.

"Stand aside, and keep quiet," he said.

"I will not!" raved the little man. "Ever since we landed, everyone's been trying by hook or crook to get us out of the land that the charter guaranteed us. We haven't given it up yet, and we won't. Now you're turning against us."

"Look, Lawrence," said Kent, "I tell you this whole area may be buried under rock or lava at any moment. Do you want to lose your lives as well as your possessions?"

"Why not?" cried Peter Lawrence. "Why not? Everything we own is here. How could we live without it?"

"Other people have," said Kent, coldly.

"Savages. Scum." The area in front of the Headquarters

Building was beginning to fill up with hurrying youngsters, and Peter half-swung toward them, addressing them as well as Kent. "Not people like us who've been gently brought up on a civilized world. We'd die out there—" and he extended a shaking hand toward the hills where, rank on silent gray rank, the Modorians stood watching.

"Shut up!" snapped Kent. The area before the building was almost full now, and he took the button from his pocket, snapping the switch and lifting it to his lips. The loudspeaker on the roof of Headquarters blasted forth his voice.

"Listen, all of you!" he said. "This is a direct order. You will pick up warm clothing and evacuate this settlement at once. Head for any open space beyond the hills, and when you get there institute a check to see nobody has been left behind. Now, move!"

But the crowd rocked hesitantly, murmuring to itself and looking toward Peter.

"Don't listen to him!" cried the little man, almost hysterically. "Don't move. Don't believe him. Go back to work! It's just another trick to get us out of here. Go back to what you were doing."

The crowd murmur rose and broke. The group eddied and began to disintegrate. On every side, people began to drift away.

"Come back, you idiots!" thundered the loudspeakers, with Kent's voice. "Will you let him shove all your heads into a noose? Do I have to order up a platoon of police to move you out by force?"

But the crowd was dispersing rapidly.

"Let him try it," screamed Peter. "We'll fight for our rights."

The last few members of the crowd broke and ran for the protection of nearby buildings. Defeated, Kent lowered the phone button and stuck it in his pocket. Peter crowed his triumph. Kent turned on him.

"May God have mercy on your soul!" he said savagely.

Peter grinned wildly; but before he could answer, the two youngsters drew both men's attention.

"*You* aren't staying!" said Branch to Judy.

"What do you mean?" she answered, between surprise and anger, "I certainly will stay if the rest of them do."

"That's what you think," said Branch bluntly. "I know Harmon knows what he's talking about. Let the rest be dumb if they want to. You and me are going where it's safe."

"I certainly will not!" said Judy; but the words were barely out of her mouth before he seized the collar of her tunic with one large hand and began to march her off in the direction of the perimeter.

"Stop!" screamed Judy. "Daddy! Help!"

Peter made an inarticulate sound in his throat and dived for a power-rifle that was leaning against the side of Headquarters. He was bringing the weapon up to his shoulder when Kent seized it and wrested it out of his hands. A single blast went skyward.

"You—" choked Peter, scrabbling desperately for the gun. "Give it back!"

"Not on your life," said Kent, grimly, pushing him away. He nodded in the direction of the dwindling pair of figures. "There go two more lives off my conscience." He held the little man off until a distant building hid Judy and Branch from sight.

Abruptly Peter stopped struggling. He stood forlorn, as if all the strength had gone out of him, looking in the direction the two had disappeared. There were sudden tears in his eyes. The tears of an old man.

"My baby," he said, brokenly. "With that—that—savage."

Kent was not feeling any sympathy for him.

"Worse things have happened to women," he said harshly.

VI

Kent stood on the hillside opposite Maker's pit, watching as a sweating crew of technicians from the repair yard struggled to sink a fifty-foot steel rod four feet in diameter deep into the rocky crust beneath his feet. Beside them an even larger crew labored to hook up an oversize generator and sounding equipment for the broadcasting of counter-vibrations through the rod.

At ten other intervals in a circle around the camp a similar job was being carried on, under the gimlet eye of the Wonder Boy, who flitted from group to group like some cherubic slave driver. The day was well advanced, and every available man with technical knowledge had been pressed into service.

Kent turned and walked away to where Charlie had set up a sort of seismographic headquarters. He was about to speak to him when he felt someone tap his elbow. He turned and saw Tom Schneider, the skinny space-communications operator.

"What is it, Tom?" he asked. The other held out a flimsy.

"Urgent," he said.

Kent turned away again.

"Stick it in your pocket, Tom," he said. "I haven't time for anything like that now." Tom reached out and grabbed him.

"I think you better read it, Kent." Kent turned an exasperated face toward him.

"Can't you take 'no' for an answer?" he demanded. "I said I didn't want to be bothered."

"You better read it," said Tom, stubbornly.

Kent sighed, and took the thing. He had expected some coded top secret dispatch from Central Headquarters. But it was nothing like that. It was from Tichi—and written out in plain language for all the world to see.

Dearest Kent:
   I've got two things to tell you. And neither one is the sort of thing that can be put very well in schoolgirl slang.

(Kent blinked and looked at the first two sentences again. This didn't sound like Tichi.)

The first I might as well put down in plain words, since it isn't even an open secret around here any more. The Colonial Office has been keeping itself informed of how things have been going for you since the colony landed—and on the strength of what's happened so far alone, a Central Headquarter's Investigation has already been started. Apparently, this business is bigger than we thought. It seems that for some time now there's been a lot of public pressure from the Outer Planets on Central Headquarters—demanding that our supreme authorities clean house in the Colonial Office—and somebody has to be thrown to the wolves. They've made up their minds it's to be you.

There's one way out of this mess; and in defiance of all polite convention I'm naming it. That is that you marry me. As son-in-law of a Supreme Council Senator, you'd be too hot to handle, and they'd have to find some other scapegoat if they have to have one.

The second is this: Do you remember the birthday party I had when I was twelve years old? You came because you were a friend of Dad's and you brought me one of those big Centaurian dolls that walk around by themselves. I was too big for dolls and I was horribly embarrassed; but I loved you so much I hid the way I felt. That same party I got you alone and asked you to wait for me to grow up so I could marry you. And you laughed and said you would and gave me a phone chip and told me to call you up in half a dozen years if I still felt the same way. You were joking, but I wasn't. All my life you've acted as if I'd never grown up, and all my life I've loved you. Well, I have grown up and the six years have gone by. I'm using the phone chip—with a little extra, since you're farther away than you thought you'd be—

(Good lord! Six years already. Why that would make Tichi eighteen, thought Kent. It wasn't possible.)

—and now you know. I just want you to understand that I'm not offering this marriage deal in a burst of childish self-sacrifice. I want you more than anything in the Universe, and you're all I've ever wanted. I'm not a child, and I'm not shelteredly ignorant—I could even tell you a few things as far as *this* world goes. And—this will rock you back on your heels—Dad agrees with me. He thinks I'd be good for you, though he won't say a word to you about it.

I would never have said a word to you, my darling. I would have gone on play-acting that I was the little girl in pigtails, if this investigation hadn't come up with only one way out of it. And now that it has, and I've spoken out, I'm almost glad; because whatever happens, at least now I know that you know. . . .

All my love

Tichi (PRSM .7:3 TKMarlowe, Wash.)

Profoundly disturbed, Kent folded the flimsy and put it in his pocket. Tichi eighteen! And this marriage stunt. Why, damn it all, he was—how old was he now?—thirty-two . . . double her age. Who would have thought she felt like that!

"Any answer?" said Tom.

Shocked back to the present, Kent stared at him.

"No," he said. "No, Tom. No answer."

"I think maybe you ought to answer," said Tom. Kent's lips thinned angrily. This was the worst of living on a sparsely populated world where everybody knew your private business and felt himself qualified to pass judgment upon it.

"No!" he snapped explosively, and turned away toward Charlie.

"I'll be around in case you change your mind," said Tom behind his back.

Kent ignored him. He was leaning over Charlie's shoulder. The lean geologist felt his presence and turned a strained face away from his instruments.

"He hits the pitch oftener all the time," said Charlie. "It's a matter of holding it. I'll guess that if he can hold it steady for ten minutes we're done for."

"That bad!" said Kent.

"Can't you feel the vibration through your feet from the rock?" Kent hesitated.

"No," he said truthfully. Charlie wiped his forehead.

"Well, maybe it's my imagination," he said. "But I don't see how we've much time left."

"Oh? How much?" It was the clipped voice of Wonder Boy, who had just come up. Charlie turned toward him.

"At a guess," he said, "two hours at the most."

"Close," said the Wonder Boy, with a sharp jerk of his head. "Take us that long at least." Charlie, sweating under the hot sun, and worried, glared at the dapper young man.

"How do you manage to stay so cool?" he said.

"I?" said Wonder Boy, calmly, turning away. "Low blood pressure." And he was gone on his way to incite his crews to greater effort.

"What is it?" said Charlie, looking after him. "Has he got steel guts or is it that he just isn't human? You tell me, Kent."

Kent did not answer him. He was thinking what the investigating committee would do to him on the basis of the first blood he spilled, and looking out over the hollow. Down below, the settlement was silent and empty. The colonists had all gone to earth inside their buildings and the hills beyond were thick with watching Modorians. Kent made a quick estimate and whistled. There must be fifteen thousand of them waiting to see what happened now.

Kent hitched up his belt and started down the side of the hill.

"Where are you going?" called Charlie.

"Maker," called back Kent, without turning his head. "I'm going to delay him, if I can. If I can't—well, one way or another I'll give us time to get the equipment set up." And his hand went half-unconsciously to the holstered gun at his side.

Kent went down the hillside and into the as yet unpaved streets of the settlement. It was like walking into a ghost town. The doors of the buildings were shut and there was no sound of life from within. Tools near the uncompleted buildings lay scattered where they had been dropped, and the general scene gave an impression of a place long deserted.

But the impression was only a surface one. Beneath it, Kent

could sense the deep terror of the colony. Fear panted sound-lessly like the breathing of a hunted animal couched in its lair. He went quickly through the settlement and breasted the hill on the far side.

The minute he came out on the hillside, he knew that something was wrong—but dared not hesitate; and so he was forced to figure it out as he walked forward. It was this that he saw—there were too many Modorians between him and Maker.

When or how they had moved to cluster around the pit, he did not know. It was possible that they had been this way for some time, and he just had not noticed. It was equally possi-ble that they had seen him start from Charlie's station and had moved while he was among the houses of the settlement. One way or another, they now barred his path—not ob-trusively, but casually, by their very presence and closeness to one another.

He saw all this as he walked the thirty or more yards from the perimeter of the settlement to a spot about a third of the way up the hill, where their ranks started. They leaned on their spears, looking not at him, but down at the settlement and over at the crews toiling under the blazing heat of the afternoon sun. They did not move as he came toward them and he saw that they must either give way, or he must shove them aside, if he was to get through to Maker at all, for there was room, but not enough room to squeeze through, between them.

Yet he could not stop and wait. He must walk forward, as suming that they would give at the last minute. He was five steps away down the hill, then he was four, then three. . . .

He walked hard against the two foremost Modorians and rebounded from them as if they had been two statues. There was not even the yielding when he touched, that softer hu-man flesh would have given.

It was only then that one of them deigned to notice him. The Modorian on his left tilted his head downward and his enormous eyes seemed to swim dizzingly before Kent's face.

"Man," he said. "Go back."

It was the final utterance. It was the conclusion, a statement beyond protest. The wild Modorians would not let him through. The knowledge that he had kept to himself ever since this conflict started had proved itself. The Modorians were individuals. Each one made up his mind for himself and they did not work together. But—and this Kent had realized silently in his heart—when the last came to the last, there was nothing to stop them all from getting the same idea and acting together, though independently. Each of the Modorians before him had made up his mind that he would not allow Maker to be interfered with. What did it matter that these were a hundred separate decisions, instead of one overall conclusion? The result was the same.

He turned away and went back down the hillside, back through the settlement and back to Charlie and the Wonder Boy. His mouth was dry and his heart pounded in his chest so strongly that he could feel and seem to hear the thud of the blood in his ears, as he walked through the silent streets. For the first time, Kent was clearly, nakedly, and unequivocally, afraid.

The afternoon was well advanced and the sun was hot upon them.

"Feel it now?" said Charlie tautly.

"Thrumming," said the Wonder Boy. "A buzzing."

"The vibrations are growing as he holds the pitch longer," said Charlie.

"How much longer with the crews?" asked Kent.

"Minutes," said the Wonder Boy. "A few."

"There!" said Charlie. His face was taut and sweat glistened on it in little beads in the lines of his brow. "See the houses quiver."

Kent looked. The settlement shimmered slightly.

"They'll be coming out soon," said Charlie. "Maybe on the next tremor. I've seen people in houses during earthquakes before."

The sun beat down, long-angled rays now, late afternoon and hot. The faces of the men were ruddy in the glare. The heat waves danced.

"I don't get it," said Charlie. The vibration coming up through the rock seemed to get into his voice, so that it appeared he buzzed the words in a monotone. "The Modorians. They'll go too. The whole area," said Charlie, "dozens of miles. Bound to collapse—Lord, you can hear it now."

They listened. Something was thrumming on the air. Was it the sound of Maker's bow, magnified and distorted by the great sounding board of the rock, or something else?

"I don't think they mind," said Kent. "The land will still be here."

"Yeah," said Charlie, hummingly, "the land."

The vibration was everywhere now. The rock, the air, the very individual molecules of each man's body seemed to dance to its tune. The eye struggled to focus and failed. Vision played tricks. The solid ground seemed to ripple and wave like water.

"They're coming out of the buildings," said Charlie, as if from a long distance off.

A weak, distant and ragged cheer came to their ears.

"Number two's hooked up," clipped Wonder Boy, his voice now strangely torn and distorted.

"Good," gasped Kent. "What about the others?"

"Coming in," vibrated Wonder Boy. "There go five and seven."

Kent tilted his head and fought his eyes to a fleeting focus on the settlement below. The colonists had indeed come out of their buildings, but the vibrations must be stronger down there, for they seemed unable to stand. They were lying flat and some were crawling. Faint screams came drifting up to the three men, wailing and distant.

The ground was really moving now. It seemed to swell and retreat under their feet and even up here on the hillside the men had to struggle to keep upright.

"One, three, four and six," buzzed Wonder Boy, distantly. He was standing over the master controls, and holding on.

The wailing from the shifting mass of color that was the village below was like the sounds from Dante's Inferno. The vibration tore and ground with angry fingers as if it would shake human flesh from human bones. Dust began to rise everywhere in great clouds, filling the air.

"—and all the rest," said Wonder Boy conclusively. "Now I'll throw the power in." His hands quivered, dancingly, as he fought with the master controls.

A new note swelled up to them from the torn and shaken ground beneath their feet. Unheard, but felt, it rose up like a wall to meet the tidal wave of vibration from Maker's instrument and the two clashed and fell to worrying each other like monstrous dogs. In their meeting and conflict there was no relief, for the earth still shook, but raggedly now, and out of tune.

"Hold on!" yelled Charlie thinly through the gathering storm of vibration, clinging valiantly to his instruments, calling to Wonder Boy. It was the ancient human battle cry in modern words. "Hold on! You're stopping him!" And Wonder Boy, clinging limpet-like to his own controls, echoed it back.

"I'm holding!"

Dust clouds rose more thickly from the quivering ground, isolating each one from the rest by a burning, opaque yellow cloud. The counter-vibrations screamed and fought, the world reeled, and then—

A break, a sudden lessening in the battle.

"Quit it!" yelled Charlie, lost in the dust. "He's stopped."

Abruptly, silence and peace returned. And they were so welcome and strange after the battle that for a moment the shaken people could not believe them and felt them somehow unreal. Then they pulled themselves together and stared through the thinning haze.

"Don't move until the dust rises," said Charlie.

VII

Like mist from the face of a magic mirror that draws aside like a veil in fairy stories to reveal unknown things, the dust thinned and passed from the face of the hollow and the distant rim of watching hills. Like a ghost growing solid and more real, the settlement came back into being before their watching eyes, the marked out streets, the buildings, the weather pylons; and it was all there, all standing and all whole.

In the streets a few people wandered dazedly, but all seemed to be on their feet and none were hurt.

Kent lifted his eyes from this to the hills beyond where, rank on rank and spears in hand, the Modorians still stood immovable and inscrutable. If any had fallen during the battle, they had gotten up again. And they waited now.

"I guess," said Kent. "It's up to me."

He went away down the hillside, loosening his gun in its holster by his side. He stepped into the settlement, and walked along its streets where the people gave him a wide berth. And he came out on the hill beyond, where the phalanx of wild Modorians had shielded Maker from him before.

They were still there; and he walked toward them.

They parted before him.

He walked through. He climbed up the narrow lane between them with the tall gray figures on each side no more than an arm's length away. He came to a little open space on the high ground around the pit, where Maker stood alone, his weapon below and behind him, glittering like some discarded toy in the rays of the late afternoon sun, gazing on the settlement below.

"Well, Maker?" said Kent, halting before him.

The Modorian did not answer, nor look down at him. His great dark eyes ate up the settlement and nothing else.

"Well, Maker?" repeated Kent, more loudly, his voice sounding blatant and huge in the silence of the waiting gray-furred crowd around them. Silence stretched out and tenseness grew brittle and thin between them. Then, slowly, without moving, the Modorian spoke.

"I will turn aside for no man, or men," he said—and, as if the words had been a talisman, he turned swiftly, his great body cat-like with the sinuous grace of his race, and flung himself at Kent, his steely arms wrapping around the man, crushing him, hurling him down the hillside.

The crowd, the ground, the rocks, the sky, whirled in one mad maelstrom around Kent as he went tumbling down the hillside between the leaping gray-furred legs of the Modorian host, and fighting for his life. The ground beat at his body with many hammers. Maker's arms crushed the breath from him and he struggled to free his right arm and draw his gun.

Hopelessly, instinctively, he fought during that wild fall down the hillside, knowing Maker was more than a physical match for any man that lived, knowing the odds were against him, but fighting anyhow. And, by some miracle, he did it; his arm came free, his hand closed about the gun butt; and, as they rolled at last toward a stop in the smothering yellow dust their fall had raised, on the level ground at the bottom of the hill, he shoved the muzzle hard against the rock-hard Modorian's side, and squeezed the button, twice.

Once more they rolled, through sheer momentum, but when they came at last to a standstill, Maker did not move, but lay limp and heavy above him. Kent fought for breath and was suddenly aware of hands that pulled the gray-furred body free.

It came away above him and he looked up to see Charlie and the Wonder Boy.

"You hurt, Kent?" cried Charlie.

"Guns!" croaked Kent, desperately, struggling to his feet and turning to face the dust cloud that obscured the hillside in front of him. "They're coming! Get out your guns!"

He faced into the wavering dust pall, his gun weaving in his hand, and the other two, tense suddenly with the implication of his words, snatched out their sidearms and stood beside him, knowing the futility of their stand, three men against thousands of Modorians, but not knowing what else to do, and acting with the direct instinct of desperation.

So they stood, expecting each next second to be their last. And the dust pall thinned before them, revealing the hillside. Even after it was gone, they still stood tense for a long minute, after all the fear and labor of the past hours, unable to trust their eyes. Then, wonderingly, they put their guns back and looked at each other as if for enlightenment.

For the slope was empty before them and the hilltops beyond were clearing like the bottom of a pond when a school of minnows melts away from a spot where the food has all been eaten. The wild Modorians with the strange understandable logic of their kind, were giving up, were retreating to the barren reaches yet untouched by man, were going away for good and leaving the human settlement alone.

Kent stood on the hillside the next morning, beside his waiting flyer, and looked down on the settlement below. To the eye it was as peaceful as it had ever been. The terrors, the troubles, the host of threatening Modorians had vanished like the night and the hills were wide and empty above it. Buildings were going up and streets were being surfaced. The weather pylons were working at last, and an artificial climate held the little hollow. Far below him he could see colonists thronging the streets in light tunics and kilts, and among them the occasional rough clothing of a prospector.

Kent grinned. One of those would certainly be Branch, for all Peter Lawrence might have to say about it. But the others would be men who three days ago were ready to turn their guns against the people they talked with. Still, their change of attitude was inevitable. Like calls to like with the strongest call in the Universe, and the men below were starved for male and female companionship and the social structure of their kind. For them the settlement was a small bit of the Earth they longed for. They would intermarry, and in time, settle down, as the civilized portions of the planet were extended.

Kent shook his head, and a sudden realization came to him of the inevitability of the whole proceeding. The situation which had loomed so large yesterday, now appeared as an incident, doomed to be forgotten in time as the march of civilization went on. He grinned a little ruefully. Now that it was all over, he felt completely useless. Modorian and colonist alike had turned away from him to their own small immediate affairs—and Maker was dead.

He frowned a little, remembering. Now that the heat had gone from his mind, he could look back and wonder on the chance that had enabled him to survive—first, the embrace of a full grown male Modorian and second, a tumble down a sixty-foot slope. The whole thing was a little too good to be true. Now, looking back on it, realization came to him. There had been no miracle about his winning. The Modorian had failed, and having failed, wanted to die. He had merely put the taking of his life in Kent's hands.

Kent was suddenly very weary. The smallness of his own importance—even to the people nominally under his control —and the greatness of the Universe came back to him. What if the Colonial Representative had been someone else? What if Maker had won and the Colonists had died? The end would have been the same. In the long run the individualist always loses to the organization. What difference whether Maker or Kent wins? Man will win, and Modorian lose—as far as the races are concerned, when the last chips are added up on each side.

Kent moved slightly, and the flimsy Tom had given him crackled in his pocket. He took it out, unfolded it and looked again at Tichi's words. The investigation committee—well, they could do little to him now, the way things had turned out. Tichi—that was something else. . . .

The great aching nostalgia of the space-weary came over him. Sooner or later everybody feels it and turns toward his home. Earth's green hills were pretty much of a myth now, as the sprawling cities ate up the open space—but there was yet a little of stream and forest and mountain untouched, and Kent felt in his heart a longing for them, too deep to be expressed.

There was nothing more for him to do here. The great first fight was over and the rest of history here would be a succession of niggling brawls and troubles. Why bother with it, when what he wanted of Earth was his for the asking?

And Tichi?

Kent laughed suddenly, out loud, at himself.

"I'm an old man," he said, to the empty Modorian landscape. "It's high time I retired."

Still chuckling, he swung himself into the flyer, drove it up off the ground and across the hollow to where Tom was setting up a subsidiary communications center.

"Hi!" said the communications man, popping out of the half-constructed building as Kent set the flyer down.

"Hi, Tom," said Kent, "you can send an answer to that message for me now."

Tom's homely face grinned.

"Right," he said. "What'll I say?"

"Just say everything's all right and that I'm coming home."

"That's all?" asked Tom. Kent frowned.

"Add 'love' to that," he said.

Tom still lingered.

"Nothing more, Kent?"

"Oh, hell!" said Kent, climbing back into his flyer. "Tell her I've just become convinced of the inevitability of things. That should keep her busy wondering—unless she starts putting her own interpretation on it.

"—but that's just what she'll probably do," he muttered half-pessimistically to the controls. Smiling, he slammed the door of the flyer behind him and lifted the machine into the air. Into the bright sky of morning, Kent Harmon headed east—and home. . . .

P: